FLOATING
AND SINKING
ON THE
SEA OF
OFFICIALDOM

FLOATING AND SINKING ON THE SEA OF OFFICIALDOM

JOHN XIAO ZHANG

Matador
9 Priory Business Park,
Wistow Road, Kibworth Beauchamp,
Leicestershire, LE8 0RX
Tel: 0116 279 2299
Email: books@troubador.co.uk
Web: www.troubador.co.uk/matador
Twitter: @matadorbooks

ISBN 978 1800463 424

British Library Cataloguing in Publication Data.
A catalogue record for this book is available from the British Library.

Printed and bound in the UK by TJ International, Padstow, Cornwall
Typeset in 11pt Adobe Garamond Pro by Troubador Publishing Ltd, Leicester, UK

Matador is an imprint of Troubador Publishing Ltd

To those brave social reformers, for the country's democracy and prosperity, you dare to challenge the old system and institutions, not hesitating to sacrifice your own interests and even life. Thanks to your struggle and pioneering efforts, your country has gradually become a democratic and prosperous society. You have set your old civilization on the path towards rejuvenation and a modern nation.

CONTENTS

LIST OF CHARACTERS

Main Characters

I.   Zhang Feng, *main hero in the trilogy and in this volume. A handsome and talented man who suffers greatly during the Cultural Revolution. After the revolution, he first becomes a scholar, and then later a political leader in his city. He is also called Brother Feng by his lovers and friends, Elder Brother by his close friends, Xiao Feng or Xiao Zhang by his family and people around him who are older than him.*

II   His close friends: in Volume 1 and this volume,

    A.   Wang Hai, *a factory director. He supports Zhang Feng in his mission to carry out economic and political reforms*

B. Li He, *a doctor. He supports Zhang Feng in his mission to carry out economic and political reforms.*

III. His lovers:
   A) Yu Mei, *daughter of a late high ranking officer and a Red Guard in Volume 1 (her name means plum blossom. Her full name is Li Yu Mei) She is also called Xiao Mei or Mei Mei by her family and lovers. In this volume, she is head of department in a city bureau.*
   B) Dan Dan, *a girl who was a neighbor of Zhang Feng (her name means peony) and his 'sister' in Volume 1. She is Zhang Feng's wife and a scholar at a university in this volume.*
   C) Qing Lian, *a former classmate of Zhang Feng and an active Red Guard in Volume 1. She is a journalist in this volume. (her name means lotus)*

IV. His personal and political enemies:
   A) Director Shen, *a high ranking official who is a rigid left-wing element set against economic and political reform.*
   B) Li Qiu, *Zhang Feng's former university classmate but also an official in the government who is a political villain.*
   C) Wang Gui, *an evil countryside militia cadre.*

Characters by Alphabet

Cai Wenge, *an ambitious villain, enemy to Zhang Feng in Volume I. In this volume, he is released from jail and sets up his own company.*

Chang Zheng, *rival of Zhang Feng and a Red Guard in Volume I, son of General Zhao Wu. In this volume, he is a friend to Zhang Feng, discharged from the army and becoming a civil officer to support Zhang Feng*

Chen Tao, *a former university classmate of Zhang Fen, an officer in city council who supports Zhang Feng.*

Dan Dan, *Zhang Feng's lover, a beautiful and talented girl. She is a lecturer at a university.*

Dan Feng, *Son of Zhang Feng and Dan Dan.*

Du Ming, *a retired general in Taiwan.*

Du Shan, *a businessman from Taiwan.*

Hai Jing, Master, *he used to be a Taoist monk who taught Zhang Feng martial arts in Volume I, with a secret identity. In this volume, he is Zhang Feng's father-in-law.*

He Hua, *a younger girl in the countryside where Zhang Feng and his friends worked as 'Educated Youth' in Volume I. In this volume, she enacts economic reform in countryside by conducting a land contract scheme.*

He, Secretary, *a secretary of the party committee of Hua Dan County.*

Hei Tou, *a local hooligan, later becoming an active Red Guard in Volume I. In this volume, he is a self-employed vendor.*

Huang Lei, *a lecturer of Jili University, Friend to Zhang Feng.*

Liang Fu, *a businessman in Hong Kong.*

Liang Hua, *a professor at the London School of Economics, supervisor to Dan Dan*

Li He, *a close friend to Zhang Feng, a doctor of Chinese medicine.*

Li Jianguo, *the late first secretary of the provincial party committee. Yu Mei's father.*

Li Li, *a friend of Zhang Feng, a Red Guard in Volume I. Her boyfriend died during the Cultural Revolution.*

Lin Jianguo, *an officer in the government who always supports Zhang Feng, a savior of Zhang Feng in Volume I.*

Li Qiu, *a former university classmate of Zhang Feng in the past, an officer who follows the evil leaders in the government.*

Li Yong, *He Hua's boyfriend.*

Liu Qi, *secretary of the Chinese Department, Jili University. A rigid left-wing element.*

Liu, Secretary, *a secretary of the provincial party committee who supports Zhang Feng politically, a subordinate of the late secretary of provincial party committee Li Jianguo.*

Lv Guohao, *director of the Jiang Cheng Daily Newspaper.*

Meng, Secretary, *the secretary of the party committee, Jili University.*

Qing Lian, *an active Red Guard who loves the main hero Zhang Feng secretly in Volume I. She is a journalist in this volume. She marries Li He, a friend of Zhang Feng*

Song Ping, *Zhang Feng's middle school classmate, a self-employed vendor.*

Sun, Teacher, *a violin teacher to Zhang Feng in the past. He was killed by the Red Guards during the Cultural Revolution in Volume 1.*

Wang Hai, *a close friend of the main hero Zhang Feng*

Wang Hui, *Dan Dan's mother.*

Wang Kai, *secretary of the city party committee who dislikes the reform.*

Wang Li, *a university student who works in a government department after graduation. She loves Zhang Feng secretly.*

Wei Wei, *a professor of the city art institute.*

Ye, Teacher, *a music teacher.*

Yu Lan, *Zhang Feng's former middle school classmate, in the same collective household while working in the countryside in Volume I, a self-employed vendor in this volume.*

Yu Mei, *Zhang Feng's lover. Daughter of the late party secretary of the province. An officer in a local government department*

Zhang Feng, *the main hero in the story. A handsome and talented young man.*

Zhang Lin, *Zhang Feng's younger sister.*

Zhang Wenbo, *Zhang Feng's father, a professor and a famous scholar*

Zhao Wu, *commander of the province military area. Father of Chang Zheng.*

PROLOGUE

In the spring of 1984, Jili City, on the banks of the Songhua River in Northeast China, is bathed in bright sunshine. Jili City is the capital of Jili Province. It is an important industrial, cultural and tourist city in China. It has many big, mechanical and chemical factories, famous universities and scientific institutes. It was also called the 'River City' because of its beautiful riverside scenery and was an agriculture province, growing sweet corn, rice, soy, sorghum and other crops. But during the disastrous, ten year Cultural Revolution, from 1966 to 1976, like all other areas in China, the economy, culture, education and social life in this city were seriously damaged. Many elites and ordinary people were persecuted cruelly and many died.

Luckily, when the Cultural Revolution ended in 1976, the new main leader, Deng Xiaoping, brought order out of chaos, corrected faulty policy and eventually, restored the whole country once more. Politically, the party removed the strict political restrictions on people which had been caused by so-called 'social class struggles' and rehabilitated millions of innocent people who had suffered political persecution during the Cultural Revolution, allowing them to regain the rights of ordinary citizens.

Economically, the new leaders realized that the socialist, centrally controlled economy was inefficient and resulted in shortages of products which made Chinese people live in poverty for many years. They started to look at the West and surprisingly, found that Western capitalist countries did not collapse like Marx had predicted. On the contrary, they had become more democratic and prosperous. The new Chinese leaders decided to learn from the West by opening the doors of their country to the outside world and carrying out economic reforms. Therefore, after the Cultural Revolution, China did not return to the simple socialism of the Soviet Union but experienced great changes in politics, economy, culture and ideology which marked the beginning of a great time in modern Chinese history. Our story unfolds against this background.

One day, in the afternoon, on the road leading to the beautiful North Mountain Park, a tall and handsome young man slowly walked towards the top of the mountain. He is the main character in our story, Zhang Feng. He was an excellent graduate of the Chinese Department in Jili University. He was already 29 years old when he enrolled because all universities in China had been forced to totally close for the ten years of the Cultural Revolution. He has just finished his Master's degree this year. Jili University is one of the top state universities in China with many famous scholars and scientists. Zhang Feng had already published quite a few articles in various state level, academic magazines, so he was well known in Chinese and foreign literary circles. That was why he was appointed as a lecturer in the Chinese Department when he finished his Master's degree. He was not only successful in his career but also in his private life. He would marry his childhood sweetheart, Dan Dan, next week.

In the wood, close to the magnificent Daoist temple, Zhang Feng sat on a huge rock to rest. From here, he could view the beautiful scenery: the wide Songhua River flowed peacefully in the distance; green willows danced genteelly in the spring wind; the great mountains beyond looked intoxicating, covered in bright sunshine. How beautiful!

Zhang Feng admired this scenery in his heart but 18 years ago, during the Cultural Revolution, there had been a horrible, political 'red storm'. His family, friends and he himself, had all suffered from ruthless, political persecution. He had lost his prestigious status as an admired and talented student and as the President of the Student Union, becoming a counter-revolutionary, avoided by everybody. Like a second class citizen, he also lost his right to Higher Education, a proper job, to join the Party and Army. And worse, he was arrested, put into jail and sentenced to death because of his criticism of the Cultural Revolution. He was saved, at the last second, on the execution ground, by his friends. It was so hard now to recall this ordeal. He sighed with emotion, comparing the past with his present situation.

Seeing a large poplar tree on the other bank of the river, his heart thumped with excitement. He remembered clearly that he had pledged his love to his first girlfriend, Yu Mei, under this tree just before the Cultural Revolution. A year before, in 1965, he had been a student in the last year of senior middle school.

He had fallen in love with fairy-like Yu Mei who was a student in another senior middle school. Yu Mei's father was a high ranking official but his own father was only a librarian and a rightist back in 1957: a political enemy of the Party. Realizing the sharp difference in their social status, Zhang Feng intended to give up his love for Yu Mei. Yet, her enduring love had emboldened him to continue their relationship. He planned to complete his Higher Education, thus entering the social elite and the upper class and gaining acceptance from Yu Mei's family. But a sudden political movement, the Cultural Revolution, like a fierce, red storm, had smashed his dream completely. He and Yu Mei were forced apart because they belonged to two different political groups: the Black and the Red. From that time on, they experienced many sorrows and joys in their partings and reunions.

However, near the end of this time, Zhang Feng lost his beloved Yu Mei because of the difficult situations caused by the political storm and from the discord that was sown by a wicked man called Cai Wenge, who not only destroyed Zhang Feng's relationship with Yu Mei, but also, plotted to have him sent to the execution ground. Unfortunately, Yu Mei's father died shortly after he regained his power. Losing both her lover and father, Yu Mei, in desperation, gave up her hopes in life and became a nun in the Taoist temple, at the top of the North Mountain.

Thinking about his relationship with Yu Mei in the past, Zhang Feng felt very sad. Actually, the purpose of his visit to the North Mountain today was to see Yu Mei again. Three years ago, when he had seen Yu Mei the last time in the Taoist temple there, she had asked Zhang Feng not to tell anyone about her decision to give up her secular life and also, not to visit her again.

But during the last three years, Zhang Feng found he missed Yu Mei all the time. Now, Zhang Feng thought he had found a reason to visit her as he would marry his childhood sweetheart, Dan Dan, next week. Dan Dan was a pretty and clever girl who had loved Zhang Feng secretly in the past but she had only been able to care for him as an 'elder sister' because she was only one year older: a marriage barrier, according to Chinese tradition. She, together with Zhang Feng, suffered terrible ordeals during the Cultural Revolution. Only after Zhang Feng had lost Yu Mei did he discover the truth that Dan Dan was actually younger than him and had loved him for so many years. She loved him so deeply, she was even willing to die for him. At last, Zhang Feng took her as his girlfriend.

After the Cultural Revolution, both of them went to Jili University. Dan Dan had also finished her Master's degree recently and was now working as a lecturer in the Department of Economy. As they were now in their mid-thirties, their parents and friends were urging them to marry sooner; thus, the wedding would be held this weekend.

Thinking about all this, he felt both bitter and sweet. He loved Dan Dan, but Yu Mei was still his dream lover. He stood up and walked towards the Taoist temple. He thought that Yu Mei might not care too much about his marriage to Dan Dan as she had probably now recovered from all the past, emotional trauma. Perhaps, he could persuade her to resume a secular life.

Walking to the gates of the temple and seeing the huge, stone lions, Zhang Feng recalled learning martial arts here with Master Hai Jing. At that time, he did not know that Hai Jing was Dan Dan's father and a counter-revolutionary. Fortunately, Hai Jing was rehabilitated after the Cultural Revolution, and interestingly, he would soon be Zhang Feng's father-in-law.

Walking into the big hall, Zhang Feng saw a group of Taoist priests sitting in meditation. He did not want to bother them so he walked to the rear of the temple.

Seeing an old priest sitting on a chair, Zhang Feng carefully asked,

"My honourable master, is the Taoist nun who came here three years ago still here?"

The old priest looked at Zhang Feng and asked slowly,

"Are you her friend? Why she did not inform you when she left here two years ago?"

"What? She has already left? Where did she go?"

"She did not tell us. She just said that her trauma had been healed and she would start a new life again."

Leaving the temple, Zhang Feng walked down the mountain and half way down, he sat on a large rock to rest. Suddenly, somebody patted him on his shoulder. He jumped up, instinctively adopting a self-defense posture.

"Hah! You have not forgotten your Kung Fu then?"

Looking at this man, Zhang Feng started to laugh; it was his best friend and brother-in-law, Wang Hai. Beside Wang Hai, stood Li He and Qing Lian. Both Li He and Qing Lian were his middle school classmates, and both of them were also active Red Guards during the Cultural Revolution. Now Li was a physician in the Province's hospital.

Qing Lian worked for the Jili daily newspaper as a journalist. She had loved Zhang Feng secretly when they studied together in middle school but she had become a fanatical Red Guard during the Cultural Revolution. At that time, she was in a constant dilemma as to whether she should love, or hate, Zhang Feng because politically, he was an 'Enemy of the People'. But when she attempted suicide because of sexual harassment from the village officer, she was saved by Zhang Feng. Since then, she had re-examined her mad and violent actions as an active Red Guard and regained her gentle and soft nature as a kind girl. She had loved Zhang Feng even more because he was also her saviour; yet she knew what her position was in Zhang Feng's heart; she had to stay in her place behind Yu Mei and Dan Dan.

In recent years, Li He had tried to pursue her. Her friends, including Zhang Feng, had also persuaded her to accept Li He's love and she had dated him quite often, but in her heart, she was still unable to forget Zhang Feng.

"Are you having a spring trip?" Zhang Feng asked them.

"Yes, yes, of course!" Wang Hai answered with a secretive expression in his eyes.

But both Li He and Qing Lian looked at Zhang Feng with confusion.

"Brother Feng, why are you here on your own? Your wedding is this weekend. Are you scared about getting married?" Li He asked.

"Did you have a quarrel with Dan Dan?" Qing Lian enquired.

"No, I am just relaxing because I have been so busy with my research these last few days. Dan Dan is arranging everything for the wedding so I do not need to worry about it."

Wang Hai said to Li He and Qing Lian,

"Could you please to go to the temple to see whether the Taoist religious rites have begun or not? Then come down to meet us after they are finished."

"Why are you not coming with us?" Li He asked, doubtfully.

"I will discuss Brother Feng's wedding with him. It will also be good for both of you to enjoy some time together," Wang Hai replied.

Qing Lian hesitated to leave but Li He took her hand and walked up with her to the temple.

After they had left, Zhang Feng asked Wang Hai,

"What on earth are you up to?"

"I could ask you the same question. What are you doing here?" Wang Hai asked, with a smile.

"I have already said that I am having a bit of relaxation here."

"Are you visiting somebody here?" Wang Hai asked, seriously.

"Do you know something about…" Zhang Feng was surprised.

"Yes, but you have not told me the truth. We are both relatives and life-death friends. You saved me and I saved you during the Cultural Revolution. Why did you not tell me that Yu Mei had become a nun in this temple three years ago?"

Seeing that he could not cover up the truth any longer, Zhang Feng replied,

"Because Yu Mei made me promise never to tell other people about her stay in the temple as a nun. How did you know about all this?"

Wang Hai told Zhang Feng that he had gone to their house this morning but only saw Dan Dan there and she looked unhappy. After Wang Hai's persistent questioning, Dan Dan had told him that Zhang Feng had secretly gone to the North Mountain that morning. She thought he was trying to see Yu Mei because she had become a nun in the temple three years ago. Wang Hai tried to comfort Dan Dan, saying Zhang Feng was not an unfaithful man. He was probably just going to see Yu Mei because he was worried about her situation and wanted to persuade her to return to ordinary life. Wang Hai then offered to go to the North Mountain to find Zhang Feng. If Zhang Feng had intended to betray Dan Dan, he would punish him.

Dan Dan felt better after listening to Wang Hai and jokily asked him, "Can you fight against him?"

Everybody knew that Zhang Feng was a powerful Kung Fu master and Wang Hai just liked to crack a joke. In order not to embarrass Zhang Feng, Wang Hai also asked Li He and Qing Lian to accompany him, telling them there were religious rites today on top of the Mountain.

After listening to Wang Hai's explanation, Zhang Feng relaxed. He told Wang Hai that Yu Mei had left the temple two years ago, probably to find a life far away from Jili City as she would have wanted to forget her sad experience here. Wang Hai said it was better for Yu Mei to leave for other place and to start a new life so that Zhang Feng and Dan Dan could enjoy their marriage. Wang Hai suggested that they should both go down the Mountain otherwise Li He and Qing Lian would blame him for cheating.

As they were walking back, Wang Hai mentioned the fortune telling picture, given to him by the old priest nearly twenty years ago, and said that the prophecy on the picture was quite accurate. It showed that Zhang Feng would move among three flowers (three ladies) in his life and the names of Yu Mei, Dan Dan and Qing Lian represented these flowers exactly. Zhang Feng said that it had all happened in the past; Yu Mei had left and Qing Lian would marry Li He and now, he only wanted to marry Dan Dan and enjoy their marriage.

He never could have guessed that those three flowers would continue to interfere with his life in the future.

PART I

A Successful Academic Career

Chapter I

A Happy Wedding

On one Sunday, decorated with lanterns and coloured streamers, a large hall of the Jili Hotel was filled with a happy atmosphere. The wedding of Zhang Feng and Dan Dan was to be held here. Standing at the entrance, they welcomed their guests. Zhang Feng's father, Zhang Wenbo, his mother, Hu Yun, Dan Dan's father, Hai Jing, and her mother, Wang Hui, were all busy with the arrangements for the ceremony and the banquet. Wearing a suit, Zhang Feng looked even more handsome than usual. With a white wedding gown on, Dan Dan looked like a beautiful peony in full bloom, which made Zhang Feng gaze at her constantly.

Looking at Zhang Feng shyly, she said,

"Why are you staring at me? Don't you know me today?"

"You are so beautiful today, Dan Dan." Zhang Feng replied.

"Am I more beautiful than…?"

Dan Dan wanted to ask whether she was more beautiful than Yu Mei but she stopped herself. She knew that Yu Mei had left the temple and this city and she would no longer interfere in the relationship between her and Zhang Feng.

The first guests included the directors from Jili University and his Department. They all admired his talent and capability and were confident that he would soon become a famous scholar. Hearing a hearty laugh, Zhang Feng knew Wang Hai was arriving. Then he saw Wang Hai in a Chinese tunic suit and his wife, Zhang Feng's sister, Zhang Lin, in a pretty, pink skirt. Wang Hai praised Zhang Feng loudly for his handsome looks and also admired Dan Dan for her devastating beauty. Zhang Lin embraced Dan Dan and said,

"Dan Dan, even ten years ago I knew you would be my sister-in-law."

Wang Hai suddenly grabbed Zhang Feng's hand,

"Brother Feng, coming into the main hall of the hotel, I suddenly recalled that you saved me from the gunfire here in the civil strife during the Cultural Revolution." Then he started to wipe his eyes.

"Do not mention such sad things from the past, Wang Hai, today is a special day of great rejoicing for Brother Feng," a voice said at the back of Wang Hai.

It was Li He, coming in with Qing Lian. She wore a bright green shirt and trousers and looked like a slender lotus. Dan Dan brought them into the hall but Qing Lian stayed with Zhang Feng. With a loving glance, she said to Zhang Feng,

"Brother Feng, you are so handsome today."

"Li He is also handsome and has such a scholarly manner," Zhang Feng replied quickly. As she moved into the hall, Qing Lian mumbled,

"How can he be compared with you…?"

A lot of guests arrived before the wedding started formally. Suddenly Zhang Lin ran into the hall and said to Zhang Feng:

"Brother, there is an impressive car just arriving with an old man in it. Maybe he is a high ranking official."

Zhang Feng felt strange because he had not invited any high ranking official today. When he got to the main entrance, he saw an old man walking slowly towards him. He started to speak to Zhang Feng before Zhang Feng could identify him.

"Xiao Feng, you do not recognize me?"

Looking carefully at his face, Zhang Feng did recognize him. He was Director Liu, an old subordinate of Yu Mei's father, the late secretary of the provincial party committee, Li Jianguo. Over twenty years ago, he brought Yu Mei to meet Zhang Feng at Fengman District, near Song Hua Lake, for a romantic holiday. On the day he drove them back to Jili City, they witnessed the beginning of the Cultural Revolution. Zhang Feng also met him at the funeral of Li Jianguo when the Cultural Revolution was over. Zhang Feng knew from the media that Director Liu was now the top leader, first secretary of the provincial party committee. He said to Zhang Feng,

"Sorry, Xiao Feng, I have come here without your invitation. But I must come because you are the saviour of Secretary Li. His spirit in the heavens asks me to congratulate you on your wedding."

"Not at all, Uncle Liu. I did not send you an invitation because I know you are very busy with your leadership work."

Walking into the big hall, Secretary Liu said,

"I hear that you have made great achievements, academically, but have you ever thought about the possibility of entering official circles? The new leaders of the Party and Government are calling for the promotion of young and well-educated officials to replace the old, poorly educated ones, in order to construct a modern and prosperous China. Secretary Li mentioned this before his death."

Zhang Feng was dumbfounded. Yes, he could still remember the suggestion from Secretary Li, Yu Mei's father, before his death. He had encouraged Zhang Feng to enter official circles to improve the political environment and to make China more democratic which would prevent the recurrence of the Cultural Revolution. But at the moment, he was following in his father's footsteps by trying to become a well-known scholar. So he said, hesitantly,

"Let me think about it, Uncle Liu."

"Do not worry, I will wait for you."

Wang Hai voluntarily acted as the host of the wedding. Giving a humorous opening speech, he asked the bride and groom to describe their feelings. Making a deep bow, Zhang Feng said,

"Thank you all for coming to my wedding. I feel like I am in a dream and I almost cannot believe that such a happy event is finally happening. Recalling the dark storm of the Cultural Revolution, we all suffered from endless ordeals and persecution, and could only work hard to survive, with no hope of having a good future and happy marriage. We should value today's hard-won happiness."

Looking at Dan Dan, he said,

"Most of you know, Dan Dan is my childhood sweetheart. Because I did not know she was the same age, I foolishly regarded her as my 'elder sister' and ignored her love for me and never guessed that she loved me. Later, I realized I had made a terrible mistake: she actually loved me so deeply she was willing to sacrifice everything and even die for me. To have such clever and beautiful lady who has such enduring love makes me the happiest man in the world."

All the guests applauded his speech warmly. Dan Dan said,

"I am very happy today, not only because I have Brother Feng's love but also because he can now make his contribution to our society with his talent and hard work. During the horrible Cultural Revolution, he was deprived of the rights of a normal citizen. We give our heartfelt thanks to Mr. Deng Xiaoping, who brought order out of chaos and gave us a bright future. Brother Feng and I are not only a couple, but also, fighting comrades, side by side. We will continue to strive for a more equal, democratic and prosperous society."

The guests applauded warmly, once again, especially Secretary Liu. Then Zhang Feng and Dan Dan kissed each other after being urged on by the guests. Dan Dan looked quite shy doing this in front of so many people. At last Wang Hai said,

"Some of you probably do not know that the groom and bride are not an ordinary couple. They are actually life-death lovers. During the Cultural Revolution, Zhang Feng saved Dan Dan twice and Dan Dan saved him once. So they are also each other's saviours."

Loud applause broke out in the hall.

A rich banquet followed. Zhang Feng had specially asked the top chef in the hotel, Master Wang, to prepare the food for his wedding. Master Wang had retired recently but he was willing to cook for the wedding after he heard about the experiences of Zhang Feng and Wang Hai in this hotel during the Cultural Revolution. It was typical North-East Chinese cuisine with some of the dishes created by him. The drinks included famous Yushu spirit and Harbin beer.

Zhang Feng and Dan Dan made a toast to the guests on every table. Seeing some guests reminded him of sad stories from the Revolution. Firstly, he saw old Principal Chang from his senior middle school. Now with a lot of grey hair, Mr. Chang had retired a few years ago. He embraced Zhang Feng emotionally and recalled the help and support they gave each other during those times.

On the table with Li Li and Chen Xing, Zhang Feng congratulated them on their marriage and recalled sadly the death of Xu Jianguo, the late boyfriend of Li Li, who died during the civil strife, and the execution of the two brothers from the Four Talents of the River City. In his memory, the big brother and the third brother had fallen on the ground in front of him and he was saved at the last second. He started to wipe his eyes. Patting his back and comforting him, Li Li said,

"That was all over in the past. Their spirits in the heavens will bless you as they know you are well and having this happy wedding."

On another table, Zhang Feng met teacher Ye who used to teach him singing in the past. She was fifty years old now and still liked to talk. She said:

"It would be so nice if teacher Sun could be here today."

Zhang Feng felt suddenly sad, as teacher Sun had been beaten to death by the violent Red Guards. He said, with grief and indignation,

"It is all because of that evil red storm, so many innocent people died."

Teacher Ye tried to comfort him and said it was all over and that such a tragedy would never be repeated.

After drinking some spirit, Zhang Feng felt a little dizzy. Dan Dan quickly came to him and gave him a cup of tea to reduce the effect of the alcohol. Seeing that the guests had all finished eating, Wang Hai asked the waiters to move the tables and chairs to the sides of the wall and said,

"Dear friends, the banquet is finished and the dancing starts now! Please dance gracefully, as much as you like."

During the Cultural Revolution, like all other entertainment, dancing had been banned. It was criticized as part of a bourgeois life style but now, people could dance any time they liked, without fear. The guests knew Zhang Feng was a very good dancer. His athletic figure and handsome face made all the ladies want to dance with him.

Music played and the guests easily formed a circle and watched the groom and bride have their first dance. Zhang Feng gently invited Dan Dan to dance the Waltz but she did not dance well. Zhang Feng had given her a few lessons before the wedding. She was a bit nervous at the beginning but gradually, she followed his steps with the help of his strong arms to guide her. Gazing at him, with deep feeling, she asked him quietly:

"Do I dance as well as she?"

Zhang Feng knew it was Yu Mei she meant. Yu Mei could dance professionally but Zhang Feng wanted to encourage Dan Dan so he said,

"You dance better than her."

Dan Dan knew Zhang Feng was cracking a joke and she pretended to be unhappy.

"Nonsense!"

Watching the graceful dancing of the groom and bride, the guests all warmly applauded. Then everybody tried to find a partner to dance with. The ladies all wanted to dance with Zhang Feng and the gentlemen wanted to dance with Dan Dan. Wang Hai got the first chance to dance with Dan Dan but

Zhang Lin, his wife, looked rather unhappy because Wang Hai used to love Dan Dan. When Li He invited Zhang Lin to dance, she felt happy again.

Qing Lian was the first to get the chance to dance with Zhang Feng. She looked very young and beautiful on that day, like a fresh lotus flower. Zhang Feng danced with her enthusiastically because he was so happy. Working in the media, she had to attend a lot of social activities so she danced very gracefully. Zhang Feng said to her,

"You dance so well."

"Because I am dancing with you!" she exclaimed.

Like a lotus in full bloom, she flushed and was intoxicated by the lively melody of the music. Her eyes were half closed and her body moved closer to Zhang Feng's chest. With tears in her eyes, she muttered to Zhang Feng,

"I am so happy right now. I wish time would stop at this moment."

Zhang Feng knew that Qing Lian still loved him, even though she would marry Li He very soon. Worrying that Dan Dan and Li He might notice their bodies so close to each other, Zhang Feng tried to move away a little from Qing Lian but she said, shyly,

"Do not worry. At least we are life-death friends."

She actually reminded Zhang Feng that he had saved her when she tried to commit suicide, and that she had saved him from being shot. Zhang Feng was moved by what she said and held her closer again, saying,

"Yes, otherwise we would not be dancing here today."

After dancing with Qing Lian, Li Li came up to dance with Zhang Feng. He asked her about her life with Chen Xing. She said Chen was a simple and honest man, a good husband, but was not romantic. He was not like Zhang Feng and Xu Jianguo, who could make women's hearts skip a beat. Zhang Feng suddenly remembered that Li Li had once kissed him when he left the chemical factory to go to university after the Cultural Revolution. He knew then that she actually loved him and regarded him as more than a younger brother. Zhang Feng quite understood the psychology of women and knew he was attractive to them but he was a faithful man, so he tried to shift the topic of conversation and asked about the working conditions in Li Li's factory.

The cheerful wedding finished later that afternoon. Zhang Feng and Dan Dan returned to their home. It was simply a bigger room in their previous student dormitory because the University did not have enough suitable accommodation for lecturers. There was no private housing market in China at that time. All employers had to wait for Government funding to build suitable properties for their employees. This meant there was always a chronic shortage of housing, and people had to wait a long time, often between five and ten years, to get basic accommodation. Zhang Feng and Dan Dan were lucky to have this simple room. The University gave these kinds of rooms to young, married teachers.

There was also a common room, used as a kitchen, for four to five families but with no gas supply, residents had to use the diesel stove to cook meals. There was no bathroom and only a public toilet. Yet Zhang Feng and Dan Dan still felt happy because they had grown up in even poorer living conditions, especially in the countryside during the Revolution. It was quite pleasant to have their own accommodation as a lot of young men still lived with their parents.

This simple bridal chamber was decorated charmingly. Sitting shyly on the bed with a red, silk quilt and looking like a peony in full bloom, Dan Dan waited for her husband's intimate caresses. They had not had sex despite being boyfriend and girlfriend for eight years because they still observed Chinese moral traditions. Feeling a little dizzy because of the alcohol, Zhang Feng sat on the chair to drink his tea. The gifts given by their friends on the table, were mostly everyday articles such as mirrors, thermos bottles, cooking utensils and clothes. He smiled and said to Dan Dan,

"There are so many gifts! There's enough for our children and grandchildren!"

"What are you talking about?" Dan Dan asked, shyly. Zheng Feng then opened the greeting cards to see who had sent them and he read the contents aloud to Dan Dan. But after opening a very special looking card, he was shocked as there were no words inside… just a painting of a white, plum blossom. 'It's from her!' he thought. It was obviously a card sent by Yu Mei.

"What's wrong?" Dan Dan asked.

"Oh, nothing, just a card sent by an old friend who I have not contacted for quite a while."

Yet in his mind, he could not control his excitement. Where was she? How did she know that he was married? Did she feel happy or bitter? To cover up his emotions, he turned on the radio. Just by chance, the famous Canton music: *A Moonlit Night in Spring on the River Bank with Flowers* was being played which had been the music accompanying Yu Mei's solo dance when they met at the Art Festival. Suddenly, the graceful dancing figure of Yu Mei rose up before his eyes. But this was his wedding night and his beloved wife, Dan Dan, was waiting for his loving caress.

Not knowing what to do, he stood up and walked to the window to open it but the bright moonlight made Yu Mei's image more real. He wanted to be immersed in his pleasant memories of Yu Mei but he did not want to let Dan Dan down. Just then, he felt a soft body touching his back.

"You miss her now?" Dan Dan said, gently.

"No, No," Zhang Feng answered, weakly.

"You are kidding me. With this beautiful music and in the bright moonlight, you are visualizing her pretty image, aren't you?"

There was no sign of anger in her voice. She carried on,

"Relax. I understand you even if I can be a jealous woman. Being unable to forget your life-death lover shows that you are a man with affection and faith. Today's wedding should have been your wedding to Yu Mei if the Cultural Revolution had not happened. Yet, she has started her new life now and she will find a good partner. Let's bless her."

Facing open-minded Dan Dan, Zhang Feng felt a bit ashamed. He knew he should love and care for Dan Dan even more and try hard to become a good husband. He carried Dan Dan to the bed, kissing and embracing her. Dan Dan closed her eyes happily and both of them entered into the climax of love.

CHAPTER II

Give Freedom to Writers

Two years had passed quickly. Zhang Feng did well in both his family life and career. Dan Dan gave birth to a healthy boy which pleased everybody in the family. The boy was good looking and would be a handsome young man when he grew up. He was named Zhang Danfeng. China started to introduce a birth control policy to slow down the increase in the huge population from the 1980s. This meant that each couple could only have one child but the Chinese tradition was to have a boy to continue the family tree. Therefore, they were extremely lucky to have a boy at that time, although Zhang Feng and Dan Dan did not care too much about this, as both of them were more Western-oriented. They spoiled their baby and always fed him well and took him to playgrounds or theme parks.

Zhang Feng also achieved more academically. He published two books and many more articles and became very well known in the academic circles of literary criticism, foreign literature and comparative literature. Because he was so exceptional, he was promoted to Associate Professor and was appointed the Deputy Director of the Chinese Department. Also, because he was a Party member, he worked as the Secretary of the University Youth League. It meant he had the chance to become an official in the Party or Government, even though he was not interested in working in a Government department as an official at that time. However, he still remembered the dying wish of late Secretary Li and the suggestion made by Secretary Liu at his wedding.

Summer arrived in the River City. On one Sunday morning, in the new, one-bed flat allotted to them by the University, Dan Dan finished her washing in their newly bought washing machine and hung the clothes up to dry in the courtyard. She said to Zhang Feng:

"It's so handy to have a washing machine. In the past, it took half a day to wash everything by hand but now it only takes an hour thanks to Wang Hai's washing machine voucher. I hope we can get a TV voucher later."

"The state owned factories are so inefficient. They cannot produce enough products, even with the huge demand from customers. I hope we can introduce some market competition one day," replied Zhang Feng.

Pointing at him, Dan Dan said, jokily,

"Be careful with your political standpoint, my Secretary of the Youth League! You seem very keen to follow the capitalist system!"

Zhang Feng smiled.

"The leaders were wrongly persecuted during the Cultural Revolution because there were no capitalist elements in the economy at all. The economy looks better now but we cannot simply follow the old ways of the centrally controlled economy which looks stable but is not efficient. There is no incentive for workers. Our life looks better than in the past, but we still need coupons to buy food and day-to-day things. If you look at the Western world, their economy has developed really rapidly in the last three decades. Marx did not realize that the capitalist countries can self-adjust their own social contradictions and build a welfare system. We should learn from the West."

Dan Dan said,

"I attended a conference on economic issues once and I saw a lot of radical, young economists calling for economic reform. But some rigid officials still insist that we cannot ever follow capitalism. We should have political reform as well. If we could have more open-minded, young officials leading the Party and Government, then we might get those reforms."

She looked at Zhang Feng.

"What do you think? Leave your professorship and become the Secretary of the City Council?"

"Let me think about it," Zhang Feng smiled.

The weather was lovely. Zhang Feng and Dan Dan put their son in his pram and walked to South Bank Park. There were a lot of people there, playing and relaxing. They noticed that people's clothes were much more colorful than during the Cultural Revolution when people could only wear blue and black or yellow army uniforms for the Red Guards. You could be criticized of having a bourgeois life style if you wore colourful and fashionable clothes. But now, women wore bright skirts or trendy shirts and jeans; men wore Hong Kong style shirts, casual trousers, and even flared trousers. People were dancing and singing on the grass. Wearing modern clothes, a young man carried a huge tape deck, playing a love song by the famous Taiwanese female singer Deng Lijun. Compared with the dull and rigid lifestyle during the Revolution, people now seemed to be happy and carefree.

Sighing with emotion, Zhang Feng said to Dan Dan,

"Those of us who experienced the storm really appreciate the beauty of the park and the nice weather. But there are still some rigid leaders complaining that beautiful music like this is unhealthy. They even criticize the new, fashionable clothes, newly released films and plays, newly published novels and poems, and say all these things are not revolutionary but examples of spiritual corruption. Luckily for us, the open-minded General Secretary of the Party, Hu Yaobang, has crushed these left-wing leaders and has said that socialist spiritual civilization should be colourful."

A sudden clear and melodious voice broke into Dan Dan's agreement with Zhang Feng.

"Ah! What a handsome little boy!"

It was Qing Lian and Li He coming towards them. Qing Lian bent down and kissed Dan Feng. Meeting their good friends like this made both Zhang Feng and Dan Dan very happy.

"We have brought a picnic with us. Let's all eat together," Qing Lian announced.

"It is the food you all like," Li He said.

They found a suitable place under the shadow of a large tree. Putting a plastic sheet on the ground, Qing Lian lifted out bread, ham, sausage, cooked eggs with spices and pork in cans from her bag. Dan Dan took some bottles of orange juice from the pram and they all sat down to enjoy the food. Zhang

Feng asked how Li He and Qing Lian had been doing recently. They said they were fine now that Li He was the Director of the Internal Medicine Department of the hospital and Qing Lian was the Deputy Director of the News Department of the Jili Daily Newspaper.

Zhang Feng asked,

"Why are you still not married?"

Looking at Qing Lian, Li He answered,

"Because she is always too busy."

"Do not delay for too long! Women sometimes have difficulty having children after 35," Dan Dan commented.

"Yes, we should marry soon. Maybe we will have a daughter and she will marry Brother Feng's son in the future, and we will be relatives," said Li He.

Caressing the little boy and looking at Li He, Qing Lian murmured,

"I may not want to marry you."

As Dan Dan and Qing Lian talked about looking after babies, Zhang Feng quietly asked Li He why Qing Lian did not want to marry him yet.

"I feel that sometimes, she is as meek as a cat, but sometimes, as fierce as a tiger, more like the violent Red Guard she used to be in the Cultural Revolution. But sometimes, I feel that maybe, there in another man in her heart."

Zhang Feng was startled at the words of Li He. He wondered whether she still loved him but surely she was aware of his status as a husband and a father. Recalling how immersed she had been when dancing with him, Zhang Feng began to worry. He tried to comfort Li He and said Qing Lian needed a bit of gentle coaxing.

Li He looked at Zhang Feng and said seriously,

"Will you try to persuade her when you have time?"

Zhang Feng noticed the hint in Li He's words and quickly promised to do it.

Zhang Feng was kept busy with his work in the Department. Dan Dan complained that he did not share the house work with her. She did almost all the house work at home in order to give Zhang Feng more time for his teaching, research and administrative work. Zhang Feng's lectures were always well received by the students because he was open-minded and not restricted by the old theories of revolutionary literature and art.

One day, he went to his elective course: 'Literature Creation'. The Department had arranged a bigger lecture hall for him as there were too many students in his last lesson. He thought that, maybe, this time, the hall would be half filled but he saw over 30 students he did not recognize, waiting outside the hall, anxiously.

"Fellow students, are you all coming to attend my lecture? Why don't you come in? You are not the Chinese Department students, are you?"

A pretty girl answered,

"Teacher Zhang, we are all from other Departments. I study in the Foreign Languages Department. We all like literature and art, so we would like to attend your lecture but the hall is very full already. Can you let us in? We don't mind standing to listen."

Other students also wanted permission to get in. Zhang Feng was moved by their enthusiasm. Entering the lecture hall, Zhang Feng heard warm applause. The hall was indeed very full.

"Thank you all for coming to my lecture. There are about 30 students from other Departments also wanting to attend. Could you please make some room for them? Thank you!"

The students inside kindly gave up some seats to these students and for those who did not have seats, they just used the stairs between the rows of seats.

Moved by the enthusiasm of the students, Zhang Feng tried to give them a good lesson. He wrote the title on the board: 'The Social Function of Literature and Art'. He told them how literature and art represented social life. Literary and art works from different periods, gave us a picture of society at that time, and described people's experiences and destinies, their sorrows and happiness. Literature and art praised the true, the good and the beautiful and condemned the false, the ugly and the evil. Literature and art could not be used as political propaganda. Hearing this point, the students applauded loudly. These young students seemed to know the country had been a cultural desert during the Cultural Revolution and literature and art had been used to advertise personality cults and false revolutionary propaganda.

Thinking of criticism of the theory of human nature by the rigid, left-wing leaders a few years ago, Zhang Feng said it was right to say that literature and art should describe the beauty of humanity. Why did the works of Shakespeare attract people all over the world? Because he created a great variety of characters, such as the melancholy Hamlet, the fatuous King Lear, the jealous Othello and the power-craving Macbeth, and endless noble and more mediocre characters. So it was not wrong to say the core element of literature and art was the theory of human nature. The students applauded loudly again at his point but Zhang Feng had noticed that Secretary Liu of the Department, sitting at the back, frowned with displeasure.

Talking about literary creation, Zhang Feng said that the works of some writers truly represented the ordeals of people during the Cultural Revolution. These works were known as 'trauma literature' or 'scar literature'.

"Yes, the Cultural Revolution was a horrible disaster. Literature can help us to draw lessons from it and to prevent any recurrence of this historical tragedy."

The students burst into thunderous applause.

After the lesson, a lot of students stayed behind to ask questions. He tried to give them satisfactory answers. When he finally left the building, a clear voice sounded behind him:

"Please wait, Teacher Zhang."

Turning back, Zhang Feng saw the pretty girl who had talked with him before the lecture walking towards him. She said Zhang Feng had given a very good lecture and also, that the University might set up an amateur Shakespeare company, enabling teachers and students who could perform Shakespeare to put on his plays. Zhang Feng said happily,

"We are thinking the same thing! We are preparing to establish a Shakespeare Association of Jili Province to get involved in performing plays at the First Shakespeare Festival in Beijing next year. You might be able to recommend some talented friends to join us."

"Can I join the company? My name is Wang Li. I am a core member of the art performing group in the Foreign Languages Department. I danced and sang in the last University art festival and also acted as the program announcer."

"Ah, yes, I remember that you danced very well and your voice was very pleasant as well. You are welcome to join our company," Zhang Feng replied.

What he did not tell Wang Li was that he associated Wang Li's dancing with that of Yu Mei during the festival. Wang Li was a good talker and it looked like she knew Zhang Feng was very good at music and art. He was handsome and talented and should be the perfect choice to perform Hamlet, she felt. Just when Zhang Feng wanted to ask where Wang Li had learnt to dance, he saw Dan Dan watching him from under a tree, not far away. He quickly said goodbye to Wang Li, and then walked over to Dan Dan.

"You are still attractive to ladies, I see, even though you are a middle aged man now."

Zhang Feng told her that this girl had attended his lecture and wanted to join the performing company.

"Then she will be able to spend more time around you."

Dan Dan knew her husband was very attractive to women but she also knew he was faithful so she was just teasing him.

"Ok, don't worry. I'm teasing you!"

She smiled at his embarrassment but then said seriously,

"Be careful when you give your lectures. Do not touch on sensitive political issues like the 'Four Basic Principles' even though the Cultural Revolution has ended. I heard from a colleague whose husband works in your Department that the Secretary, Mr. Liu Qi, did not like your lecture. He said that you are making yourself conspicuous by acting differently."

The 'Four Basic Principles' were to uphold socialism; to support the people's democratic dictatorship; to uphold the leadership of the Communist Party and to support Marxism-Leninism and Mao Zedong Thought.

"No wonder he frowned when the students applauded my lecture today. There are still some rigid, left-wing leaders who do not like political reform which would make our country more free and democratic. The truth is, they do not want to lose their privileges."

Thinking for a while, he continued,

"It looks like I should be sure to attend the political and ideology forum in the University next week. But I have to go anyway because of my post as the Secretary of the Youth League."

Walking arm in arm with Zhang Feng, Dan Dan said,

"It is alright. Just be a little bit more careful. We are the social elite now but not in the Five Black category. My husband did not even fear the bullets during the Cultural Revolution, let alone a few rigid left-wing leaders!"

The Five Black category included the political enemies of the Revolution.

"Dearest wife, can I have braised pork with soy sauce this evening?"

"Greedy again? Be careful you don't get a pot belly, otherwise, no ladies will talk to you!"

"I do not care, as long as I have you as my beautiful wife."

They left the campus, cheerfully.

A week later, the big conference hall in Jili University was full of staff, lecturers and officials. This was a forum organized by the Propaganda Department of the provincial party committee. The top leaders wanted to know the reactions and feedback from people to the new political policies. There were two different political groups in the party: the open-minded reformers and the rigid, left-wing elements.

Before the meeting started, Zhang Feng met his former university classmate, Li Qiu, who now worked in the Propaganda Department since his graduation. He was an overcautious person and always obeyed his superiors. He greeted Zhang Feng warmly and introduced another official in his fifties.

"Zhang Feng, this is Director Shen of our Department. He will lead today's conference."

Strangely, Shen did not shake hands with Zhang Feng, and just said coldly to Li Qiu,

"Let's go, the meeting will start soon."

They went in. Zhang Feng could not understand why Director Shen had treated him so coldly. A lady called out behind him, just as he was entering the hall.

"Brother Feng! Will you deliver a speech today?"

Turning back, Zhang Feng saw Qing Lian, in a blue suit. She looked very smart. Qing Lian told Zhang Feng that she had come to the forum to gather news for a report. She always looked very happy whenever she met Zhang Feng. He just treated her as his younger sister. They entered the hall together and Zhang Feng's colleagues greeted him and also looked at Qing Lian with envy.

The University Party Secretary started talking first. He told them that the main purpose today would be to collect the opinions and feedback for new policies implemented since the economic reforms had started. He emphasized that there would be no political punishments like those in 1957; everybody would be free to give their opinion.

Surprisingly, Secretary Liu Qi in Zhang Feng's Department stood up first. He fiercely criticized the bourgeois spiritual corruption against the leadership of the Communist Party. He said, some people with ulterior motives, had tried to cut down the banner of Chairman Mao and attack the leadership of the Communist Party in the name of reform and democracy. Probably seeing Zhang Feng, he continued that somebody had tried to promote the theory of humanity and had asked for more freedom for writers, ignoring the leadership of the party. Hearing this, Zhang Feng felt very angry but Qing Lian held his arm tightly when he tried to stand up to speak. She wanted to calm him down.

At this moment, a teaching and research director from the Chemistry Department, Mr. Huang Lei, stood up to refute the opinion of Secretary Liu. Zhang Feng and Huang Lei got along very well with each other because both of them were members of the sports teams before graduation, and both were open-minded, young men. Huang Lei said that somebody still wanted to have a personality cult and to suppress the democratic atmosphere with the excuse of struggling against capitalism and spiritual corruption. The Central Committee of the Chinese Communist Party had already indicated clearly that it was Mao Zedong who had launched the Cultural Revolution wrongly and caused the ten-year disaster. Why was it still necessary to have his banner? Was it because some leaders were not happy with the liberation of ideology and intended to go back to rigid Stalinism, and not allow the free development of different artistic forms and styles? After Huang's speech, some speakers supported his opinion but others did not agree but it looked as if there were more in favour.

At last, Zhang Feng could wait no longer to stand up and talk. He said the evil influence of the Cultural Revolution remained even though it had ended. Some people were not happy with Deng Xiaoping's policy of opening reform and the liberation of ideology. Their hidden purpose was that they did not want to give democracy to the people in order to keep their privileges. He reminded the audience that the initial political proposition of the Chinese Communist Party was to establish a democratic new China and not a feudal dynasty with a dictatorship. The leadership of the Party could stay as it was but democracy had to exist inside the Party and also, be extended to ordinary people outside the Party. People should have freedom of speech but not political punishment. The country would not be prosperous without freedom of thinking.

The audience burst into thunderous applause as Zhang Feng finished his speech. The left-wingers looked unhappy with dull, long faces, especially Director Shen. In the excitement, Qing Lian stood up to applaud. A lot of young people also followed her, giving Zhang Feng a standing ovation.

Chapter III

Who Presents This Flower?

After the conference was finished, Zhang Feng and Qing Lian met Huang Lei in the corridor. The two men embraced each other warmly and praised each other's speeches.

"Just wait for tomorrow's report in the Jili Daily! I am so pleased that so many people support the reformers!" Qing Lian said.

Zhang Feng and Huang Lei asked Qing Lian not to mention their names in the report.

"Don't worry. It is not 1957 any longer and the Cultural Revolution is over."

Patting Huang Lei's shoulder, Zhang Feng said,

"Yes, both of us would be denounced as 'rightists' if we were back in 1957."

"Not just the two of us! Over half of the audience today would have been called 'rightists'," Huang Lei smiled.

They talked about their work and arranged to play basketball at the weekend.

Back in the Propaganda Department, Director Shen asked Li Qiu,

"Your former university classmate, Zhang Feng, was in the limelight today. What did you think about his speech?"

Li Qiu had noticed that Director Shen was unhappy about Zhang Feng's speech so he said,

"Zhang Feng is an arrogant man. He has been influenced deeply by Western capitalist ideology."

"Do you know, I worked in the recruitment office of the Education Department in 1977, when the country had just restarted higher education exams after the Cultural Revolution had ended. I opposed his acceptance as he'd had political problems. Sure enough, it seems that he still hates Chairman Mao. It would be very dangerous if he is appointed as a high ranking official; the Party would collapse under his leadership," Shen said.

The next day, Zhang Feng prepared to go to the University after lunch. With a newspaper in her hand, Dan Dan walked in.

"Look at today's Jili Daily! The front page is a report on your conference yesterday with the head line: 'Support Ideology Liberation and the Reform Movement.' The report specially mentions your speech. This article is a head-on blow to the left-wing group."

Zhang Feng was happy and asked Dan Dan to pass the newspaper to him but she held onto it and asked,

"Please answer me a question first. Did Qing Lian write this report?"

"Yes, it should be her, as she attended the conference and sat next to me."

Dan Dan pretended to be unhappy.

"Why is she always so close to you? Do not forget, she will marry Li He soon."

Zhang Feng gently patted Dan Dan's shoulder.

"My dear wife, why are you jealous? We are all old friends. When you think that she used to be an active Red Guard during the Cultural Revolution but now, she is thoroughly criticizing that mad movement… It can't be easy."

Dan Dan smiled and passed the newspaper to him.

"Yes, because you saved her and then influenced her, she regained her tender and kind nature. During the Revolution, Yu Mei was your girlfriend, I was your 'elder sister' and Qian Lian was like a female servant. But now, Yu Mei has left, I became your wife and then Qing Lian moved one step nearer and became your 'sister'. So she has every right to get close to you. But my woman's intuition tells me that she still loves you so you should look out for yourself."

Zhang Feng hugged and kissed her.

"Alright, alright! I only have you in my heart." Dan Dan closed her eyes and enjoyed his caress.

In the Director's office of the Jili Daily, Director Lv Guohao was talking to Qing Lian.

"Qing Lian, I asked you to keep a balance between the two different arguments but you have only focused on the opinion of the reformers and under-reported the views of the left-wing. We will be in trouble now. A phone call from the Propaganda Department has criticized your report; they will investigate the journalist responsible. If the worst happened, you might lose your post of Deputy Director."

Qing Lian said, indifferently,

"I do not care about this post."

Mr. Lv was an open-minded person. He actually wanted to protect Qing Lian.

"Do not worry. I will contact Secretary Liu, the first secretary of the provincial party committee. He used to be the subordinate of late Secretary Li and also suffered during the Cultural Revolution. He is very different from Director Shen; he will support the reformers."

Two days later, Dan Dan told Zhang Feng about Qing Lian's problem. Dan Dan had a good female friend whose husband worked for the provincial party committee. Through her husband, Dan Dan discovered that Secretary Liu had spoken highly of this report but did not criticize it. Secretary Liu had said the Party should support democracy and create a relaxed, political atmosphere. Different political opinions should not be suppressed any more. He also criticized the actions of the Propaganda Department.

"It looks like Secretary Liu shares the same viewpoint as you. No wonder he is encouraging you to enter official circles," Dan Dan said. "If most top leaders are as open-minded as he is, our country has a promising future. Then you do not need to worry about your 'sister' Qing Lian!" Dan Dan said, jokingly.

"Of course, I am pleased it has worked out the right way," Zhang Feng replied.

Zhang Feng had been very busy recently with setting up the Shakespeare Association of Jili Province, which would be the first, province-level, association in China. Both traditional Chinese culture and Western culture returned to people's lives after the Cultural Revolution. Among all of Western literature and art, English and French literature were particularly attractive to Chinese readers. Shakespeare's works were especially regarded as the pearl in the art crown.

In China, his dramas attracted millions of readers and theatre fans. In Zhang Feng's two volume books: *An Introduction to Shakespeare,* he determined that the reason why Shakespeare could be accessed by Chinese people was, firstly, the poetic representation in his drama. China is a country with a longstanding poetic tradition. Secondly, the deep philosophy in his writing. Philosophy is at the core of Chinese culture. And thirdly, and most importantly, the beauty and the variety of his characters which reflected all of human nature. This especially attracted Chinese people after the Cultural Revolution as the literary works during that period could only represent revolutionary policy and the leadership of the party. All the characters followed the same revolutionary pattern. Shakespeare was a lighthouse in China's 'Renaissance of Literature and Art'.

A lot of teachers and students waited in a big room behind the stage of the University auditorium. They all wanted to play in 'Hamlet' which Zhang Feng's performing company would produce in the forthcoming first Shakespeare Festival of China, to be held in Beijing. Zhang Feng was one of the organizers. He had invited Professor Wei Wei from the provincial art institute to direct this play. Sitting on chairs, Zhang Feng, Wei Wei and another two judges conducted auditions to select actors and actresses. Those auditioning were all fans of the performing arts and were keen to get a part. It was not difficult to select people for minor parts but it was much harder to fill the major roles.

A clear voice broke into the conversation between Zhang Feng and Professor Mei,

"Teacher Zhang, may I play Ophelia?"

A pretty girl came up to the table.

"Is it you, Wang Li?" Zhang Feng recognized her.

She was the student from the foreign languages department who had attended his lecture recently. She had actually mentioned on the day that she would like to play a role in a Shakespeare play.

Professor Wei was interested in her offer. He asked,

"Why do you think you are suitable for the role of Ophelia?"

"I am a keen fan of Shakespeare. I can recite a lot of famous lines in Shakespeare drama in either Chinese or English. I am good at singing and dancing and a member of the University art company."

"Very good!"

Zhang Feng, Professor Wei and the two other judges all felt very happy.

Professor Wei asked,

"Can you perform a speech from 'Hamlet'?"

"No problem."

She performed Ophelia's sorrowful speech from Scene I, Act III, after she sees the madness of the prince,

"O, what a noble mind is here o'erthrown!

The courtier's, soldier's, scholar's, eye, tongue, sword:

The expectancy and the rose of the fair state,

The glass of fashion, and the mould of form

The observ'd of all observers, quite, quite down."

While reciting, she portrayed the inner sorrow of Ophelia through actions and emotional feeling. She entered so deeply into the role that tears streamed down her cheeks.

"Excellent!" All the judges started to applaud.

Wang Li got this role straight away. To Zhang Feng's surprise, Huang Lei also came to the auditions. He said, he had been a fan of arts and performing since his childhood and he used to be a member of a children's performing group. He got the role of Horatio after an audition and he was very pleased.

They had still not found a suitable person to play Hamlet and were feeling a little anxious. Professor Wei gazed at Zhang Feng for a few minutes and smiled.

"We do not need to bother about this any longer. Hamlet is already here!"

The other two judges also looked at Zhang Feng.

"Yes, Teacher Zhang is the best person to play Hamlet."

"Do you know, Teacher Zhang is not only a famous Shakespearean scholar but also, an excellent musician and artiste. Twenty years ago, when he was a student in senior middle school, he used to sing solo, play the violin and conduct the orchestra, and he won three gold medals. By chance, I was one of the judges at the art festival," said Professor Wei.

"That all happened in the past but I really fancied that one day, I might play Hamlet after reading Shakespeare's works which I secretly borrowed from a close friend during the Cultural Revolution," Zhang Feng said, humbly.

"Fine! Teacher Zhang is tall and handsome, refined and cultivated, versed in both expressive literature and martial arts. He is the best person to play the role of Hamlet!" Professor Wei exclaimed.

During the next two months, under the direction of Professor Wei, Zhang Feng and the other members of the company rehearsed seriously, in the evenings and at weekends. Zhang Feng contacted the directors of some drama and theatre institutes in Beijing to borrow scenery and props for the play so that they only needed to take their costumes with them when they travelled to the capital.

Everybody worked hard during the rehearsals. With the explanation of the characters and their motivations from Zhang Feng, as a Shakespearean scholar, and with the direction of Professor Wei, the actors and actresses quickly perfected their roles. During their breaks, Wang Li and Huang Lei quite often discussed their understanding and representation of the characters.

Zhang Feng noticed that Wang Li treated him as her beloved prince during the rehearsals and at other times, her soft eyes still exuded tenderness and love towards him. Zhang Feng knew of his attraction to women but he also knew how to deal with it. He told Wang Li that she did not need to be so immersed in the role of Ophelia outside the rehearsals.

"I am an actress following the performing theory of 'Experimentalism' by Stephen Schiff. I cannot step out from my role, even outside the rehearsal," she said, jokingly, and then continued, "I know you have a beautiful wife. Do not worry. I am just trying to find out how to get along with my future boyfriend, if he is as handsome and talented as you."

Then she made a wry face and ran away.

Zhang Feng laughed at her funny words.

"A naughty girl. She is still a child."

The time came for the first ever Shakespeare Festival to be held in Beijing. Saying farewell to Dan Dan and his family, Zhang Feng travelled to Beijing with his company. Looking at the endless green fields from the window of the train, Zhang Feng recalled his experience of the Revolutionary Tour to Beijing during the Cultural Revolution. He described it to Wang Li and Huang Lei. They listened to him with great interest, as both of them had been very young back then.

After arriving in Beijing and passing the Tian An Men Square, the memories of rescuing Yu Mei there during Mao's

Red Guards interview welled up in Zhang Feng's mind. He wondered where she was now and if she was doing well. He hoped she would find a good man and enjoy her new life.

The first Shakespeare Festival began grandly in Beijing. This was a great Chinese event, embracing Western culture after the Cultural Revolution. The Chairman of the International Shakespeare Association came to the Festival. Mrs. Thatcher also sent a letter of congratulation. From the Western point of view, this was a very important step for China, giving up its rigid, 'closed door' policy and joining the international community.

A total of 20 Shakespeare plays were performed in Beijing and Shanghai at that Festival. Zhang Feng felt very excited every day. Apart from watching performances, there were also a lot of seminars. Zhang Feng met some famous Shakespeare scholars and exchanged academic knowledge with them.

Zhang Feng performed their 'Hamlet' on the last day before the Festival ended. It attracted special attention as it was the only play performed by an amateur theatre company. A lot of famous figures in theatre circles and Shakespeare studies attended the performance.

Behind the certain, Zhang Feng could see the theatre was filled to capacity. Professor Wei encouraged the company actors to concentrate on their roles and imagine that this stage was the old castle in Denmark where this thrilling, historical tragedy happened. The performance ran quite smoothly. The audience applauded loudly after Act I. In Scene II, Act II, Zhang Feng recited Hamlet's words with his sonorous and powerful bass voice,

"What a piece of work is a man! How noble in reason! How infinite in faculty! In form and moving, how express and admirable! In action, how like an angel! In apprehension, how like a god! The beauty of the world! The paragon of animals!…"

To the audience, these lines evoked the beauty of humanity and the creativity of human nature. This was just what China needed for its economic and political reform; the rigid left-wing had suppressed human nature in the country and made people there like slaves, without creativity and independent thought. With a sympathetic response to Shakespeare's thinking and the appreciation of Zhang Feng's excellent performance, the audience applauded warmly.

When Zhang Feng finished the lines in Scene I, Act III, " To be or not to be, that is the question:…", the audience burst into even more warm applause as these lines were very well-known to Chinese readers and audiences. The performances of Wang Li, Huang Lei and the other actors were also well received. At the end of the play, the audience gave a standing ovation to Zhang Feng's company. Zhang Feng and his fellow actors took three curtain calls before the audience left the theatre.

Behind the stage, they were all about to remove their stage makeup and costumes when suddenly, a student actor shouted,

"Teacher Zhang's wife is coming!"

Turning his head, Zhang Feng saw Dan Dan walking towards him with a bunch of flowers.

"It is you! How did you come to Beijing?" Zhang Feng said, surprised.

Dan Dan pretended to be unhappy.

"Why? Can I not come to Beijing? I came specially to watch your performance. I presented flowers to you 20 years ago at the art festival as your 'elder sister', but now, I do it as your wife!"

Zhang Feng embraced Dan Dan and kissed her warmly. All the members of the company started to applaud.

Wang Li murmured with envy,

"She is lucky to have married such an excellent man.'
Suddenly, another female voice was heard,

"Congratulations on your superb performance, Brother Feng!"

This time it was Qing Lian. She presented a bunch of fresh lotus flowers to Zhang Feng and explained to Dan Dan,

"Our newspaper is very interested in this Festival and sent me to cover it for a news item. Look, I took many photos of your performance."

She pointed at her camera. Dan Dan and Qing Lian walked towards each other.

At that moment, a theatre attendant came up to Zhang Feng with a bunch of lilies in her hand and asked him,

"Are you Mr. Zhang Feng? There is a lady here who asked me to hand this bunch of flowers to you." She added, quietly, "She was a very beautiful lady."

Zhang Feng was not surprised to have female fans but when he looked at the flowers more closely, he found a piece of plastic plum blossom (fresh plum blossom only appears during the winter time). He was shocked and wondered if it could be her: Yu Mei. Why had she not come to see him? He really wanted to chase after her but stopped as Dan Dan and Qing Lian were there.

He explained to them,

"It is nothing. These are flowers sent by a Shakespeare scholar in the drama institute."

He put the piece of plastic plum blossom into his bag and gave the bunch of lilies to Wang Li who held the flowers from Dan Dan and Qing Lian.

On the last day of the Festival, Zhang Feng attended some of the academic seminars. Outside the conference room, there were some book stands, selling Chinese translations of Shakespeare works and books on Shakespeare studies. Among them were the two volumes of Zhang Feng's *An Introduction to Shakespeare.* They attracted the attention of more and more readers. Some readers found him and asked him to sign their copies.

During the lunch break, a member of staff from the publishing company came to him and said,

"Professor Zhang, all copies but one of your books have sold out. We just received a phone call from a lady who said she wanted to order 100 copies but she must have one signed copy. So I have come to ask for your autograph on this last copy."

One hundred copies? How strange. Nobody would buy so many copies in this way unless it was for university reference or libraries. But why a signed copy?

He wrote his name carefully on this last copy of his book and sat on a chair in the corridor. Suddenly, he felt his heart beating faster. Was it her again? She had sent him the flowers and now she had bought up all his books! Feeling both happy and sad, he was lost in thought. He felt happy because she still missed him, and also, she must have returned to society and begun a new life. He felt sad because she did not want to meet him. Was it because she did not want to affect his life with Dan Dan?

Two days later, Dan Dan and Qing Lian left Beijing. Zhang Feng and his company were also on the way back to the River City. In the train, everybody was talking and laughing but Zhang Feng sat there as if in a trance.

Wang Li touched his arm and said quietly,

"Teacher Zhang, are you still thinking about the female fan who sent those lilies to you?"

"No, no, I just miss my family and my son," Zhang Feng replied, quickly.

"Lilies represent love. Ordinary fans would not give you lilies. I heard the theatre staff saying that the fan who gave you the flowers was a very beautiful lady. Could she be your previous girlfriend?" Wang Li asked, secretively.

"Why do you think that?" Zhang Feng asked, surprised.

"There are many female students and staff on campus who love you, even though you are already married. There are a lot of stories about your experiences in the past which would make a good book! I heard that your first girlfriend and you were life-death lovers but a villain ruined your relationship and she went to the Taoist temple to become a nun. They also said she left the temple and returned to secular life. Is it possible that she still misses you and cares about you?" Wang Li asked.

Wang Li's words touched Zhang Feng's mind. He flushed.

"If I were her, I would visit you openly. I would try to have a platonic kind of love with you so I could at least be your female intimate, even if I could not live with you."

Fearing that others may be listening to their conversation, Zhang Feng made a gesture to ask her to be quiet and said,

"You are still a little girl. You do not understand what love is."

"How can you say that? Ophelia understands deeply the happiness and sorrow brought about by love!" she murmured.

They both laughed.

CHAPTER IV

Should I Marry Him?

Two days after returning home, Dan Dan passed a copy of the Jili Daily to Zhang Feng as he was preparing his next lesson.

"Your sister, Qing Lian, has done very well for you. She fully reported your activities during the Shakespeare Festival with a whole page in their supplement. Look at this enormous photo of you, as the Prince of Denmark, which is going to affect the sleep of a lot of women!"

"I don't care as long as my wife sleeps well," Zhang Feng replied, jokingly.

Dan Dan kissed him with pleasure and gave him a card.

"Look at this: an invitation to attend Qing Lian's wedding this weekend in a hotel next to Song Hua Lake."

"Very good! They should have got married much sooner. They have delayed for so many years. Luckily, Li He is a patient man; otherwise, he might have tried to find another woman. He could easily get a young and pretty girl with his high social status." Zhang Feng said.

Dan Dan pretended to be unhappy.

"You men all have the same problem. You focus too much on women's appearance. Will you try to find another woman when I get older and have lost my beauty?"

Zhang Feng smiled.

"My wife is a peony fairy and will never get older."

Dan Dan patted his shoulder.

"You just flatter me. OK. I am going to buy a present for them and have your suit dry cleaned. We should dress formally for our old friends' wedding."

On Sunday morning, surrounded by green mountains, the Song Hua Lake sparkled in bright sunshine. Opening the hotel room window, Qing Lian gazed at the beautiful scenery in front of her. Today was her wedding to Li He but she did not feel excited. It had not been easy for Li He to woo her for so many years. Urbane and with good status, he could easily have found another young and pretty girl to marry. The problem was that he did not make her feel any passion nor make her heart beat faster. Maybe, this was because she always compared him with Zhang Feng. Zhang Feng had all the excellent qualities which led women to be infatuated with him but he was married, with a family, plus, he was a faithful man. He could only ever be her dream lover.

"Sister Qing Lian, you should have your makeup on and be in your wedding dress!" exclaimed an attendant.

Looking at her watch, she realized it was already ten o'clock. The wedding started at 12.00 noon. She followed the attendant to the wedding hall. Li He was very busy there, arranging the decorations, furniture and banquet with his parents and colleagues.

At noon, he and Qing Lian stood at the entrance to welcome their guests. In her beautiful, white wedding dress, Qing Lian looked very young and lovely with lily-white skin and willow-leaf shaped eyebrows. Li He gazed at her and told her how beautiful she looked but Qing Lian only wanted to hear such things from Zhang Feng. Wang Hai and Zhang Lin arrived first, with their flowers and a red bag in their hands.

Wang Hai said, loudly,

"Living conditions are so much better now. We won't be giving you mirrors or thermos bottles! We will give you money so you can buy anything you like."

"Do not talk about money. We are just pleased that you have come," Li He said.

Qing Lian's colleagues from the newspaper and Li He's colleagues from the hospital came, one by one, but Qing Lian felt anxious because Zhang Feng and Dan Dan had not yet arrived. She wanted to make her entrance to the wedding hall under the gaze of Zhang Feng. Then, she would finally give up her love for him and become his 'sister'.

After a little while, Dan Dan came rushing in.

"Sorry, our son had a fever last night. He is better this morning but Zhang Feng had to take him to his parents' home and then he will come here. He said not to wait for him as he may be late."

Qing Lian looked disappointed but Li He did not pay too much attention to this. It was already12.30 and Zhang Feng had still not turned up. The wedding host asked the groom and bride whether they should start now. Qing Lian still wanted to wait for Zhang Feng but Wang Hai said carelessly to them,

"Today is your wedding. It does not matter if Brother Feng comes late. Let's start now."

The wedding began cheerfully. Li He and Qing Lian described their love for each other.

Wang Hai chipped in,

"Do you know that they belonged to two different rebellious factions during the Cultural Revolution and fought against each other?"

Noticing the embarrassment on the faces of Qing Lian's parents, Zhang Lin explained hastily,

"Do not listen to Wang Hai's nonsense. They were just having fun with each other."

But for those who had experienced the Cultural Revolution, it was clear that the fighting between the two factions had never been about having fun: it was a real, life or death kind of fighting.

The host quickly changed the topic and asked whether the bride and groom had any common hobby. Qing Lian looked absent-minded and continued to watch the entrance. She was very nervous waiting for the appearance of Zhang Feng, like a bride waiting for her father to hand her to the groom.

Following the new Western style of ceremony, the host asked Li He,

"Mr. Li He, are you willing to marry Miss Qing Lian?"

"I will," he answered but when the host asked Qing Lian the same question, she suddenly put her head in her hands and ran into the waiting room on one side of the hall. All the guests were astonished.

Li He explained, hastily,

"She has been very nervous and tired these last few days and this has now triggered a headache. She should be fine after a rest."

Then he followed her into the waiting room.

While all the guests waited anxiously, Zhang Feng entered the wedding hall, hurriedly, and apologized for his delay. Not seeing the bride and groom there, he asked,

"Where are Li He and Qing Lian?"

At this moment, Li He came out of the waiting room and said to Zhang Feng, in a fluster,

"Brother Feng, Qing Lian has a headache because she did not sleep well last night. She feels a bit better now after taking some medication. Can you use Qing Kung to treat her like you did for me before?"

He took Zhang Feng into the waiting room with a meaningful look and then he left Zhang Feng and Qing Lian together. Seeing Qing Lian, resting on the sofa in her wedding gown, Zhang Feng asked gently,

"What's the matter Qing Lian? Do you have a headache because of nerves?"

Wiping her eyes, she stood up, and asked,

"Why are you so late?"

She let Zhang Feng sit on the sofa and suddenly, leaned on his shoulder, and burst into tears.

"Brother, you are my spiritual rock. Do you think I should marry him?"

"Of course you should. He has loved you for so many years. He is a good, responsible man and will be a good husband."

"I know this but he is not the man who makes my heart beat faster. Will I have a happy life living with a man I do not love?"

She suddenly flushed, plucked up her courage and said,

"Brother Feng, something has been in my mind for many years. I must tell you today. You knew I started to love you when we were in middle school. Unfortunately, we became political enemies but you disregarded past grudges and saved me when I tried to kill myself. You also reformed me through persuasion and helped me regain my kind nature. Since then, I not only regard you as my saviour but also, love you again deeply but even I know this is only one-sided. You have your childhood friend, beautiful Dan Dan as your wife, and you probably still miss your life-death lover, Yu Mei. My wish now is only to be your 'younger sister'. I would be happy if I could see you, help you and talk to you from time to time. To have this pleasure, I am willing to live alone as a single woman."

Not realizing that Qing Lian had been totally frank and told him her most secret thoughts, Zhang Feng tried to persuade her,

"My dear sister, we should all have a partner and family, otherwise, we will feel lonely when we get older. There is a distance between the ideal and reality. It is good that you have a man who loves you and wants to live together with you. Looks and manners may be important during the early stages of a relationship but care, patience and responsibility are more important when you have a family."

Qing Lian thought this over and asked,

"In that case, should I marry him?"

"Yes, my judgement won't be wrong. Li He and I have been intimate friends for many years."

Qing Lian wiped her eyes using the tissue given to her by Zhang Feng.

"Alright, Brother Feng, I will do as you say because you gave me a second chance of life but you must promise that I can still be your friend and can meet you, talk to you, after I am married."

"You will be my good, younger sister forever."

Finally looking happy and kissing Zhang Feng suddenly, she cried,

"Then I will go and be the bride in today's wedding!"

She left the room, leaving Zhang Feng to wipe the lipstick from his face.

Seeing Qing Lian coming out of the waiting room, everybody breathed again.

Wang Hai said to Zhang Feng,

"Brother-in-law, can you give me the same treatment next time I get a headache?"

Actually, only Li He, Dan Dan and Zhang Lin knew what had really happened in the waiting room. They understood the complex relationship between Qing Lian, Li He and Zhang Feng.

The wedding continued smoothly. The banquet which followed was also very rich, and the cooked, fresh carp from the lake was especially liked by all the guests.

Afterwards, the guests sent the bride and groom off to their wedding chamber and then left the hotel. Zhang Feng, Dan Dan, Wang Hai and Zhang Lin stayed in the hall slightly longer. Li He and Qing Lian drank some more and it was clear they had something on their minds. When they said goodbye to this last group, Zhang Feng noticed a sad expression in Qing Lian's eyes.

After leaving the hotel, Wang Hai and Zhang Lin went to the train station. Zhang Feng told Dan Dan he would like to have a walk around the lake. He had not been to this lake for many years. Walking along the banks and looking at the vast expanse of water and the green mountains, Zhang Feng suddenly recalled a sweet holiday here with Yu Mei, twenty years ago. He and Dan Dan had sat down for a little while, on a stone bench, under a tree. Zhang Feng tried to find the same place where he and Yu Mei stayed many times during their holiday. In the end, he found it but the trees there had become very tall and now towered over them. How rapidly the time has passed, he thought to himself.

"What are you thinking?" Dan Dan asked.

"I used to swim here in the summer time," he replied.

"Did you meet her here before the Cultural Revolution?" Dan Dan asked.

"You mean, did I date Yu Mei here? How did you know that?"

"It was your sister told me that you had a holiday with Yu Mei here a year before the Cultural Revolution," Dan Dan said.

"Yes, soon after that, we were parted because of the changes in our political status: I belonged to the Black and she to the Red."

Leaning on Zhang Feng's shoulder, Dan Dan said,

"I can understand the emotional trauma caused by everything. Yu Mei is a good girl. I actually quite like her and regard her as my sister. If we lived in the past, when China allowed polygamy, you could have married both of us. Even married Qing Lian as well"

"Oh, what are you talking about? You are speaking nonsense!" Zhang Feng replied, immediately.

"I am teasing you but you might have thought about this, especially when you tried to comfort her during her father's funeral."

Zhang Feng hugged Dan Dan and kissed her.

"Can you shut up now, my naughty girl?"

"Sometimes, you behave like a little boy!" Dan Dan smiled.

Then, arm in arm, they waked along the huge dam to the train station.

Autumn soon arrived. One day, Zhang Feng received a phone call from his previous university friends, telling him that there would be a reunion of their classmates from all over the country next Sunday, at a venue in the city party committee building. Zhang Feng was very pleased as he had not seen them for five years since graduation. There were over 60 students in his class and they were all excellent academically, although their political attitudes were very different.

Next Sunday morning, Zhang Feng went to the venue in the city party committee building. Chen Tao, a former classmate who worked there as a secretary in the general office arranged this reunion. Entering the room, he saw over ten of his previous classmates tidying and arranging the venue and he quickly joined them. They all greeted him warmly. Zhang Feng was a very popular and most excellent student back at university, with his handsome looks and his position as the President of the Student Union and leader of the art group and sports team. A lot of girls loved him back then and felt it was a pity he already had Dan Dan as his girlfriend.

Chen Tao came up to him to shake his hand. They'd had a good relationship in the past as Chen Tao came from an intellectual family. His parents also suffered during the Cultural Revolution, so Chen Tao had the same, open-minded, political standpoint as Zhang Feng. Zhang Feng thanked him for organizing this reunion. Li Qiu, from the Propaganda Department, also came up to Zhang Feng and praised his speech in the political forum at the University.

Zhang Feng thought he was a toady and said,

"Your Director Shen did not like my speech, did he? He even criticized the report in the Jili Daily."

Li Qiu looked embarrassed.

"It is normal to have different opinions about reform."

Zhang Feng did not want to talk to him. He and Chen Tao joined the other students decorating the room.

Near lunch time, most of the classmates and friends had arrived. Many came from other provinces. As Jili University was a top state university, the graduates had been assigned to jobs and positions all over the country. In Beijing, some of them worked in different Government departments. In other cities, they worked in Party and Government organizations, media, research institutions or taught in universities like Zhang Feng. They greeted each other warmly, exchanged working and private experiences and talked about the new changes brought about by the economic and political reforms.

After enjoying the meal and drinking, they became more relaxed and casual. They recalled interesting things which had happened in the past at the University. Some young men told the women that they had secretly loved them during their studies but dared not say so. The women laughingly said it was a pity that their husbands were not as good as they might have been. Quite a few girls came up to Zhang Feng and told him that they still loved him. Some of them even said they were still single because they compared all their potential partners with him. Others cracked jokes saying they would quickly pass on the news to them if Zhang Feng ever got divorced.

One single woman said,

"Do not count on him ever getting divorced. His wife is much more beautiful than me."

Zhang Feng was in a good mood, so he did not mind their jokes. He told these single ladies that he would try to introduce some good men to them.

It was about 4 o'clock in the afternoon and some classmates from distant cities prepared to leave. At this moment, some of those who worked in Central Government started to talk about political reform in the country which interested Zhang Feng. One of them said that the Party had learnt the lessons of the damage caused by the personality cult of Chairman Mao during the Cultural Revolution. The new leadership, led by Deng Xiaoping, clearly wanted to prohibit any personality cult inside the party and the Government, to improve democratic practice and to listen to the opinion of the people. This meant big progress in political reform.

Zhang Feng, and a lot of his classmates, remembered the sensational events which had happened last year, during the parade on Tian An Men Square, to celebrate the 35th anniversary of the establishment of the PRC. A group of students from Beijing University were holding up a poster with a greeting to Deng Xiaoping: 'How do you do, (Deng) Xiaoping', which was taken by a photographer and published in the People's Daily, causing a nationwide sensation. On one hand, the poster showed the support of the people for the new policy of economic and political reform. On the other hand, it showed that people used a simple and honest way to express their love and esteem for their new leader, not like the fanatical: 'Long Live Chairman Mao' slogans. A classmate recalled how, if somebody had dared to use this way of addressing Chairman Mao during the Cultural Revolution, they would have been beaten to death on the spot.

The abolition of the lifelong post system was another major political reform. In the past, the Party and Government officials kept their posts for life. This affected the leadership which could not be changed or recycled meaning new policies were not introduced to reflect the changes in society. After the abolition of this system, officials were forced to retire when they reached the age limit of 60 or 65, bringing leadership succession to the benefit of the whole country.

At this moment, a young man from the general office of the Central Party Committee said, secretively,

"I have some internal information to tell you."

He explained how, recently, the Central Committee of the Party was preparing to promote some young, well-educated officials to replace the old, poorly educated ones. The old officials were so powerful during the civil war but not good for modernization of the country. The selection could be made from Party and Government organizations but also, from universities and institutions as long as the candidates were Party members with Higher Education qualifications and the fearless spirit of a path-breaker. His talk aroused some warm discussion. Chen Tao said,

"Our Brother Feng would be a very good candidate!"

All the classmates agreed with his opinion. They believed Zhang Feng would be a very good official, able to carry reforms forward but Li Qiu said it would be a pity because he was already successful in academic circles. Actually, he worried Zhang Feng's promotion might affect his own political future.

Zhang Feng said humbly,

"No, No, I am fine just teaching and doing research. I am not the right person for official circles."

A few classmates, who worked in the Beijing Party and Government Departments, said the situation in official circles was very different from that during the Cultural Revolution. You had to work hard to get promotion. If you just drank tea and read newspapers in your office every day, your position would be lost.

Then his friends guessed what post Zhang Feng might be assigned. Chen Tao said Zhang Feng was a Secretary of the Youth League which was equal to the status of a Section Chief. If he was assigned to work in the Party, or a Government Department, he should be Director of a Bureau. A female colleague said Zhang Feng could be a Deputy Mayor or a Deputy Secretary of a city party committee. Other classmates also tried to guess the possible posts Zhang Feng might obtain but Zhang Feng thought they were all joking. It would not happen to him as he still intended to become a full professor and famous scholar, like his father. He did not realize that a political promotion was going to come very soon.

Part II

Joining Official Circles

CHAPTER I

Do You Still Remember the Last Words of Secretary Li?

One week after the reunion, Zhang Feng received a phone call from the office of the university party committee. He was told that the Party Secretary, Meng, wanted to see him. Zhang Feng thought Secretary Meng would talk about his administrative work. It might be a good chance to ask to be relieved of his post as Secretary of the Youth League in order to concentrate on his teaching and research. After all, it was quite rare for a professor to have such a political administrative post.

In the office of the university party committee, Zhang Feng met Secretary Meng who was due to retire in a few years' time. He admired Zhang Feng because he had done well both academically and in administration.

Asking Zhang Feng to sit down and giving him a cup of tea, Secretary Meng said,

"I know you are very busy with your academic work. Being Secretary of the Youth League at the same time must be an extra burden."

Zhang Feng was happy and said,

"I really want to resign from this job. Have you got another person in mind to replace me?"

Secretary Meng said with a smile,

"You will not only have to quit from the post, but also, from your Deputy Director of Department role and your professorship."

Zhang Feng was surprised.

"What? Is this a punishment? Is somebody trying to capitalize on my weak points? Has Director Shen informed on me?"

"Don't worry. Nothing like that has happened. It is not 1957 and the Cultural Revolution is over. Nobody can randomly inform on others politically."

Then he told Zhang Feng it was a good thing for him. He said the party central committee wanted to promote and appoint young, well-educated, capable officials, with intelligence, in cities and provinces at different levels. They were going to replace all the incapable and poorly educated officials.

"After consultation, the provincial party committee has drawn up a list of candidates, which includes you. I was told that you were highly praised. I received a phone call from the Organizational Department of the province and was told that you would be appointed as the Deputy Secretary of the city party committee, in charge of the Reform Office, dealing directly with economic reforms in different areas. If you would like to take this post, I will reply to them or, if it's a surprise, you can have a few days to think about it."

"Yes, Secretary Meng. It is a surprise! May I talk about it first with my family and friends?"

"Of course you can. Actually, I would like to keep you in our University. My original plan was to have you follow in my footsteps. In the future, you might have become the Vice Chancellor, or Chancellor, because you are very capable. You have already contributed greatly to the reputation of our University. However, as Party members, we have to obey instructions from the official, higher levels of the Party," Secretary Meng said.

Back home, Zhang Feng told Dan Dan first. She said she had already predicted this would happen.

"Do you remember what Secretary Liu said at our wedding about his wish for you to become an official in the Party or Government? I guess this time he has recommended you."

"I know I have the capability to be a good official but I still feel sorry about leaving my academic career," Zhang Feng said.

"It would be more meaningful to make our society more equal, democratic and prosperous rather than publishing a few more academic books," Dan Dan replied.

Thinking for a while, Zhang Feng agreed.

"Yes, the reason why we suffered so much during the Cultural Revolution is because we did not have a sound political system which would prevent personality cults and dictatorships. If more officials, like us, are open-minded and persist in democracy, we could prevent the possible recurrence of such political disasters. I still remember the last words of Yu Mei's father, the late provincial party secretary, before his death. He hoped that I would become an official and that I would be able to contribute to the economic and political reforms."

They decided to consult their parents. Zhang Feng rang his parents, saying there was an important issue to discuss with them that evening. His mother invited them for dinner and said she would cook Zhang Feng's favourite braised pork with soy sauce. That evening, they went to their parents' house with their son and smelt something delicious coming from inside as soon as they opened the door. The dining room was quite full, with Zhang Feng's father, Zhang Wenbo, his mother, Hu Yun, Dan Dan's father, Hai Jing, her mother, Wang Hui, and Wang Hai and Zhang Lin were also there.

"This is lively!" Zhang Feng exclaimed.

His father, Zhang Wenbo, said,

"We will have a big family dinner tonight and a family meeting to discuss your future."

Wang Hai said, casually,

"My dear brother-in-law, do not forget to promote me to the post of factory director after you become the Deputy City Secretary."

"Nonsense! I have not even taken the post yet but you're already trying to look after your own interests!"

Looking at the appetizing dishes on the table, Dan Dan announced, happily,

"I will give up my diet today and start again from tomorrow."

"You don't need to lose weight as you are not fat," Zhang Lin said.

Zhang Wenbo and Hu Yun had cooked braised pork with soy sauce and steamed, braised pork. Hai Jing and Wang Hui had made popular Northeast boiled pork with bean noodles and pickled Chinese cabbage and deep fried eggplant 'box' with minced pork. Zhang Lin had brought roasted pork head meat and preserved duck eggs.

Wang Hai said,

"Hai, we have a dinner here that looks like a feast for the Chinese New Year celebrations!"

All of them sat down to enjoy the delicious dinner and to talk about recent changes brought about by the emerging reform policies. When they got to the fruits and tea after the meal, Zhang Wenbo said,

"OK. Let's start the meeting of our family 'political bureau'. We will each give our opinion on Xiao Feng's proposed new career. I would like to give my opinion first. I would actually quite like him to follow in my footsteps and become a famous scholar but looking back at my own life and the twenty years from 1957 to 1977, like most intellectuals, I suffered from terrible political persecution. Why? Because the left-wing leaders were engaged in class struggles and their personality cult and did not give people democracy. We desperately need reform to change our political system. If most of our leaders and officials are well educated and open-minded reformers who try to make our society more equal, democratic and prosperous, and are not just bothered about their own power and privileges, then our country has a promising future." Taking a sip of tea, he continued,

"Being concerned about our country's future and being involved in political practice is one of the key ideologies of Confucianism. Throughout modern Chinese history, we can see that many revolutionaries strove for bright future for our country by following this ideal, even if they were seemingly also influenced by Western political ideas.

Everybody agreed with him, especially Hai Jing who also suffered terribly during the 1957 anti-rightist movement and the Cultural Revolution.

Wang Hai also said, excitedly,

"Only people who dare to think and dare to act, like Brother Feng, can really push the reform movement forward. Economic reform has been carried out too slowly in the Northeast area compared to the South. Recently, one of our middle school classmates visited the village where we used to work and saw the farmers still farming lazily, without incentives, earning very little money and with little food. In the cities, we still need coupons to buy food and other daily necessities. In the factories, workers do not work hard as everything is arranged by bureaucratic officers under the centrally controlled economy. I heard that, in Shen Zhen City, they have started free market trials and the factories there have become very efficient and productive. But the leaders here are very cowardly. They are frightened of reform because of the influence from the left-wing. Join official circles bravely, Brother Feng, and make an all-out effort to change the situation. As an official in charge of the reforms, you can directly push economic reform forward!"

Listening to Wang Hai's speech, Zhang Feng nodded his head and said,

"You have made a very good point which is just what I have been thinking."

Dan Dan said,

"A country must improve its economy first and create more of a middle class which is the foundation for a democratic system."

Zhang Lin joined in.

"My sister-in-law deserves her profession as an economist. She has made a very good point."

In the end, Zhang Feng announced,

"Since everybody supports me, I will join the city leadership and try to do a good job for a few years. If I fail, I will return to my academic work."

All the family members applauded warmly.

Next day, Zhang Feng rang Secretary Meng and told him that he had accepted the new post in the city. Secretary Meng said he was glad to know Zhang Feng would follow the Party's instructions but at the same time, he also felt sad because Zhang Feng would be leaving the University.

Zhang Feng said,

"Secretary Meng, I will try the new job for a couple of years. If it does not work out, will you welcome me back?"

Meng said of course he would. Then he asked Zhang Feng to go to his department and the Youth League to resign his jobs there. After that, he could report to the city party committee and start his new job.

Back in his department, his colleagues all congratulated him on his promotion. Only Secretary Liu Qi seemed cold. Zhang Feng did not care as he took such a reaction for granted from the rigid and conservative leaders and officials everywhere. The female department secretary passed a letter to Zhang Feng.

"Professor Zhang, this is your letter."

Seeing the stamp on the envelope was from Beijing, he thought it might be a letter from the Shakespeare Association. However, he was surprised when he opened the envelope and read the letter. The letter was printed, not handwritten:

"Congratulations on your new job. Please work hard to make our country and society better. Don't forget the hardship and suffering of the past and the people who shared those experiences with you. Don't let the historical tragedy of the Cultural Revolution recur and don't let young lovers

* 61 *

suffer the pain and sorrow felt in their parting and reunion ever again."

There was no sender's name and no signature but Zhang Feng knew for sure that this was a letter from Yu Mei. How did she know so much about his situation? Why did she not give him her contact details? The flower and purchase of his book in Beijing during the Shakespeare Festival showed that she lived in Beijing so why didn't she want to meet him? These were painful thoughts but at the same time, he felt more determined than ever to take up his new post.

A few days later, he reported for duty at the city party committee. Secretary Wang Kai and Mayor Gong met him. Secretary Wang was an official from the countryside without the benefit of a good education. Mayor Gong was a well-educated official and a good talker. They assigned and explained his tasks, saying his job was very important and risky because there was no existing policy to follow. He needed to explore a way in which to carry on the economic reforms and they would support him in his work. The Director of the Organization Department told him he would have two assistants. One was a demobilized army officer who used to work in the Jili military army and his post was as Director of the Reform Office. They would try to find another assistant for him with the post of Deputy Director of the Reform Office.

Zhang Feng asked,

"May I have comrade Chen Tao from the city party office in this post? He is a former university classmate. We have a very good relationship and that will create good co-operation in our work."

The Director answered,

"No problem. I am sure he will be happy to take this post as it is a promotion for him."

The Director also showed Zhang Feng his office which was next door to the Reform Office. The Director said they would furnish it well but Zhang Feng said that was not necessary; he only needed simple chairs and a table.

Two days after this, he started his new job formally. He got to his office quite early to see a woman in a smart dress cleaning the office.

Seeing Zhang Feng, she said,

"Good morning, Secretary Zhang. My name is Wei Li and I am your work secretary. I have a duty to arrange your daily working programme and prepare documents for you."

Zhang Feng thanked her politely but surprisingly, Ms. Wei said that he did not need to thank her as this was her job. Zhang Feng realized that this was officialdom and he was no longer in his previous academic circles so he should behave differently. At that moment, somebody knocked on the door and a middle aged, military looking man came in.

"Good morning, Secretary Zhang. My name is Lin Jianguo. I have just reported to my post as the Director of the Reform Office."

After saying this, he smiled rather secretively at Zhang Feng. Looking at this man, Zhang Feng felt he was familiar. Suddenly, he remembered this was Secretary Lin who had been in the Army, 18 years ago. He had rescued Zhang Feng from execution at the last second.

"Secretary Lin! It is you! My saviour!"

They embraced each other and talked warmly, as they had not seen each other for so many years. Lin told Zhang Feng that he had worked for General Zhao Wu for many years until Zhao retired last year. He had also resigned from his position as a regimental commander that year, requesting, instead, a civil job in Jili City, his hometown. Zhang Feng asked about the situation with Chang Zheng, the son of General Zhao Wu, and also, his old rival for Yu Mei. Lin said Chang Zheng had done quite well in the Army. He was a division commander now. At this moment, Chen Tao came in.

"Hi, Brother Feng, my prediction comes true! You are a high ranking officer now. Thank you for recommending me for the post of Deputy Director of the Reform Office."

Zhang Feng introduced Lin and Chen to each other then he patted their shoulders and said,

"I am so happy to have two powerful assistants. One is capable and the other is intelligent. Let's join our efforts to do a good job."

CHAPTER II

To Feed Ten Billion People Well Is the Biggest Political Achievement

The first meeting to discuss reform in the countryside was held in the Reform Office as soon as Zhang Feng took up his post. Zhang Feng sat in the host's chair and Lin Jianguo and Chen Tao sat next to him on his left and right. The people who attended the meeting included heads and secretaries from different counties and the head of the city agriculture office. Zhang Feng explained that the main purpose of this meeting was to discuss the progress of reform in the countryside, to acknowledge achievements and highlight problems. Being modest, he asked about each attendee's experience of their work.

Seeing his easy manner, the local officials felt relaxed. They started to talk about the situation and problems in their area. Some of them said that after the Cultural Revolution, farmers were able to concentrate on farming but production still relied on the weather. Without incentives, farmers still did not work very hard although they worked together to earn points. The yield was still quite low. In some years, they still relied on grain from the Government if there were natural disasters. Zhang Feng thought that the situation had hardly changed from the time when he worked in the countryside during the Cultural Revolution. This was not good.

"I used to work in the countryside during the Cultural Revolution. At that time, farmers worked within an indiscriminate, egalitarian system and farmers had no incentive to work hard. Is it any better now?"

An outspoken county head said,

"Exactly the same. Collective ownership and distribution. You will get the same whether you work hard or not."

Before the meeting, Zhang Feng had discussed the background with Lin and Chen. They had talked about the contract and free market style policy in the 1960s during natural disasters and the similar policy in An Hui Province in recent years. They all believed this was a good way to give farmers incentives to work. But they also knew that there was a heated debate inside the Party and Government about the political legitimation of this policy. The rigid, left-wing leaders insisted that this policy would damage socialist, public ownership and was a step towards capitalism. But Zhang Feng thought they should break down the rigid, economic structure and find a practical way to improve the economy.

Chen Tao asked the heads and secretaries,

"Have you heard of the output contract policy in the South? Any of you intend to try it?"

A few of them said immediately that they dared not try it as the central People's Daily had said that this contract policy betrayed the concept of public ownership. It was a capitalist policy.

The head of Hua Dan County added,

"There is an audacious person in our area. She is a women's team head and a party member in Heng He Commune. She has tried the output contract in her village and always argues with the local leaders. She says socialism means people should have enough food. Do you think she is very bold?"

His words attracted the attention of Zhang Feng.

"Heng He Commune? That is the place I used to work as an educated youth. What is her name?"

"I think it is something like He…He…"

"He Hua?" Zhang Feng asked.

"Yes! He Hua. Do you know her?"

"I worked with her 15 years ago in the same production team," replied Zhang Feng.

Knowing Zhang Feng had once worked in the fields made all the local officers happy because they knew his experience could help them improve the living conditions of the farmers.

After the meeting, Zhang Feng decided to go to Heng He Commune to investigate He Hua's actions. If it was workable, he could spread it to his city. Both Lin and Chen wanted to go with him but Zhang Feng asked Lin to accompany him as he was strong and good at Kung Fu so it would be safe. Chen stayed behind to deal with office work.

To find out the truth, Zhang Feng did not contact Hua Dan County and Heng He Commune, but went directly to He Hua's village. They did not drive but travelled by train and dressed like ordinary people, not high ranking officials. On the way to Heng He Commune, Zhang Feng talked to Lin Jianguo warmly and asked him not to call him 'Secretary Zhang', just 'Xiao Zhang' would do. Lin Jianguo agreed but in the office, he would still prefer to call him 'Secretary Zhang'.

They arrived at Hua Dan County after a couple of hours. Having not been there for over ten years, Zhang Feng saw very few changes in the county town. There were only a few more buildings on the street. They took the bus to Heng He Commune and paid a few Yuan to a groom for a carriage ride to He Hua's village. On the way, Zhang Feng told Lin his story and experiences of working as a farmer in the village. They also watched the farmers working in the fields on both sides as they passed by.

It was getting quite dark when they arrived at the village. It was just the same with many straw and mud houses. Zhang Feng still remembered the location of He Hua's house but when they got closer, they could hear somebody crying inside. Zhang Feng knocked on the door gently. A tall boy opened the door, wiping his eyes. Recognizing the boy as He Hua's younger brother, Zhang Feng asked,

"Is this He Hua's home?"

The boy replied in fear,

"What are you doing? You have already arrested my sister. Is that not enough?"

Zhang Feng was surprised and asked,

"You say your sister has been arrested? Why?"

Seeing the boy dared not speak, Zhang Feng explained that they had come to help He Hua and that he used to work here over ten years ago and had a good relationship with her. Listening to Zhang Feng, the boy looked more relaxed and happier. He told Zhang Feng that He Hua had tried to bring in the land contract but the officers in the brigade and commune had disagreed. He Hua argued with them, but the malicious head of the commune militia, Wang Gui, had arrested her yesterday. The boy said the team leader, Pan, and accountant, Song, would know more about this incident and he could take them to their houses if Zhang Feng wanted to know the details. Zhang Feng still remembered Leader Pan. He and Lin went together to Pan's house.

Opening the door and looking closely at Zhang Feng, Leader Pan was surprised. Warmly shaking hands with Leader Pan, Zhang Feng said,

"Do you still remember me? My name is Zhang Feng. I worked with you over ten years ago in your team as an educated youth."

Looking carefully again, Leader Pan said,

"Yes, I remember now. You worked very well in the fields because you were such a powerful man."

Obviously, he still remembered the competition between Zhang Feng and Lieutenant Wang to see who could carry the heaviest bags. He also remembered that Zhang Feng was recruited as a worker in the chemical factory. Zhang Feng did not mention that he was a high ranking officer now. He just told Leader Pan that he worked for the city council and had come here to investigate something. Then he introduced Lin Jianguo to Leader Pan. When Zhang Feng asked about He Hua's problems and her arrest, Pan sighed and said,

"He Hua is a good girl. She always works hard for our team and tries to improve the living conditions of the farmers. She has a boyfriend who is an educated young man but from a landlord's family. He Hua is already in her thirties now but she puts off her wedding because of her concern for the interests of our farmers."

Zhang Feng asked why she had been arrested.

"It is just that evil head of the commune militia, Wang Gui, he used to be a lieutenant of militia here. He always focuses on attacking other people politically and not on farming issues.

This time, He Hua and our team were trying the land contract to improve production. Other leaders in the commune warned us not to follow capitalist ways but Head Wang treated it as a counter-revolutionary event, saying that contract policy was going against the late Chairman Mao's instructions and then he arrested He Hua. This is actually personal revenge because he used to woo her but was rejected by her. He hates her now because she has a boyfriend."

"I remember. That guy always tried to find fault with me when I worked here. He really is a villain," Zhang Feng said.

Zhang Feng comforted both Leader Pan and He Hua's brother and said he would stay overnight with his assistant, and tomorrow, he would go to the commune to rescue He Hua. Leader Pan was pleased and arranged for them to stay in his house and served them supper.

The next day, Zhang Feng and Lin got up very early and walked all the way to the commune. It was about 8 o'clock in the morning. After asking about the location of the militia, they walked to a big yard surrounded by a few, small houses. Zhang Feng saw a middle-aged man quarrelling with three militiamen who were holding rods in their hands.

The man asked,

"Why did you arrest my girlfriend? What crime has she committed? The only thing she has done is to give the farmers more grain and food."

A militiaman shouted,

"Get out of here! Son of a landlord! You dare to try and rescue her, a counter-revolutionary woman! We will beat you with this rod!"

The young man still tried to argue with them but he was beaten to the ground. Zhang Feng guessed that this young man was He Hua's boyfriend and he and Lin rushed to protect him, helping him to his feet.

Zhang Feng said seriously,

"Why on earth are you beating people so easily?"

They looked at Zhang Feng and Lin. They knew they looked like people from the city but not somebody of status or importance because they were dressed normally, without cars and personal assistants.

"Who are you? What are you doing here?"

Zhang Feng said,

"We have come from the civic council to investigate the issue of He Hua's arrest."

"Do you have a reference letter? You look like her accomplice who has come to rescue her. Get out of here! Otherwise, we will not be so easy on you."

Zhang Feng was very angry.

"Why are you being so unreasonable? You're like gangsters!"

Hearing Zhang Feng say they were gangsters, they brandished their rods at Zhang Feng and Lin Jianguo. Zhang Feng warned them to stop but they continued more fiercely.

Lin Jianguo shouted,

"If you do not stop, we will defend ourselves!"

Zhang Feng had not used his Pili boxing for a long time so he said to Lin Jianguo,

"Jianguo, show them our skill in martial arts!"

Lin Jianguo had been a boxing and martial arts master in the Army. In just a few seconds, they had beaten the three men down to the ground.

He Hua's boyfriend applauded their fighting but one of the militiamen shouted, loudly,

"Help! Help! Somebody has come to rescue the prisoner!"

Suddenly, a group of militiamen ran out from the yard with guns. Zhang Feng recognized the leader as the former Lieutenant Wang, now the head of the commune militia.

Zhang Feng said politely,

"Are you Head Wang? We have been sent by the city council to investigate the land contract matter. Seeing your militiamen beating this young man without any reason, we tried to stop them but they also started to hit us, so we had to defend ourselves."

Gazing at Zhang Feng, Head Wang recognized him and said,

"Are you the student who worked in my village many years ago?"

"Yes, I was in that competition with you, do you remember?"

Looking at Zhang Feng's dress and with a sinister expression, Head Wang said scornfully,

"I remember you went to work in a chemical factory. You say you come from city government? You do not look like an officer in this humble kind of dress. Do you have a reference letter? You do not even have an official car with you."

Lin Jianguo said,

"To investigate matters in a local area, we don't need a reference letter."

"Who knows whether you are swindlers or not. Shut them in a room and interrogate them later!" Head Wang said.

"Call your commune secretary to come here," Zhang Feng said.

"He is in a meeting and has no time to deal with swindlers," Wang replied.

Lin Jianguo said angrily,

"Do you know to whom you are talking?"

He wanted to reveal Zhang Feng's true identity but Zhang Feng made a gesture to stop him.

The militiamen shut them in a small room inside the yard. He Hua's boyfriend, Li Yong, told Zhang Feng about He Hua's suffering. He said most of the commune leaders did not want to arrest He Hua and only one of them, who was a relative of Head Wang, supported Wang's desire to punish He Hua. Head Wang was actually taking some kind of private revenge. He hated He Hua for having a relationship with another man. Li Yong told Zhang Feng that Head Wang was a really sinister despot in the area and constantly bullied and oppressed ordinary people. Some of his assistants were local hooligans. They bribed him to get their posts in the commune's militia. Hearing this, Zhang Feng said with bunched fists,

"His arrogant days will end soon!"

Zhang Feng did not want to waste time and he asked Lin Jianguo whether there was a way out of the room. Lin used to be a scout in the Army. After searching the walls and windows, he said,

"I've got a way to get out."

He prised open the back window with the small tools he carried in his pocket. They quickly jumped out from the room and ran towards the commune party committee building. As they got closer, they heard shouts behind them.

"Catch them! They are escaped criminals!"

Seeing Head Wang and his assistants chasing them, Zhang Feng said,

"Let's run fast!"

They ran into the big yard of the commune party committee and knocked at the door of the main office and rushed into the room. Lin Jianguo locked the door from the inside. There were six local officers in the room who all looked scared. Hearing the shouts outside, they thought these men were going to kidnap them.

Zhang Feng asked,

"Who is the commune party secretary?"

"I am." A man in his fifties with a beard replied.

"We have come from the city party committee to investigate He Hua's arrest but your head of commune militia arrested us without any reason. Please sort out this problem for us immediately."

At that moment, Head Wang knocked at the door fiercely and shouted,

"Secretary Yang, open the door! They are swindlers. We need to arrest them!"

Knowing Head Wang and his militiamen were outside, the leaders felt relaxed.

Secretary Yang asked, coldly,

"You say you have come from the city party committee? Why did I not receive any phone call from a high level office? Do you have a reference letter?"

Lin Jianguo replied,

"Why do we still need a reference letter? The Cultural Revolution is over."

Secretary Yang asked,

"But how can you prove that you have been sent by the city party committee?"

Angrily, Lin Jianguo pointed to Zhang Feng and said,

"This is the…"

But Zhang Feng stopped him as he did not want to put pressure on the lower level officers with his high ranking post. Also, the local officers might not know his name as he had only just been appointed.

He said to Secretary Yang,

"It is easy. You just make a phone call to your county secretary and ask him to come here. Somebody here wants to see him."

Zhang Feng's idea was if Secretary He came, everything could be resolved easily, including rescuing He Hua and punishing Head Wang. Secretary Yang rang Secretary He and asked him to come straight away. Secretary He was confused as he had not received any information from the city party committee but he said he could be here in 20 minutes.

Head Wang was still knocking at the door loudly. Zhang Feng asked Secretary Yang to explain to Head Wang that Secretary He would be coming soon to identify them. Wang said angrily,

"Ok, I will wait for 20 minutes then I will shoot them if they really are swindlers!"

A lot of people had gathered on the street outside the yard to see what was happening. One of the commune leaders recognized Zhang Feng. He had made a very good impression on him in the past. He had actually supported Zhang Feng's application to university during the Cultural Revolution. Zhang Feng had not told him about his post as the Deputy Secretary of the city party committee. This leader also told Zhang Feng that Head Wang was very unpopular as he was a villain and was hated by ordinary people. He also told the other leaders he knew Zhang Feng was a decent person and not a swindler. Secretary Yang said they would know the truth very soon.

After about 20 minutes, the noise of a Jeep could be heard. The door was opened and Secretary He and his assistant came in. Head Wang and his militiamen also tried to rush in but were blocked by Secretary He's assistant. Seeing Zhang Feng,

Secretary He walked over to him immediately and shook hands with him, saying,

"Secretary Zhang! How come you are here? I would have sent somebody to welcome you if I had been informed of your arrival."

Then he said to the commune leaders, sternly,

"You are behaving very badly! This is Secretary Zhang from the city party committee. Why are you treating him like this? No seat for him? No cup of tea for him?"

Secretary Zhang from the city party committee! All the commune leaders were scared because they had never seen such high ranking official in their village before. They hastily offered up their seats and made tea for Zhang Feng and his colleagues, apologizing to them. Secretary He invited Zhang Feng to dinner but Zhang Feng politely declined. He told Secretary He that he had two urgent things to deal with: to punish Head Wang and rescue He Hua. Then he told Secretary He what had happened to him that morning.

Hearing about the bullying behaviour of Head Wang, Secretary He was very angry indeed. He said he had already received many letters of accusation describing Head Wang's poor conduct but had not yet found time to deal with this. So today, he would make a decision on behalf of the county party committee. Then he opened the door, stood with Zhang Feng by his side, and said seriously to Head Wang and his followers,

"Wang Gui, you have been audacious enough to hit and shut out Secretary Zhang of the city party committee today. Admit your guilt!"

Head Wang looked frightened after hearing that Zhang Feng was a high ranking official. Secretary He then said to the people standing around,

"I announce, on behalf of the Hua Dan county party committee, that Wang Gui has been sacked from his post as the head of the commune militia. He is also expelled from the Party. We will investigate further the criminal things he has done to hurt ordinary people."

The people nearby burst into loud applause and Head Wang collapsed on the ground. Secretary He was a leader who liked to act decisively.

"Secretary Zhang, let's go and rescue He Hua."

A few militiamen who did not like Head Wang led the way for Zhang Feng, Secretary He and Secretary Yang to the small, dark room in which He Hua was imprisoned. They could hear a woman's cry inside. After the door was opened, He Hua's boyfriend, Li Yong, came to her and comforted her,

"Do not cry, He Hua. Look who came to rescue you!"

Zhang Feng walked up to her.

"How are you, He Hua? I haven't seen you for so long."

Raising her head and looking at Zhang Feng, she seemed to be searching her memory. Suddenly, she took hold of his arm and said,

"Brother Zhang, is it you?"

"Do not call him Brother Zhang. He is our city party committee secretary now," Li Yong said.

He Hua was surprised.

"Really? I knew many years ago that Brother Zhang would be a great man of important social status one day."

Zhang Feng knew it was not the time to recall past experiences; his main task was to improve the living conditions for millions of farmers in the countryside. Saying farewell to Secretary He and Secretary Yang, he and Lin Jianguo returned, with He Hua and Li Yong, to He Hua's village.

The next day, Zhang Feng held a meeting to discuss the land contract situation with He Hua, Li Yong, Leader Pan and another 20 team members. Zhang Feng asked He Hua to talk about the details of the plan. He Hua said, their plan was to allocate the whole 100 acres of land to individual members so each family would get about five acres of land each to grow crops. The ownership of the land still belonged to the village production team, so the plan would not be against the principle of public ownership. The team members only got the right to manage their land.

After the harvest, each family would deliver tax grain to the state and grain to the team and all the rest of the grain would belong to them. This meant the more they grew and harvested, the more grain they would have for themselves. They also made a plan to share farming tools and livestock. Zhang Feng was very happy after listening to He Hua's plan as this would give great incentives to the farmers and push them to work very hard.

He said to the team,

"The purpose of the Communist Party in launching the Communist Revolution was to give people better lives. Poverty is not the outcome of socialism. Why don't we use such good methods to feed our millions of farmers and people in the cities?"

Leader Pan handed a paper to Zhang Feng excitedly. It was a collective contract for this plan, with the signatures of all the team members and their fingerprints. The contract stated that all members would share the legal responsibility. If there were any negative legal issues, they would share them. In case the leaders of the team were arrested or put into jail, the other members would look after their family and raise their children.

After reading the contract, Zhang Feng had tears in his eyes. He wondered why it was so difficult for honest farmers to feed themselves and earn some money. He also admired the courage of these farmers.

Leader Pan said,

"We were actually just about to make our petition to the commune when He Hua was arrested but luckily, Secretary Zhang came to help us!"

Zhang Feng explained that he completely supported their land contract plan. To make the situation permanent, he would return to the city to discuss this issue with other leaders, and try to legalize this plan and policy. At the same time, he would promote it to more production teams, allowing more farmers to carry on this effective way to increase their grain output.

He said farewell to He Hua and the other team members the next day and returned to the River City.

Chapter III

I Offer My Post as Political Collateral

The next day after Zhang Feng returned to Jili City, he held a joint meeting with the city party committee and city government to discuss the land contract plan in the countryside. The resolution had to be found soon because the spring ploughing season was approaching. The main leaders of the city, plus the members of the Reform Office, all attended the meeting.

Zhang Feng delivered a report about the investigation in Heng He Commune and gave details of the significance and feasibility of the land contract plan. He also described the benefits of this policy in some areas of Southern China. To stop the left-wing leaders from voicing their opposition using Chairman Mao's collectivization model, Zhang Feng said the Chinese Communist Party took the land by force from the landlords and distributed it to the farmers after the liberation.

But later, the Party asked the farmers to return the land because the policy of public ownership was introduced. Farmers were organized into collective working units as production teams, production brigades and even the vast communes.

However, the problem was that agricultural production in China was still fairly low with no mechanization, only manual tools and domestic animals and without the resources to form big, modern farms. To rigidly organize them into co-operative farms would cause major problems. The main difficulty was the lack of incentives for the farmers themselves. They got the same return whether they worked hard or were very lazy. Zhang Feng described his recent experience in the countryside to prove his point.

Zhang Feng's report aroused much interest and warm discussion. Some of those attending the meeting said his report was very convincing because of his professorship but the First Secretary of the city party, Wang Kai, coughed and said,

"We cannot compare ourselves with Secretary Zhang because he is well-educated. But today's meeting is not an academic one. We need to agree a policy and consider political principles. In the past, Chairman Mao asked all farmers in the country to learn from Da Zhai village because they were the perfect example of collective ownership. Chairman Mao, before his death, strongly opposed Liu Shaoqi's individual farming and land contract policy. So, to me, this land contract plan is a politically backwards step and a move towards capitalism."

After his speech, those who were willing to support Zhang Feng dared not talk because Wang Kai was the foremost leader in the city. If anyone wanted promotion, they must obey his words. But Zhang Feng did not care as his intention in being an official was to benefit ordinary people and not for personal gain.

As he was trying to refute Secretary Wang's opinion, Mayer Gong said,

"Both Secretary Zhang and Secretary Wang's speeches are reasonable. We have started the reform movement and we should be practical and realistic and give up rigid rules and regulations. So, if any practice or policy can improve people's living conditions, why not try them?"

His speech was tactful. He did not offend Secretary Wang but his words pleased Zhang Feng. After his intervention, both sides gave their opinions. Yet, after a whole day's discussion, they still had not reached a common understanding.

A Deputy Mayor suggested that it would be better to delay the decision making and wait until Central Government gave a clear instruction but Zhang Feng was anxious because this was a big issue concerning the crucial interests of the farmers and ordinary people in the city. These officials could sit and read newspapers and drink tea all day long but ordinary people had to endure the torments of hunger and poverty. Having discussed this with Lin Jianguo and Chen Tao, he decided to see Secretary Liu of the provincial party committee.

The next day, Zhang Feng went to Secretary Liu's office. Secretary Liu smiled at him and asked him to sit down.

"I knew you would come to see me. What happened? Is it becoming difficult?"

"I did not realize that there are so many hard-headed officials in our leadership team and that it would be so difficult to change the existing system," Zhang Feng admitted.

"That is why we need well educated and open-minded young officials like you. I have read your land contract plan. It is a good one. It has been used in the South but there are still disagreements in the central party committee. You must know that reform will not be plain sailing. There will be struggles between reformers and the rigid left-wing guys. The Cultural Revolution ended 10 years ago now but there are still leaders using Chairman Mao's policy to suppress people. In agriculture, we learnt from the Soviet Union's collective farms and organized the people's communes. That brought about disasters at the end of the 1950s. Although we are back to production team levels, the farmers still have no incentives. Alright, let me to discuss this matter with other provincial leaders, then I will let you know what to do next," Secretary Liu said.

A few days later, another meeting was held. Secretary Liu and other provincial leaders also attended the meeting. The atmosphere in the room was very tense. Zhang Feng once again explained the details and the potential benefits of the land contract plan. Then the leaders on both sides gave their opinions. Director Shen and Secretary Wang were the two who opposed the plan most vigorously. In the end, everybody looked at Secretary Liu to see what he would say.

"Hearing your opinions, I think those who support and those who oppose all have their reasons. Reform is an experiment which needs to be tried out and explored. How can we build a modern country without giving up the unbending rules and regulations of the past? We should not use political arguments to suppress the people. Our provincial party committee completely supports Comrade Zhang Feng's plan."

Most of the delegates warmly applauded his speech.

Secretary Liu continued,

"But the burden on Zhang Feng's shoulders will be very heavy. He must face a lot of difficulties. Our decision is to try this plan in just four production teams in Heng He Commune for one year. If the outcome is good, we will extend it to other communes. If this trial goes badly, we will learn lessons from it."

"Somebody has to bear the political responsibility!" Said Secretary Wang.

"It will be a political responsibility," Shen also said seriously.

Hearing the political threats from these two hard-headed guys, Zhang Feng stood up.

"I will offer my post as political collateral. I will resign from my post if the plan fails."

Then he picked up the contract from He Hua and her team and showed it to the officials.

"Look at this contract with all its signatures and fingerprints. These twenty farmers use their land and lives as a guarantee to carry out the land contract plan. Why are they ready to risk everything for this scheme? Because they do not want to endure poverty any more. The existing situation is they cannot deliver tax grain to the state, they do not have enough food to eat and no money. Their houses are poor and their clothes are ragged and patched. Comrades, they helped the Communist Party to overthrow the National Party and established a new China. But forty years have passed and they still live in poverty. Can we ignore this as party officials? Please look, the last fingerprint on the contract is mine. I will not ask for grain and money. I only bear the legal and political responsibility for them. If the plan fails, I will not only have to resign my post, I may even go to jail!"

His speech provoked warm applause.

Secretary Liu stood up excitedly and said,

"This is great! You are a really great man!"

Everyone stood up to applaud, except Director Shen and Secretary Wang, who sat there with long faces. Chen Tao couldn't help wiping his eyes.

Spring in March is still chilly in Northeast China. In He Hua's village, Zhang Feng, Lin Jianguo and Chen Tao, together with Secretary He from Hua Dan County, and Secretary Yang from the commune, held a mobilization meeting for the implementation of the land contract plan. Zhang Feng announced the decision from the city and provincial party committee that the plan would be carried out in four production teams in the commune over five years, with the possibility of an extension if the outcome was good. The farmers involved all applauded loudly. Standing next to Zhang Feng, He Hua kept wiping her eyes. Secretary He and Secretary Yang also promised that the county and commune would help the teams with chemical fertilizer, tools and seeds.

After the meeting, Zhang Feng asked Leader Pan and He Hua to discuss distribution of the land and preparation of the spring ploughing season with the teams. All of them felt very confident about implementing the plan and were determined to eliminate poverty.

After meeting with the other three teams, Zhang Feng went back to He Hua's village which he regarded as his second home because of the shared emotional experiences he'd had with He Hua and the other villagers there. Zhang Feng remembered He Hua had loved him during the time he was farming there but because of the big difference in age between them, he had only treated her as his younger sister. At that time, he and Dan Dan would give her lessons using old school textbooks. He could see she was a capable, country girl and keen to make progress. This time, she had really showed her courage and ability to follow a radical path which others were scared of.

Back in He Hua's home, Zhang Feng saw she was cooking lunch. Looking at Zhang Feng and his assistants, He Hua felt happy.

"Brother Zhang, no, Secretary Zhang, please have lunch here."

"Do not call me Secretary. Please still call me Brother Zhang. I would like to talk to you more and would love to have lunch with you."

He Hua looked a bit embarrassed.

"But I do not have seafood and meat like people in the city, only steamed corn buns, coarsely ground maize and potato soup. I could kill a chicken and cook it for you."

"No, no! Don't kill a chicken! Your food is good enough for me."

Lin Jianguo and Chen Tao also said a rustic meal would be very nice. Zhang Feng helped He Hua to cook. He picked up firewood, fired the stove and peeled the potatoes skillfully.

"Brother Zhang, you still remember how to cook country meals!"

"I learnt from you."

Then he told Lin Jianguo and Chen Tao about his experience in the village during the Cultural Revolution. Chen Tao listened to him with great interest as he was ten years younger than Zhang Feng and had not been sent to the fields to work as a student during the Cultural Revolution. Lin Jianguo knew the countryside well because he grew up there. They all enjoyed the food.

Zhang Feng said the good thing was that the village had fresh grain from last year's harvest but in the cities, the grain was stored in warehouses for many years so the taste was not as good. There was no wheat or rice in the villages so the farmers could not have dumplings here. He Hua said she would have the money to buy wheat flour if the land contract plan worked. Zhang Feng congratulated He Hua for having a boyfriend and said Li Yong was an honest and kind young man with an education. He also asked when they would get married and He Hua answered, shyly, that the wedding was delayed because of the new plan.

"We will have our wedding if we have a successful harvest this autumn."

Zhang Feng was very pleased and said,

"We will definitely come to your wedding."

It seemed that Lin Jianguo wanted to say something to He Hua as well but he waited until they said their goodbyes.

"Sister He Hua, do you know Secretary Zhang wrote a 'military pledge' for the land contract plan? He will suffer a severe political penalty if the plan is unsuccessful. He might even lose his post."

He Hua was very surprised.

"Oh my god, Brother Zhang, you really are ready to risk everything for a better life for us. Do not worry. We will try our best to make the plan successful. Not only to protect your post but also to win a promotion for you."

Zhang Feng replied with a smile,

"My post is not important. I can always go back to my university if the worst happened. The most important thing is to feed the millions of farmers who are struggling and give them a better life."

Before he left, he assured He Hua that she could ask him for help if she ever faced difficulty. He then gave her five Yuan for the lunch but she declined firmly. Zhang Feng said,

"I know you and your brother just had some grain last year and no money at all. This little amount is just for you to buy soy sauce and vinegar."

Lin Jianguo and Chen Tao also persuaded He Hua to take the money. She thanked Zhang Feng and was reluctant to say goodbye to them.

A week later, Qing Lian knocked at Zhang Feng's office

door. With her slim figure and beautiful face, she attracted the attention of a lot of men in the corridor. Zhang Feng gave her a seat and asked his secretary to make her a cup of tea.

After the secretary had left the room, Zhang Feng asked,

"How is your life after marriage? Are you happy? You should feel happy living with a man who loves you so deeply."

"Just so, so," she replied, drily.

She asked about the situation with the land contract plan and said she would write a report on it to boost this policy. Zhang Feng was pleased and gave her a detailed explanation also telling her about He Hua's story.

Qing Lian suddenly asked,

"Was that the pretty village girl who loved you when we were in the fields?"

"How did you know this? You did not work in my production team."

"We were not on good political terms at that time, but I still cared about your private life," Qing Lian answered, shyly.

"All of this is over. She has a boyfriend now. They will marry this autumn if they have a good harvest."

"That is great! Tell me about their wedding and I will go. It will be a very good story for my newspaper."

Before she left, Zhang Feng exhorted her not to mention him too much in her report and to write more about He Hua and her team members.

With an emotional glance, she said,

"Just wait for the report, Brother Feng."

A few days later, Dan Dan passed the newspaper to Zhang Feng.

"Look at this report! Your 'sister', Qing Lian, seems to be always trying to do something for you."

Looking at the paper, he saw a report on the front page with the headline: 'The farmers carry out reform in the countryside. Secretary Zhang supports them fully and is their rock.' The report greatly praised He Hua's team for daring to try the land contract in order to increase output and improve their living conditions. It also mentioned how Secretary Zhang Feng had ignored criticism from the left-wing group and supported the farmers' actions. "I asked Qing Lian not to mention my support too much and to focus on He Hua's courage, but she forgot."

Dan Dan said, jokingly,

"It is good to have a few more female friends. He Hua was very happy to meet you?"

Dan Dan still remembered that He Hua had loved Zhang Feng when they were working in the fields, but at that time, Dan Dan was only Zhang Feng's 'sister'.

"My dear wife, you are my greatest supporter when it comes to my reform work, not other people. Don't forget to tell me about the economic developments in Japan, South Korea, Taiwan and Singapore in the last three decades when you do your research project."

Dan Dan said with a smile,

"Fine! You only think of me when you need help. Now read the report written by your 'sister', Qing Lian. Is she enjoying married life?"

Before Zhang Feng gave an answer, she added,

"She probably says it is 'so, so'."

"How did you know her answer?"

Zhang Feng was very surprised.

"Apart from economics, I am also an expert in emotions!"

"Maybe you should also have a job as a marriage consultant!"

"Maybe," she smiled.

It was nearly April. Sowing time was approaching. Zhang Feng and his assistants went to He Hua's village. They could see many farmers working in their fields, ploughing, loosening the soil and putting manual and chemical fertilizer on. Zhang Feng felt excited as normally, at this time of year, farmers were still idling their time away inside. He saw entire families also working in the fields to help the farmers. They all greeted Zhang Feng who asked them why they had started to prepare for sowing so early this year. They said this year was different. They had been allotted their own land. The final harvest would determine how much grain they could have for themselves after delivering the tax grain to the state and the collective grain to the team. That was why they must work very hard. Zhang Feng was very pleased to see the incentives created by the land contract. In one field, Zhang Feng saw the notorious lazy bones, Wang Feng, who greeted him. He asked Wang Feng why he was working so much harder now.

"I dare not be as lazy now or I would not have enough grain to eat if my land only produces a small amount plus, the other villagers would laugh at me."

Zhang Feng encouraged him to work hard.

Arriving in He Hua's field, Zhang Feng could not find her at first. Another farmer told him that she was helping Old Sun loosen the soil in his field. Walking to Old Sun's field, Zhang Feng saw He Hua and her brother helping the old man breaking up the soil. It was clear that she wanted all the team members to have a good harvest, not just herself. Zhang Feng was moved by her kindness. He and his assistants all took off their coats to work together with He Hua. Zhang Feng worked quickly and thoroughly and his efforts were praised by Lin Jianguo and Chen Tao.

He Hua said,

"Do you know, when Brother Zhang worked here in the past, he obtained the highest possible three thousand working points every year!"

Lin Jianguo and Chen Tao nodded their heads to praise him.

After finishing the work in Old Sun's field, Zhang Feng and his assistants went to He Hua's field to help her. After a moment, Chen Tao noticed that He Hua seemed to have something to ask Zhang Feng but clearly did not want to bother him.

Chen Tao asked her,

"Sister He Hua, do you have something to ask Secretary Zhang?"

He Hua said quietly she had a small problem and she did not like to bother Zhang Feng but he overheard their conversation.

"It is nothing major," explained He Hua, "we just have a shortage of chemical fertilizer and we want to buy some from the county but the agricultural bureau told us that the amount available was limited. They are giving priority to the production teams without land contract plans. Also, the commune has some improved variety of seeds. We would like some but the person in charge has refused to give us any because he is a relative of the evil Wang Gui."

Zhang Feng felt very angry. It was obvious that these guys were deliberately making things difficult for He Hua's team. They did not want farmers to have land contracts because they had a rigid way of thinking and also, they would lose some of their privileges if the farmers got richer. Zhang Feng wanted to go to the county and commune straight away, but Lin Jianguo and Chen Tao said it would be better to let them resolve these problems alone as Zhang Feng had other things to deal with. In the end, Lin Jianguo went to the county to find Secretary

He and resolved the fertilizer matter and Chen Tao went to the commune and asked Secretary Yang to sort out the seed problem. They stayed there overnight with Zhang Feng in Leader Pan's home.

The next day, Lin Jianguo and Chen Tao made their way back. Zhang Feng, He Hua and Leader Pan were discussing some issues about the contract. Lin happily told them the chemical fertilizer problem was resolved. He had found Secretary He first, and Secretary He went to the county agriculture bureau and told them they must sell the fertilizer to He Hua and the other teams under the contract plan. He criticized the officer there for his negative attitude towards rural reform. The officer was scared and promised to send the fertilizer to He Hua's team the next day. He Hua and Leader Pan were very happy.

Then Chen Tao was back before lunch time with his good news. He had found Secretary Yang in the commune. Yang went to the seed station and asked the head to send the improved seeds to He Hua and the other teams straight away. He would lose his post if he continued to make trouble for He Hua and the other teams. The seeds were sent out immediately and would probably arrive that afternoon. He Hua and Pan kept thanking Zhang Feng and his assistants for their help.

Zhang Feng smiled and said,

"Not at all! This is also my project. Do not forget, my fingerprint is also on your contract!"

Everybody laughed.

Chapter IV

A Good Harvest – Never Seen in 30 Years

The warm wind in May turned the fields and mountains green around Jili City. Zhang Feng kept thinking about the progress of the land contract in He Hua's team and so he decided to visit them. To move around more quickly and conveniently, the city had given him a Jeep as it was more powerful on bumpy roads in rural areas. Lin Jianguo drove the Jeep because he had used one quite often in the Army. They drove to the commune and met Secretary Yang. They borrowed a horse and cart and Lin, once again, offered to drive.

On the way to He Hua's village, Zhang Feng noticed that the seedlings in the fields on both sides of the road were not looking healthy because of the dry weather recently. He started to worry about the effects of the weather on He Hua's crops but when they arrived at her village, he was surprised to see that the seedlings in her team's fields looked very healthy and much taller than in the other fields. Hearing the sounds of happy laughter near Leader Pan's home, Zhang Feng saw Pan, He Hua and some of the other villagers walking to the fields to start weeding.

Seeing Zhang Feng and his assistants, they all came up and asked,

"Brother Zhang, what do you think of our crop seedlings?"

"Excellent!" Zhang Feng replied.

"How could they not be like this? The way we treat our crops is just like the way we look after our children!" Leader Pan said.

"We did not work like this when we worked collectively for the team. It did not matter when you cut back a seedling, but now it is different. Losing one seedling means getting less grain for yourself," another villager added.

Zhang Feng felt very pleased after listening to them. He said he would go to the other teams in the afternoon but first, he would like to help He Hua and her team weed their fields. He asked Lin and Chen whether they were able to do this job. Lin said he had done some weeding before but Chen had never done it. Zhang Feng and Lin helped Hu Hua with the weeding and shovelling and Chen Tao helped He Hua's brother to sharpen the tools and feed the domestic animals.

While working, Zhang Feng talked to He Hua. He said he used to be able to do this kind of work very quickly in the past, but now, he needed to be very careful not to damage the seedlings. He Hua also said that the feeling of responsibility for the crop was different now compared to in the past. Zhang Feng praised He Hua's boyfriend and said he was a good boy. Looking at Zhang Feng, He Hua flushed and said her boyfriend could not compare with Zhang Feng, though he was a kind young man. Zhang Feng said he would wait for their wedding in the autumn.

Summer came around very quickly. The strong sunshine produced a lot of heat and there was a drought in some areas of the Jili countryside. One weekend, Zhang Feng decided to visit He Hua's village but he did not want to bother his assistants. He asked Wang Hai whether he could drive a Jeep. Wang Hai said there was no problem and he also wanted to visit the village where he had been sent with Zhang Feng during the Cultural Revolution. Dan Dan wanted to visit the village as well and see the countryside where she used to work as a farmer. Zhang Feng decided on a tour of the countryside. They went to the city council in the early morning and just before they drove away, Qing Lian ran up to them and shouted,

"Wait for me!"

"This is a weekend. Why not stay home with Li He and relax," Zhang Feng said.

"He has his own things to do but I want to go to Heng He commune to collect background information for my future report," Qing Lian said.

Wang Hai spoke loudly,

"Get on then! We will all go to the countryside together again!"

Everybody laughed.

Wang Hai drove quite fast and they arrived at He Hua's village before lunch time. Looking at the dense, green growth of the crops, they felt amazed as the crop here was double the height of that in the fields of the other teams.

Wang Hai was surprised and shouted,

"Oh, my god! It is so different between the teams, those with the land contract and those without."

After finding He Hua's team, Zhang Feng saw they were watering the fields with water from the stream outside the village. The river was lower down the fields around the village, so the farmers never bothered to collect water from there for the crops in the past. But now, it was different. Leader Pan told Zhang Feng how the hot weather had made the fields very dry so the crops needed water. The villagers carried the water from the stream for watering the crops, even though it was quite hard work. The management of the land was their own responsibility, not the team's.

Zhang Feng asked Wang Hai,

"Can you still carry a water bucket?"

"No problem!"

"I remember, in the past, in your student collective household, it was always Brother Zhang and Brother Wang carrying heavy water buckets, up to 40kg per bucket!" He Hua said.

Zhang Feng and Wang Hai took off their coats and carried water buckets to the field, walking several hundreds of metres each journey. Dan Dan and Qing Lian helped to fill the buckets with river water. All of them worked very hard and were soaked with sweat.

During lunch time, He Hua served some tasty pancake rolls to Zhang Feng and their friends. She said she had bought a pancake pot recently, so she could cook delicious Shang Dong style pancakes now.

"Oh, this is so delicious," said Wang Hai.

Zhang Feng reminded him not to eat too much. He Hua said that was no problem as there was still quite a lot of pancakes at home. She asked her brother to fetch some more. Ha Hua sat next to Dan Dan and they recalled their experience of being there in the past.

He Hua said,

"Sister Dan Dan, you still look very beautiful and not at all like a woman in her thirties. You are very lucky to be married to Brother Zhang. You make an excellent couple, endowed with both beauty and talent. Actually, even back then, I noticed you were not really his 'sister'."

"How did you know this?" Dan Dan asked.

"Countryside girls also have their intuition. Because when you looked at Brother Zhang, the expression in your eyes did not look like that of a sister," He Hua smiled and continued,

"Why did you prefer to be known as his 'sister'?"

Dan Dan really wanted to tell He Hua that at that time, Zhang Feng's girlfriend was Yu Mei but their relationship had ended tragically. Dan Dan changed the topic quickly.

Qing Lian seemed to remember something. She asked whether Head Zhang of the production brigade was still a leader. Pan told her he had died of cancer five years ago.

"Evil people will have an evil ending. He harassed me a lot in the past, and I almost died because of his harassment."

Zhang Feng recalled how he had saved Qing Lian when she tried to commit suicide. His actions moved her and changed her from being an insane Red Guard back to the gentle and kind woman she used to be.

Before Zhang Feng and his friends left, they visited the poor, straw-mud house where they had lived during the 'students' exile' in the Cultural Revolution. Recalling their hard life as the 'Educated Youth', they were filled with many emotions. He Hua said the villagers would build better brick houses with more money if the land contract plan was successful.

Zhang Feng said,

"I will build a bungalow here for my retirement and enjoy a rural life."

Everybody thought he was just joking. He did not know at the time that it would really come true, thirty years later.

Autumn came at last and farmers in different counties and citizens in the city were all keen to know the result of the land contract plan. Good news was delivered to the city party committee: 'An incredible harvest – never seen before!' Chen Tao jumped from his chair. All the officials in the Reform Office applauded warmly. Zhang Feng was very calm because he knew the harvest season was very short and sudden, heavy rains could damage the matured crops.

"All of us will go to Heng He Commune tomorrow to help the farmers gather in their crops," he announced. "At the same time, we can calculate the crop yield for our report. You will not go in vain! There is delicious rustic food waiting for you!"

His colleagues laughed.

Early next morning, Zhang Feng took 15 people with him to Heng He Commune. When they arrived, they were met with a wonderful harvest scene: huge bundles of corn cobs on corn stalks, plump-eared red sorghum, bent on their stalks and enormous soybeans swaying in the wind. Sighing with emotion, Zhang Feng and Lin Jianguo said they had never seen such wonderful crops.

On the threshing ground, Zhang Feng saw the villagers busy gathering in their produce. Seeing Zhang Feng and his companions, He Hua ran to him, embracing him and bursting into tears. Zhang Feng patted her and asked what had happened.

She suddenly started to laugh.

"Brother, I am so happy! We have succeeded!"

Seeing this moving scene, the people around them all applauded warmly. Leader Pan asked Zhang Feng why he had brought so many officials here.

"They have come here to help you harvest the crops."

Pan said that Zhang Feng really understood the farming seasons.

"Secretary Zhang has brought his companions here to help with our harvest today. We need to entertain them well. For this evening's supper, you should at least have a braised chicken with mushrooms." Zhang Feng said,

"No, no. You can only eat chicken during the Chinese New Year's celebration." He Hua replied,

"Brother Zhang, you are still looking at old calendars. If you go to our homes now, you will see flocks of chickens and ducks, even herds of sheep and pigs. Do not forget, our contract encourages us to raise domestic animals on private plots. In the past, you were criticized if you raised more than a few chickens."

People around her laughed.

Zhang Feng waved to his colleagues,

"Let's start work then!"

They were all busy with different activities. Zhang Feng asked his male colleagues who was up to the strenuous farm work of gathering in corn, sorghum and soybean. For those who could not do the farm work, they helped the women to load the crops on carts and sent them to the threshing ground. Seeing Zhang Feng quickly cutting down the crops with his sickle, his colleagues praised his skill.

After a busy working day, more than half of the villagers' crops had been gathered in. He Hua and Leader Pan said they felt more relaxed now as the rest could be done over one or two days. Zhang Feng said he and his colleagues would help some more tomorrow, up to lunch time. Once he knew the average yield per Mu (an area of land equal to 667 square metres), he would go back and report to the city council.

Next day, at about lunch time, Zhang Feng returned to the threshing ground after working in the fields. He Hua burst out, cheerfully,

"Brother, we have finished the calculations for the yield of the first ten households. The calculation for the rest of the ten households looks very similar. Brother Zhang, both you and Director Lin used to work in the fields. Can you guess the possible average yield per Mu for our harvest?"

Zhang Feng mused,

"In Northeast China, the average yield for corn is about 400kg per Mu, for sorghum, about 300kg in a good year, soybean? About 150kg per Mu."

Lin gave a similar answer. Just then, Leader Pan came in and after hearing the estimates from Zhang Feng and Lin Jianguo, he said, with a smile,

"Xiao Zhang, no, Secretary Zhang, what you said about past yields was correct, but not this time. He Hua, tell them the final number."

He Hua excitedly picked up a piece of paper and read,

"The average crop yields for our first ten households are: corn, 700kg per Mu, sorghum, 400kg per Mu, soybean, 230kg per Mu. For other oil plants, like sunflowers, the yields are also much higher than before but we have not bothered to calculate them."

Zhang Feng and his colleagues were speechless on hearing this information.

Zhang Feng asked,

"Did you just do one calculation?"

Leader Pan smiled and said,

"We also did not believe it at the beginning but we got the same results over three checks."

All the people on the threshing ground hailed their success.

"I did not realize we could get such an incredible harvest!" Zhang Feng exclaimed.

"I have been farming all my life but I have never got, nor heard of, such a high yield!" cried Pan.

Zhang Feng continued,

"We are extremely happy. We did not sweat in vain. Please carry on with the harvest and then report the final results to the county agricultural bureau. They will come to check and report the final calculations to the city council. We will expect an on-site meeting about the success of the land contract plan in your village. Officials from all counties and communes will come to the meeting. The outcome, I think, should be that having this land contract plan will extend to all villages in our province. Millions of our farmers will have more grain, more food and more money!"

All the villagers clapped their hands, cheerfully.

In October, a grand, on-site meeting to review the land contract plan was held in He Hua's village. Mayor Gong, Zhang Feng and officials from all communes and counties attended the meeting but the hard-headed, left-wing leaders, like Director Shen, Secretary Wang and Zhang Feng's former classmate, Li Qiu, did not come. Qing Lian came happily with a lot of journalists and photographers. As a leader in charge of implementing the plan, Zhang Feng formally announced the outcome achieved by He Hua's team.

He explained that with the final checks by the city agricultural bureau, He Hua's team had achieved an unprecedented harvest and a very high yield which had never been seen before. It was the first time in many years that they had fully delivered the tax grain to the state and delivered the full amount of collective grain to the team. After all this, the amount of grain to be kept for themselves was three times the amount of previous years. After selling extra grain, oil seed and some domestic animals to the state, the average income for each household was 500 Yuan, compared to 50 to 100 Yuan in past years. Sometimes, they made no money at all in bad years. Half of the village households had been able to start renovating their homes with the extra income. Zhang Feng said the other three production teams using the plan had also achieved very similar harvests. His speech evoked warm applause.

He Hua also delivered a speech on behalf of the team. She was too excited to say much and in the end, she just said,

"We are saying goodbye to poverty at last! We will have a better life now!"

Then she specially thanked Zhang Feng for his support without which, they would not have succeeded and they would still be suffering extreme poverty. Everyone gave Zhang Feng a standing ovation. The farmers from other teams and other communes also shouted,

"We want the land contract plan! We want the land contract plan!"

The local leaders said they would not delay any longer and would start the plan from next year.

A deep male voice boomed out at this moment,

"Don't you worry that you are following capitalist ways?"

The voice belonged to Secretary Liu of the provincial party committee.

Zhang Feng was surprised and asked,

"Why are you here Secretary Liu? Are you in Beijing for a conference?"

Liu replied, explaining more fully,

"Nothing is more important than this meeting. The ultimate task of the Communist Party is to give people a better life. My countrymen, friends and colleagues, we all see the benefit of the land contract plan. Why did we not dare to do it before? Because of the influence of rigid, Soviet Union socialism and the example of Da Zhai village which still controlled our minds. Social practice proved that these policies were not workable in our country. We must follow practical and realistic ways, not dogmatic ways. To carry out reform, we must bravely explore new ways to make life better for our people. We desperately need powerful officials, like Zhang Feng, to succeed."

Then he declared that the land contract plan would be extended to all the counties in the province. People in the meeting burst into thunderous applause.

After the meeting had ended, Zhang Feng and He Hua excitedly took Secretary Liu and other leaders to visit some households in the village. They saw that all the granaries were full, with some grain sacks even stacked in yards, waiting for new storage to be built. In He Hua's house, Qing Lian took a photo of her holding a huge bundle of corn cobs. In Leader Pan's home, Zhang Feng and Pan held up an enormous bundle of sorghum and Qing Lian quickly took a photo. Seeing flocks of chickens and herds of pigs and sheep, Secretary Liu asked whether the farmers were allowed to raise such numbers of domestic animals. Some farmers explained how they would have been punished for doing this in the past as it was seen as a form of capitalism. Secretary Liu gave a bitter smile and shook his head, meaning it was stupid.

Three days after Zhang Feng returned home, Dan Dan passed a copy of the Jili Daily to him, saying,

"Look! You are really in the limelight now! The Jili Daily has used a whole page to report your on-site meeting and the reaction from the other counties and cities to the success of the land contract plan. Do you know that the farmers have composed a ballad about you saying: 'If you want a good harvest, go find Secretary Zhang'? There are also some large photos of you in the paper."

Zhang Feng turned to the second page of the paper and saw the photo taken of him with Leader Pan. The next photo was the one of He Hua holding the enormous bundle of corn.

Dan Dan said,

"Your sister, Qing Lian, is a very good journalist, using photos of a handsome man and beautiful girl to attract the attention of the readers!"

"I told her not to take my picture but to take photos of the farmers instead, but she did not listen to me."

"Because it gives her an opportunity to keep a large photo of her Brother Feng!"

"What are you saying? She has a husband now!" Zhang Feng said.

Yet Dan Dan's guess was really right. At this moment, Qing Lian was gazing at the photo she had taken of Zhang Feng and had hidden it in a place where Li He would not find it.

A few days later, Zhang Feng was called to a meeting in the office of the city party committee. He thought it must be a meeting to discuss the work for the next stage as all the leaders of the city party and local government were there. But suddenly, the Head of the provincial personnel department entered the room. Everyone felt surprised because his appearance usually meant there would be some personnel appointments.

He firstly talked to the leaders casually and then he turned to Zhang Feng.

"You do not need to worry, Secretary Zhang, your post is

safe because the land contract plan has been successful but you were really good at making jokes."

"I did not make a joke about it. I was very serious as I knew that trying out the land contract plan would be very risky."

The Head of personnel said,

"We desperately need officials like Secretary Zhang who dare to take risks in order to carry out reforms. I will now announce the decision of the provincial party committee. Comrade Zhang Feng has been appointed as the Mayor of Jili City. Mayor Gong will take the post of Secretary of the Jili party committee. Secretary Wang will become Head of the city people's congress."

This appointment really surprised Zhang Feng as he did not expect promotion for his efforts and achievements. All the leaders supporting him applauded his appointment warmly but Secretary Wang looked very embarrassed as he was being demoted.

Secretary Gong said to Zhang Feng, happily,

"Mayor Zhang, we will work well together."

At the same time, in the office of the provincial propaganda department, Li Qiu was speaking ill of Zhang Feng. He said Zhang Feng had won his political bet this time and got a promotion but was giving himself airs and becoming cocky.

Shen said,

"Hai! Being in local government is like being in a gambling house. You may win or lose. Just wait to see how far he will be carried by his success."

One week later, on a morning when Zhang Feng was not in his office, Lin Jianguo quietly went in and put a letter on his desk. Zhang Feng returned to his office in the afternoon and saw the letter without a stamp. Feeling curious, he opened the letter. He felt his heartbeat quicken when he saw the familiar writing of Yu Mei. 'At last, she writes to me directly.' he thought but he was disappointed as there was no return address and no signature. Her letter read:

"Dear Brother Feng, can I still call you this? Congratulations, you have won your initial success and have been promoted to the post of Jili City Mayor. I hope you can go even further as my father wished before his death. Bless you forever!"

After he had finished reading the letter, he thought about Yu Mei painfully. Where was she? How was she doing? Had she found a man who loved her deeply? Why had she not given her contact details? Was she worried that it might make Dan Dan feel unhappy? No, she is an open-minded woman and she would not be jealous about such contact. He was gratified that Yu Mei missed him which meant she must still love him.

Before winter arrived, Zhang Feng, Dan Dan, Wang Hai, Li He and Qing Jian all attended He Hua's wedding in her new house. Everybody believed Li Yong was a good husband. Wang Hai warned him, jokingly, that if he treated He Hua badly, all of them, as her brothers and sisters, would punish him. Li Yong replied hastily that he would look after her carefully for the rest of his life. He Hua killed a pig and cooked many delicious dishes such as braised pork with bean noodles. The guests said they would never find such fresh and delicious cuisine in the city.

He Hua told Zhang Feng that she had a new idea to further improve the living conditions for the farmers there. She wanted to set up village-township enterprises to earn more money for the villagers because farming alone was not enough. She had heard some village-township enterprises had started in Southern China and provided wonderful incomes for farmers. She, together with Li Yong, planned to set up an oil press factory, plus local specialty products like wood fungus and honey. Zhang

Feng was happy after listening to He Hua's proposals. He had just started to consider reforms in commercial and industrial areas recently and he told He Hua to act bravely and always asked him for help if she faced any difficulties. He joked that he could put his fingerprint on any future contacts.

Dan Dan asked,

"How many posts do you have?"

All the wedding guests laughed.

PART III

Economic Reform in the City

Chapter I

The Rising of the Self-Employed Vendors

Winter was coming. One day, Dan Dan was at home because she was not teaching that day. Her son, Dan Feng, was cared for by her parents and Zhang Feng's parents. The most enjoyable thing for retired people to do in China was to look after their grandchildren. Dan Dan wanted to do some shopping and left the house with a shopping bag.

The house they had moved into recently had been allotted to them by the city council as Zhang Feng was now the Mayor of the City. It was a pleasant house in the area reserved for high ranking officials. Just by chance, its location was very close to the house where Yu Mei's family used to live when her father, Li Jianguo, was the First Secretary of the provincial party committee.

Initially, Zhang Feng was not keen on moving in. He did not want to become a member of the privileged social class, as at that time, ordinary people had great difficulty finding places to live. There were very long waiting lists for council apartments which gave many people a great deal of stress. When Zhang Feng found that he could see Yu Mei's previous home from this new house, he quietly agreed to move in. Dan Dan actually realized the reason why he had changed his mind later because sometimes, she could see her husband staring at that house, blankly.

Leaving her home, Dan Dan enjoyed a beautiful white world of snow and ice. The roads were covered in thick snow and the rime covered trees swayed in the wind. Her marriage to Zhang Feng was happy. Her son was cute and her husband was attentive to her. She was doing well in her teaching and research work but recently, she could feel Zhang Feng had been treating her more politely, like in the kind of brother-sister relationship which they'd had in the past but not in a romantic way any longer. Sometimes, he even forgot her birthday.

She knew he was very busy with his leadership role and responsibilities and she also understood that living together as husband and wife for long could diminish the initial passion of lovers. Yet, her intuition told her Zhang Feng still missed Yu Mei although Dan Dan never doubted his loyalty to her. She knew it was very difficult for Zhang Feng to forget his life-death lover, Yu Mei.

In the grocery shop, not far from her home, she bought noodles, Canton sausages and pork ribs. It made her happy that she did not need to buy food with coupons any longer. After the land contract plan had spread to the whole country, food supply became sufficient and richly varied. The food coupon system had been totally abolished recently after 30 years and now, you could buy everything you needed if you had money. A family could sit down together for pork dumplings any time, not just during the New Year festival.

After finishing her food shopping, Dan Dan noticed a lot of street vendors selling clothes and small electrical appliances nearby. She remembered some friends had told her that good quality, digital watches could be bought here so she walked over.

When she got closer, she saw a dark, fat man quarreling with a man and a woman. The dark man said,

"This place is mine. I was here yesterday."

But the other two people said,

"The places do not belong to anybody. Whoever comes first gets the spot."

The dark man became very rude and started to wave his clenched fists at the other two sellers.

Dan Dan tried to stop him.

"You must be able to come to an agreement because you are all in the same business."

The dark man turned back to look at Dan Dan and was about to tell her not to meddle in other people's business but he was suddenly startled as he recognized her. She also recognized him. He was the notorious hooligan from the time of the Cultural Revolution and a fierce Red Guard who had killed and injured a lot of people and was sentenced to ten years in jail. Zhang Feng once told her that he and Wang Hai had seen him selling ice-cream after his release.

Dan Dan said,

"Are you Hei Tou? You did a lot of evil things during the Cultural Revolution. Why are you still so nasty?"

Hei Tou could not remember exactly who Dan Dan was but he was worried she might dig up more of his past so he said to the other two sellers,

"OK, I will find another place."

Then he walked away with his bag.

Dan Dan also recognized the other two street vendors when they tried to thank her for her help.

"Are you Yu Lan and Song Ping?"

They had been Zhang Feng's middle school classmates and had lived in the same collective household in the countryside during the Revolution. Dan Dan used to see them quite often when she visited their collective household during that time. They had not gone to university and so, did not have regular jobs. Dan Dan was very sympathetic and asked about their existing situation.

After returning to the city, they had worked in restaurants and as cleaners, but had earned very little. Recently, they had started to sell goods on the street stalls. They travelled to Guang Zhou City to buy clothes and electrical appliances made in Hong Kong, then brought them back here to sell but it was not an easy job as they could not do it during bad weather. The most difficult thing for them was the constant harassment from the City Management Officers because street selling was still illegal. If they were caught by the officers, they would be fined and their goods would be confiscated.

Dan Dan sympathized with them and felt that the Government should help these people. They worked hard to sell something which could not be bought from state shops. It was probably those hard, left-wing leaders who persisted in public ownership and thought that street vending was a capitalistic way to do business. Dan Dan wanted to help them so she bought three digital watches from them. Song Ping and Yu Lan kept thanking her.

Just after Dan Dan had paid them, they suddenly heard shouts,

"Run away! The city management officers are coming!"

All the vendors quickly packed up their stalls and ran away. Seeing Song Ping and Yu Lan hastily packing up their goods, Dan Dan bent down to help them. Just then, a group of management officers rushed up to them.

"Stop! You are caught! Nobody can run away!"

Then they loaded their truck with the products from the stands and took all the vendors to the City Management Office.

Pointing to Dan Dan, Yu Lan said to the Head of the officers,

"She is not a seller. She is a customer who bought our products."

"What customer? I saw her tidying up your stall."

Dan Dan wanted to argue with him but she also wanted to help Song Ping and Yu Lan, so she went along to the City Management Office with them. Hei Tou had not been caught as he ran away very quickly. Song Ping and Yu Lan did not know Zhang Feng was now the Mayor of the City as they did not have time to read newspapers nor listen to the radio. If the officers had known that Dan Dan was the wife of the Mayor, they would have released her straight away.

In the City Management Office, a Deputy Director gave an admonitory talk to the sellers. He told them that all street vendors were just social rubbish who idled about and did not want to work properly. They continued to try and sell even after being caught, so this time, he would punish them severely.

Dan Dan disliked what he was saying.

"Could you please refer to the facts? These sellers have earned their money through hard work. They sell products to customers who cannot buy them in the state shops. So what's wrong with that?"

The Deputy Director looked at Dan Dan, and asked,

"Who are you? You look like a lady with status. Why are you involved in street selling? Have you been divorced by your husband recently?"

Dan Dan was really angry now. She had not realized there were such unreasonable government officials.

"Do you want to know who I really am? Give me the telephone."

The Deputy Director was becoming nervous but he pretended to be confident. He asked an officer to hand the phone to Dan Dan, saying,

"You want to find a 'back door' way out but I won't put up with this."

Dan Dan did not want to use her status as the wife of the Mayor to suppress them. She really wanted to help the sellers. So she did not ring Zhang Feng, but rang Lin Jianguo instead.

"It that Jianguo? It's Dan Dan. I am in a bit of trouble. Can you come?"

Lin Jianguo was worried and asked,

"Where are you?"

"I am in the City Management Office. I have been caught street selling."

Li Jianguo knew Dan Dan was joking.

"Please wait there and I will come straight away!"

Then he drove to the City Management Office quickly with two assistants.

The Deputy heard Dan Dan's words and thought she could not possibly be married to a high-ranking official so he said, with a wicked smile,

"Are you trying to find some officer to plead mercy for you? It depends on how high his rank is."

Dan Dan ignored him. She told Song Ping and Yu Lan not to worry. Somebody would come to rescue them.

Lin Jianguo entered the City Management Office in a rush. Seeing Dan Dan and the other sellers standing in the room like criminals and surrounded by thug-like officers, he was very angry.

"What are you doing here? Why have you arrested these people?"

The Deputy Director recognized Lin Jianguo and said, politely,

"Director Lin, these people were street selling and breaking the law. They did not listen to our instructions so we caught them and will fine them and confiscate their products."

Seeing Lin was a high ranking official, Song Ping pointed at Dan Dan and said,

"She is not a seller. She is our old classmate who wanted to buy something from us but this officer arrested her as well."

One of Lin's assistants said, angrily,

"You dare to arrest the wife of Mayor Zhang!"

"Wife of Mayor Zhang?"

All the officers of the City Management Office were frightened.

Dan Dan said, calmly,

"I do not want to talk to you as the wife of the Mayor. I am just a lecturer at the University, a normal citizen. You should not treat these sellers as criminals even if they have done something wrong. Central Government is discussing whether to legalize street selling by self-employed people. They are a vulnerable social class and we should show some sympathy for them."

Lin Jianguo said to the Deputy Director,

"Ask your Head, Li, to come here!"

Head Li was just passing this office by chance so he entered the room.

"Who wants to see me?"

Seeing Lin Jianguo, he immediately said,

"Oh, it is Director Lin! Come to my office and have a cup of tea!"

Most officials in the city knew Lin Jianguo was a favourite assistant of Mayor Zhang and they did not want to offend him.

Lin Jianguo said,

"Forget the tea and please resolve this matter first."

After Head Li discovered what had happened with the street sellers, he said to the Deputy, angrily,

"What are you doing? The city council already told us not to interfere with street vendors until there is a clear policy on the matter. Release them immediately and return their products to them!"

Then he apologized to Dan Dan again and again.

Lin Jianguo said to the sellers,

"Do not worry. The city council is discussing your business. You are all legal workers. We will help you."

The street vendors were very pleased and applauded. Dan Dan told Song Ping and Yu Lan that Zhang Feng would do his best to help their business and improve their living conditions. They said they were very pleased that Zhang Feng had become the Mayor. Even when they lived in the collective household in the countryside, they predicted that one day, Zhang Feng would be a man of special social status. They took their products and left the office happily. Lin drove Dan Dan back to her home.

When Zhang Feng returned home that evening, his first words to Dan Dan were,

"My dear wife, I am so sorry you felt frightened today."

Dan Dan said it did not matter for her. She just did not realize that young people who did not get a chance to go to university had such a hard life. At the same time, as an economist, she thought the Government should legalize and also, standardize the business of self-employed street vendors. She suggested the city council might set up a free market to provide places for their stalls.

Zhang Feng patted his leg and said happily,

"Oh, my dear wife, I should give you a post as my economic adviser! We are discussing this very matter in a few days. Firstly, we must decide how to legalize the business of these sellers, secondly, how to manage their business. Your suggestion of setting up a free market place is a very good idea."

Dan Dan smiled.

"Do I deserve a reward then?"

"I can cook you a delicious meal this evening."

"You just like eating. I need to go on a diet as I have put on weight."

"Then what else do you want?" Zhang Feng asked.

Dan Dan flushed and said quietly,

"How long have we not…"

Zhang Feng suddenly understood what she meant. He embraced and kissed her, and said,

"Well, let's have some nice, intimate time tonight."

Dan Dan shut her eyes and enjoyed the caresses of her husband.

One week later, Zhang Feng held a meeting with the Reform Office and the City Industrial and Commercial Bureau to discuss policy for the self-employed vendors. Some officials who disliked these sellers, said they were just bad people without proper jobs, some were even newly released criminals. They specially mentioned the notorious Hei Tou. Other negative points brought up included the idea that their business was against the principle of public ownership as they worked privately. They insisted that street vendors disturbed traffic and affected street hygiene.

Lin Jianguo and Chen Tao both talked about this issue. They believed that most of these vendors were in a vulnerable social class, such as students returning from the countryside after the Cultural Revolution. They had suffered a hard life already so they should be helped to improve their living conditions. It was not a bad thing to make some money. Their business supplemented that of the state shops and they sold efficient, new goods to customers, just like farmers selling their grain and livestock in free markets. Their business was actually complementary to public ownership.

Summarizing the main points of the meeting, Zhang Feng said that industrial and commercial reform should now be on the agenda. In order to modernize the country, the Government must learn from marketization and not follow the Soviet Union's unbending, centrally controlled, economic system. The business of the self-employed vendors could boost consumption and improved consumption would stimulate production, which was a positive thing. If the state shops continued to sell the same goods for year after year, how could a prosperous China ever emerge? Most officials agreed with him.

"I have discussed all of this with Secretary Gong. In order to manage the business of these sellers, we have decided to build an indoor market, using city funding. Vendors can erect their stalls inside this market but they will need to apply to the Industrial and Commercial Bureau for a license first. It means they can run their businesses legally."

The officials at the meeting all said it was a good proposal which would help to legalize and standardize this business. Some of them even said they would tell their relatives and friends to apply for the license.

Zhang Feng's proposal was reported to Director Shen by Li Qiu. Shen felt he had seized upon Zhang Feng's mistake and reported what had been proposed to the provincial party committee saying that Zhang Feng always intended to follow capitalistic methods to enact reform. But his complaint was rejected by Secretary Liu who said the central party committee had discussed this matter recently with a positive outcome. The new policy would encourage this business and give guidance to the vendors because trading, production and employment would all benefit.

Director Shen said, angrily,

"Zhang Feng dares to act in this way because he has Secretary Liu protecting him like a political umbrella. The good thing is that Secretary Liu will retire in the next few years and then we will see whether he dares to oppose me again."

Getting such support from Secretary Liu, Zhang Feng and his colleagues were very happy and they started to act quickly. They went to the construction site every day to supervise the progress of the company constructing this huge, indoor market so quickly and so well. In three weeks, a huge, metal arched shelter covered with plastic sheeting stood on the site. It was the new trading market for the self-employed vendors to sell their goods. The citizens praised it for its attractive appearance and its huge space. The city council then announced that street vendors who wanted to sell in this market could apply for a license to the City Industrial and Commercial Bureau.

On the morning of the first day of applications, Zhang Feng said to Lin Jianguo that he would like to see how many people would apply because he was worried that the application procedure was too formal and off-putting. Arriving at the City Industrial and Commercial Bureau, they were surprised by the scene in front of them. There was a very long queue from the entrance of the office to the distant river bank, with roughly 200 people in the queue. Zhang Feng was pleased and asked Lin how many stands this market would hold. Lin said there would be about 250 places. Zhang Feng said in that case, it would be almost full with these first applications.

Just then, a young man left the office in a rush and shouted,

"A license! I have a license now! It is the first license in our city!"

It was Song Ping, Zhang Feng's former middle school classmate who had been caught by the City Management Office together with Dan Dan.

When he saw Zhang Feng, he shouted,

"Brother Feng! No, Mayor Zhang! I have a license now!"

At that moment, Yu Lan also came out of the office, and said to Zhang Feng,

"Brother Feng, my license is the second one!"

Zhang Feng congratulated them and people all around thanked Mayor Zhang for his help and support. They said they would work hard to supply the best quality goods to the citizens. Zhang Feng also encouraged them to work hard. Song Ping and Yu Lan asked Zhang Feng and Dan Dan to visit their stalls in the new market for something good and fashionable.

One week after the market had opened, Zhang Fang wanted to visit the stalls to see for himself how well it was going. In the morning before he left home, he told Dan Dan that she could meet him there at 12.00 noon if she also wanted to buy something there.

Just as Zhang Feng, Lin and Chen were ready to leave for the market, Qing Lian suddenly arrived.

"Brother Feng, wait for me!"

"You also want to visit the market?" Zhang Feng asked.

"Of course! Self-employed vendors are the pacemakers of commercial reform. I need to collect information for my article."

She always dressed smartly when she came to see Zhang Feng; a point which was noted by Lin and Chen but not Zhang Feng.

Arriving at the market, Zhang Feng saw a sea of people. All the stalls were full of superb collections of attractive products: fashionable clothes, modern electrical appliances, bags and shoes – all the things which could not be found in the state shops. The market manager told Zhang Feng that all the places were let out and there was a long waiting list. Zhang Feng said it was very good and asked the manager to make more places available to the sellers on the waiting list.

They made a special point of visiting the stands of Song Ping and Yu Lan and could see their stalls were full of attractive goods. Many customers were buying something from them. They greeted Zhang Feng and his colleagues warmly. Qing Lian also talked to them and took a photo of Song Ping's license as the number '001' was quite significant.

Zhang Feng asked Song Ping,

"Is it better than selling on the street?"

"It is not only much better, I am having difficulty counting up the money I have made here because there is too much of it!"

"Does that mean you will be a man with ten thousand Yuan?" asked Zhang Feng, quietly. (A man with ten thousand Yuan would be regarded as a rich man at that time.)

Song Ping replied,

"Almost! My neighbours used to look down on me and my girlfriend's mother is always pushing her to leave me but now, she is saying that her future son-in law is a man with ten thousand Yuan. She is already arranging our wedding. An old lady next door to us was always saying how proud she is of her son-in law because he works as a butcher in a state shop but she is very quiet now!"

Zhang Feng laughed loudly at this. Qing Lian suddenly grabbed Zhang Feng's arm and asked him whether a nice skirt which she had found on Yu Lan's stall suited her. She held the skirt up to her chest to show him. Her behaviour seemed very intimate to him and people close by thought she was Zhang Feng's partner.

Suddenly, the voice of Dan Dan was heard,

"Let me have a look. He does not understand clothes."

Seeing Dan Dan next to her, Qing Lian quickly behaved herself and asked,

"Sister Dan Dan, do you think this skirt suits me?"

Dan Dan said it was very suitable and praised Qing Lian for her slim figure. Dan Dan complained that Zhang Feng did not care about her figure any longer since she had become fatter after giving birth to her son. She said, with a little jealousy, that all men liked slim women. Qing Lian noticed her jealousy, so she quickly changed the conversation topic.

Attracted by the exciting and colourful products, they all bought something. Dan Dan bought a Mandarin gown and Zhang Feng bought a tape recorder to play music to his son. They suddenly heard a husky voice,

"Good afternoon, Mayor Zhang and Madam Zhang!"

Turning around, Zhang Feng saw Hei Tou there. He was selling clothes he had got from Hong Kong. Zhang Feng asked how his business was going.

"Thanks to Mayor Zhang, my business is not too bad."

"If you behave like a decent person and work hard, society will accept you again," said Zhang Feng.

Hei Tou kept bowing to thank him. After walking out of the market, Zhang Feng saw the Director of the Commercial Department talking to the managers from five, major state shops.

"Mayor Zhang, what should we do? The free market is flourishing but our managers in the state shops are losing business now."

Zhang Feng said,

"But this is a good thing. We cannot make progress without pressure. The state shops should enhance their marketing strategies and should not rely on official supplies. You must expand your channels to replenish your stock and also set up the rewards system. Lin Jianguo has said we will discuss reform for state enterprises soon and you could make some suggestion to help us."

CHAPTER II

Do You Want to Become a Business Woman?

He Hua was very busy these days. After the success of the land contract plan, the villagers no longer had to worry about their food but compared with people in the city, their income was still low. Their clothes, accommodation and cultural life were still very poor. Because transport was awkward and unreliable, especially for those who lived in the mountain areas, many farmers never left their own counties during their life time.

He Hua discussed this with Li Yong. They believed that income from agriculture was quite limited and if they could only set up some enterprises, like people in cities did, then there would be more money to improve living conditions. There were more labourers than the farm land needed in most villages so if some factories and workshops were established, employing the extra labour, the whole village would benefit.

The easy way to do this was to process agricultural products and create businesses like an oil press factory. They could get ten times the income selling soybean oil than selling just soybean. They could buy the machinery needed, build a workshop and hire a skilled operator to press the soybean from their own land, then sell the oil to the commune and county shops. A workshop would also process the famous honey found in their mountain area. In the past, villagers only had a few beehives as a hobby but now, they could manage many more hives and process the honey themselves, bottling it and adding their own labels. Other specialties, like mushrooms and wood fungus, could also be processed and sold. Leader Pan and the other team members all liked He Hua's proposal.

Keen to get richer, He Hua and her followers quickly started the plan. Over the next few months, the oil press workshop produced the first lot of soybean oil of very high quality. Everybody agreed to put He Hua's symbol (her name means lotus) on the bottles. The oil sold very well in the commune and county shops and customers liked the oil, saying it was both good and cheap. Their specialties also sold well and soon they had earned back the cost of starting up and started to make a profit. All the villagers were very pleased.

One day, He Hua and another two other villagers carried 20 boxes of the soybean oil to the commune shop on a cart. On the way, He Hua said that one day, they might be able to build a road connecting their village to the outside communes and counties. This would improve access greatly meaning people would be able to transport their products on trucks and lorries.

After arriving at the commune shop, they told a shop assistant that their oil was available but they did not realize that the manager had told the assistant never to buy oil from He

Hua. This was because the county commercial department had told them He Hua's business could damage the income of state enterprises. He Hua was quite angry and tried to argue with him but he still refused to buy any. Disappointed, He Hua and her friends rested under a big tree.

Suddenly, a strange voice sounded behind them,

"Ha, ha! Can't you sell your oil? Just go back to your workshop and wait for bankruptcy!"

Turning back, He Hua saw the evil Wang Gui, who had arrested her over the land contract and had been fined by Secretary He. He Hua realized that Wang Gui had a few relatives working in the commune and in the county leadership. It must be them trying to ruin her business.

He Hua said to him angrily,

"Wang Gui, you really are an evil snake, always biting innocent people."

Wang Gui looked triumphant.

"Nobody can save you, not even your Brother Zhang!"

'Brother Zhang!' He Hua thought. 'Why not contact him? He told me that I could ask for his help if I was faced with any difficulty.'

She still had his phone number with her. Ignoring the harassment from Wang, He Hua found a public telephone and called Zhang Feng's office, but he was not there. His secretary told her that Zhang Feng was visiting some counties to investigate the issue of village and township enterprises, and he would be in Hua Dan County tomorrow. The secretary said she would inform Zhang Feng of He Hua's request and would ask him to go to the Heng He Commune tomorrow at lunch time. He Hua was very pleased and found a small hotel to stay in overnight.

Next day, at about lunch time, He Hua heard the noise of a Jeep outside the yard of the Commune Party Committee. She saw Zhang Feng jump out and he ran to her straight away.

Shaking hands with Zhang Feng excitedly, she said,

"Brother Zhang, I am so sorry to bother you again."

Then she told him about her new business and how somebody had tried to ruin it.

Patting her shoulder, Zhang Feng said,

"Don't worry, sister. I have come just at the right time. I can help you."

He turned to Secretary He who had just walked up to him,

"Lao He, He Hua is an example of the land contract plan you set up. She is always moving forward and she is trying to run new village and township enterprises. But now she has got some difficulties and she needs your help."

Secretary He was quite familiar with He Hua so he asked her what had happened. He Hua told him how the shop had refused to buy her oil to sell.

Secretary He said angrily,

"These guys are always trying to impede the progress of reform. Let's go to the shop."

He Hua drove her cart to the shop together with Secretary He and Zhang Feng. In the shop, Secretary He criticized the manager seriously and asked him not to follow incorrect instructions. He said Secretary Zhang had just brought in the new policy from Central Government. The new policy stated that the business of the village and township enterprises followed the idea of collective ownership, not private ownership and their business would stimulate the reform of state enterprises. They should be firmly supported.

The manager was in a panic and said to He Hua,

"Unload your carriage! I will pay you right now and buy whatever you have left later!"

He Hua and her friends unloaded the cart happily and Zhang Feng also helped them. Holding up a bottle of the oil, Zhang Feng said to He Hua,

"'He Hua brand!' This is very good! You have your own brand, He Hua! Not only are you good at farming, you are also a good business woman!"

He said he would buy a few bottles for Dan Dan and Qing Lian who would also help to promote her products. He was sure that using He Hua's oil would make the dishes cooked very delicious. He Hua wanted to give some bottles to him, but Zhang Feng insisted on paying her. Secretary He also bought two bottles oil.

At noon, Zhang Feng politely declined the invitation from Secretary He for lunch and instead, he ate with He Hua and the two other villagers in a small restaurant. He wanted to know more about her new business as this was the reason why he had come down to the countryside, mainly to investigate village and township enterprises like this.

While eating, He Hua talked to Zhang Feng about another big plan. She told him that although the land contract plan gave farmers more grain, their income was still low. In most areas, the situation was still that there were too many labourers and not enough land. Having village and township enterprises would give farmers more money and also, resolve the employment issue. Apart from the oil press and specialty workshops, she also wanted to set up a brickyard to make bricks and tiles, which could help farmers to build better houses and improve their accommodation.

Looking at Zhang Feng, she said,

"Big Brother, I have an even more ambitious plan. I would like to build a sandstone road to connect our village and the commune which will provide much better transportation. Our products could be carried much faster and in larger quantities."

"Oh, my sister! It is a pity you live in the countryside! I should give you a post in the city agriculture department to deal with town planning schemes," laughed Zhang Feng.

"No, no, brother! I am not the person for an official post. I would be more than satisfied if I could just build a new, modern village."

"Good idea!" Zhang Feng replied. "A new, modern village. Yes, that will be a wonderful plan to change the poor and backward villages into new, modern villages."

They started to discuss the plan to build a road. He Hua said she planned to borrow money from the county and organize the workers from different production brigades along the route. Zhang Feng said he could also get a loan from the city agriculture bank. He Hua was very pleased and said she would like to write another official pledge like she had done last time for the land contract. She promised to finish the road project in six months. At the same time, she would build a brickyard to produce bricks and tiles and increase the output of the oil and specialty workshops. She would try to get her villagers earning about 1500 Yuan annually per household.

"Should I put my fingerprint on this contract?" Zhang Feng asked.

All the people around him laughed.

After returning home, Zhang Feng told Dan Dan about He Hua's proposal. Dan Dan said she was going to an academic conference to discuss the progress of the economic reforms so she would like to know more about He Hua's plan. Zhang

Feng also called Qing Lian to his office and gave her a bottle of soybean oil made by He Hua. Qing Lian looked very happy and thanked him, with emotion.

"Would you put an advertisement in your newspaper for He Hua's products?" Zhang Feng asked.

"No problem. It would be very easy. A report by me will be the same as a free advert."

Zhang Feng then asked how she was getting on with Li He.

Pulling a long face, she said,

"Feeling dull. He treats me well, like a good husband but I just regard him as a good friend, with no passion."

Zhang Feng suggested they should have a child together.

"Have a baby with him? The baby would not be as cute as your son."

Two days later, Qing Lian published a report in the Jili Daily, with the title: 'The Rise of Village and Township Enterprises'. The report described He Hua's story and how she had set up her oil press workshop and also outlined her proposal to build a road to the village, set up a brickyard and build a new, modern village. This report attracted the attention of the public. A lot of state companies offered to help He Hua's team to build the road and the brickyard. Many shops in different regions ordered their oil and specialty products from her. He Hua rang Zhang Feng to say her supply could not keep up with the growing demand now.

Over the next few months, Zhang Feng, Lin Jianguo, Chen Tao, Dan Dan and Qing Lian visited her village to monitor the progress of all the projects. Seeing that the road was almost half completed and the brickyard was nearly finished, they were very pleased.

Six months later, once He Hua and her team had finished their projects, Zhang Feng organized a huge official visit. All the leaders from communes and counties, journalists, Dan Dan and Qing Lian all went and many cars and buses were needed to take them. After arriving at Heng He Commune, they found their way to He Hua's village. At the start of the road was a large sign with the words, 'Happy Road'. Everybody said this was a good name for the road. Driving on this wide and flat, sandstone driveway, felt wonderful. The road ran across mountains and valleys and extended into the distance like a huge dragon.

Qing Lian couldn't help shouting,

"It is so wonderful!"

They could see a lot of trucks and lorries driving towards He Hua's village to load up with products.

Secretary He said,

"It is so efficient! They do not need to use horse and carts any longer."

Arriving at He Hua's village, they saw a fork in the road. One led to the village and the other led to the factory and workshops. He Hua was waiting at the side of the road and she invited the visitors to see the brickyard first. They saw many trucks in a long queue waiting to load bricks and tiles. Yi Yong ran up to the visitors. He was the head of the brickyard and he explained that the soil nearby was very good for making high quality bricks. There was a high demand for these materials as many farmers wanted to build improved houses of brick and tile and bricks were needed to build workshops. Their bricks and tiles were cheaper than those from the state yards and were of a good quality. That was why the demand exceeded supply. The visitors were pleased to know this.

They also visited the oil press workshop and specialty workshops. He Hua said the businesses kept expanding and they needed more workers. They had recruited some farmers from nearby villages and these new workers were pleased to have the extra income.

An official from the Industrial and Commercial Bureau asked,

"I have heard that you not only created these businesses but that you have also built a new, modern village. Can we visit it?"

He Hua replied,

"Of course you can. Please give us your opinion and suggestions."

Then she led the visitors to her new village.

After the visitors had got out of their cars and buses by the threshing ground, they were very surprised to see a beautiful village. There were rows of modern, brick and tiled houses with large yards, modern grain barns and pigsties and tap water for the villagers. He Hua said the city construction company had helped to build the road and also, helped to build a water tower so that the villagers did not need to collect their water from the wells. Leaders from different communes and counties praised He Hua's modern village highly and also expressed their desire to support the village and township businesses.

One officer from another county asked He Hua,

"I heard you wrote a pledge for all these plans. Is that true?"

"Yes, I did it with Mayor Zhang." Then she spoke to Zhang Feng,

"Mayor Zhang, I promised to improve the living conditions of my team members through running the village enterprises, and I also tried to achieve the goal of increasing their annual income to an average of 1500 Yuan. I have achieved this goal now. By our most recent calculations, our team members' annual income has reached 2000 Yuan."

Her words aroused huge surprise. A head of a city bureau said,

"My god! My annual salary is under 2000 Yuan. Can I come to your village and work here?"

People around him laughed loudly. Qing Lian and her colleagues could not stop taking photos.

A few leaders of commercial bureau from other counties said to Zhang Feng,

"Mayor Zhang, the businesses of the village and township are booming, but our state enterprises are facing difficulties now. Some managers of the state brickyards have complained to us that He Hua's business affects their sales because of the competition. Some of them are even facing bankruptcy." Zhang Feng replied,

"That is not a bad thing. The state-run enterprises must increase their sense of marketing competition because of economic reform. They have become used to the state monopoly, so they are inefficient, with huge amounts of waste and outdated equipment. Central Government has started to consider reform of state-run enterprises and there will be new policy very soon. You can ask these heads with you to think about how they could improve their production."

After the visiting group had left, Zhang Feng, his assistants, Dan Dan and Qing Lian stayed with He Hua and Li Yong for dinner. Zhang Feng and his friends all congratulated Ha Hua and Li Yong for their achievements, praising their will and energy.

"He Hua, sister, do you want a child? You have been married for over one year now," Dan Dan said.

"We are too busy to have a family," replied He Hua.

"Women over 35 sometimes have difficulties having a baby. Li Yong comes from a family with only one son in each generation."

Li Yong said, honestly,

"I don't mind. It is up to her."

Everyone laughed. Qing Lian changed the topic quickly as she had not made up her mind yet whether or not to have a child with Li He.

He Hua's success encouraged farmers in other regions to set up their own village and township enterprises. Because these businesses were collectively owned, they did not go against the principle of socialist public ownership. People said they wore a red political hat. These enterprises boosted the Chinese economy greatly and contributed almost 30% of the country's GDP at that time which also helped to improve the living conditions and employment of the farmers.

This was the second stage of economic reform in China, after the first stage of the land contract scheme had proved to be so successful. The third stage, a more important stage, was to reform the thousands and thousands of state-run enterprises. This would be a much harder political and economic battle in the modern Chinese history of the 1980s.

CHAPTER III

On Tian An Men Square

The businesses of self-employed vendors and those of village and township enterprises were all flourishing but the reform for state-owned enterprises was being carried out with great difficulty because of issues with ownership, price-setting and employment. There were great differences in opinion between the main leaders. Director Shen, who had always disliked Zhang Feng, now became the Head of the Provincial Commercial Bureau and his follower, Li Qiu, became a director of a department within the Bureau. They strongly opposed the reform proposals for state enterprises, saying that Jili Province and Northeast China was the main industrial base in China, built up in the 1950s with the help of Soviet Union. There was no need to change. But Zhang Feng argued that these enterprises had a lot of problems: inefficiency, huge waste, no incentives for workers, no responsibility for the directors. The Head of the Provincial Industrial and Commercial Bureau also said that even though the Cultural Revolution had ended ten years ago, these state enterprises still made very little profit; sometimes, even losses. They should be reformed. Seeing the big difference in opinions, Secretary Gong suggested that the Reform Office should investigate the existing situation and then report back to the city council. The council would discuss the matter again.

The next day, Zhang Feng, together with Lin Jianguo and Chen Tao, went to Wang Hai's motor vehicle factory. Wang Hai was the Deputy Director there. He had done well over these last few years to be promoted from a workshop director to the Deputy Director of the factory. He always tried to improve production but decisions had to be made by the higher authorities, especially since this was the first motor vehicle factory in China controlled directly by the Mechanical Ministry in Central Government. There were too many rules and regulations to observe. Entering the motor workshop, Zhang Feng heard quarrelling and he saw Wang Hai criticizing a few young workers.

"What are you doing? You play poker during workhours? The conveyer belt has a problem but you did not report it to the maintenance workshop."

A young man wearing a hat replied, cockily,

"Director Wang, you don't need to concern yourself with this. It does not matter whether we produce more or fewer motor vehicles. I still get 60 Yuan salary per month and you are still the Director."

Wang Hai was angry and started to blame him. Zhang Feng rushed in to stop Wang Hai and asked him to persuade these workers politely instead of shouting.

Seeing Zhang Feng, Wang Hai relaxed and said,

"Brother Feng! Why did you not tell me you were coming?"

"I have some big things to discuss with you. Let's go to your office first."

Wang Hai turned to those young workers and said,

"Each of you must make a statement of self-criticism to your workshop director. We will start reform soon and you will suffer if you carry on behaving like this."

Behind Wang Hai's back, those guys made wry faces.

On the way to his office, Wang Hai told Zhang Feng that the leader of that group of young workers was a relative of Director Guo who ran the factory. He had got his job through the 'back door' and was lazy and badly behaved and did not listen.

Seeing a stack of waste steel sheets, Wang Hai sighed,

"There will not be waste like this if we start having production contracts as there will be clear quotas. Then the workers will be more careful."

Zhang Feng patted his shoulder and said,

"Very good. The purpose of my visit today is actually to investigate the situation of state enterprises like this and find practical ways to introduce the production contract scheme. It looks like you already have some ideas!"

Wang Hai replied, happily,

"Oh, it will be great! I have fancied introducing the production contract scheme for a long time as it means we will earn more money and can improve our lives."

He and Zhang Lin had had a baby recently so they desperately needed more money.

Zhang Feng said to him,

"But reform in state-run enterprises is going to be more complex and risky than the land contracts and village and township enterprises."

Wang Hai patted his chest and said,

"I am not worried about that. Remember, that bomb could not even kill me during the Cultural Revolution!"

Lin and Chen joined in with their laughter.

In the Director's office, Zhang Feng held a temporary meeting with all the officers in the factory. Lin Jianguo firstly talked about the basic scheme of the production contract and tried to get some feedback from the officers. He said the basic principle was that the factory would have a fixed quota. They would guarantee to turn over profit to the state and then keep the additional profit. In short, the factory was responsible for its own profit or loss. For example, if the factory had a quota to produce 20,000 trucks annually, the profit from the sale of over fulfilled orders of trucks would belong to the factory. The factory had its own right to manage the production, to handle materials, workers and sales.

Zhang Feng explained,

"It means the factory could get more income but it also takes risks as well. You will need the capability to manage the production and marketing competition. You should be brave, but also, careful."

Wang Hai said, immediately,

"Excellent, we will do it!"

But Director Guo shook his head and said,

"No, it will not be so easy and is too risky. We have not even met the production quotas set by the state over these last few years. How could we over fulfil orders?"

Wang Hai replied,

"If we have the power to manage and straighten things out, then we can give all the workshops contracts and get rid of the lazy workers and rely on the capable and hard-working workers instead. We also need the right to sell extra trucks to the market. Then we will be able to do it."

The other two Deputy Directors also supported Wang Hai. Director Guo said he would not get involved in the scheme. It meant he would only get his salary but no bonus.

After two weeks, approved by the Provincial Party Committee and the Mechanical Ministry, the first production contract scheme began in the Jili Motor Vehicle Factory. It caused a sensation in the city and the province.

Qing Lian wanted to visit Wang Hai's factory to collect information for her report. Li He also wanted to go as he had a day off and he missed Wang Hai. They travelled by tram to get there. It was a huge complex; no wonder people called it 'the city of motor vehicles'. At the reception, Qing Lian showed her journalist's license.

The elderly receptionist said,

"You can look around. It is very different now. The workers all come in on time and do a lot of overtime. Everybody works harder now."

Walking into the assembly workshop, they saw workers operating on the conveyer belt and the brand new trucks coming down the belt, one after another. In the car workshop, they saw the famous 'Red Flag' make of cars under assembly. This car was used for the parade during the National Day celebrations in Beijing. Li He asked a worker what rank an official must be to drive this car. The worker said they must at least be a state minister. He explained that this car was still made manually and only 100 were built a year.

Near the Director's office, they suddenly heard the fierce noise of fighting and saw a group of workers inside and outside the office. They could hear Wang Hai shouting.

Qing Lian said,

"It looks as if Wang Hai is in a fight with somebody."

She quickly took out her camera and added a flash lamp and then started to take photos. The young workers were startled.

Li He shouted,

"Make way for us, we are journalists!"

When Qing Lian and Li He entered the room, they were shocked by the scene in front of their eyes. A few young workers were attacking Wang Hai with stools and Wang Hai was defending himself with a broomstick. He stumbled over a chair and fell. Qing Lian aimed her camera at these men and took photos of them.

Li He shouted to them,

"Put down your stools! You are breaking the law!"

These men thought it was the police so they immediately stopped. Li He helped Wang Hai to get up. Just then, another Deputy Director who supported Wang Hai came into the room and shouted,

"What are you doing? Do you want to kill Director Wang?"

The leader of this group who was also Director Guo's relative said,

"Why are we being made redundant? Isn't this still a socialist factory?"

Wang Hai, now sitting on a chair, said angrily,

"The main function of a socialist factory is to create wealth for the country but it is not a place for idleness."

The Deputy Director said,

"Your workshop director already explained to you that the production contract scheme will place capable and hard-working people in key positions, but the lazy and stupid ones will be laid off. The redundancy list was discussed by your director and the old workers collectively."

"You did not listen to me!" Wang Hai cried. "I told you there are three choices for you! Firstly, you can choose to go to less skillful sectors, like the after-service department. Secondly, you can go on a training course to improve your skills. Thirdly, you can buy up your service and have three years' salary as your redundancy compensation. Then you can work as a self-employed vendor and become a 'ten thousand Yuan household'."

The leader of the group said,

"I won't stay here any longer. I will get my redundancy compensation and become a 'ten thousand Yuan household'!" Then he left the room.

A few of his close friends also followed him. The rest of these young workers said they preferred to re-train or work in the after-service department and left the room as well. Qing Lian and Li He asked Wang Hai what had happened.

"That relative of Director Guo tried to hassle me," explained Wang Hai. "He did not work, he was very lazy and caused trouble quite often. Nobody liked him. So with this new scheme, his name was put on the redundancy list. He hated this and tried to make trouble for me with his close friends."

Li He and Qing Lian laughed and asked him,

"Is it more difficult to be a Director than head of a collective household in the countryside during the Cultural Revolution?"

Wang Hai said this post could not compare with the other one. Qing Lian asked him about the achievements and problems of the production contract scheme. Wang Hai gave her some details.

A few months later, the factory was flourishing. Wang Hai predicted it was likely they would not only fulfil the state quota to make 20,000 trucks, but also, would produce 5,000 extra trucks. After the reserved funding for technical improvement, they could expect a large of bonus for everybody. The workshop directors said they did not need to push their workers to work harder now because they could not stop working. The workers voluntarily did overtime as they tried to increase the quantity and quality of their product. If they over fulfilled the quota, they would get a bonus.

When Wang Hai and Zhang Lin went to Zhang Feng's home for dinner, Wang Hai told them excitedly that if everything went well, his bonus would be enough to buy a commercial, three bedroom apartment. At that time, there was a very small commercial housing market as most people had to wait for a rented, council house. Commercial houses and apartments were very expensive and ordinary people could not afford to buy them. Zhang Feng asked Wang Hai how much bonus he would get. Wang Hai's reply surprised him.

"Oh, my god! Your bonus is more than my three years' salary as a Mayor!"

Wang Hai said to Zhang Lin, proudly,

"What do you think? You made the right choice to marry me many years ago. At that time, I was only a worker, with just a diploma from the Open University. I was very nervous when I met your parents to ask for their permission to marry you. Fortunately, I had Brother Feng as my guarantor."

"Don't get dizzy with your success!" laughed Zhang Lin.

"Keep away from those pretty female university graduates in your factory!"

Wang Hai said hastily,

"Do not listen to nonsense. Brother Feng's Pi Li boxing is still waiting for me." All of them laughed.

After dinner, Dan Dan, Wang Hai and Zhang Feng discussed the long term plans for the factory. Dan Dan said although the situation looked good, more competition would come along with the further development of China's economy, so she suggested that Wang Hai should develop new products to meet the demands of the market and not just make the same old make of motor vehicle. Also, he needed to expand into new markets and not just rely on the markets arranged by the state. The right to set the price was also important, otherwise it would affect profits. After listening to Dan Dan's points, Wang Hai suddenly saw the light, and said,

"Oh, my good sister-in-law! You really deserve your post as an economics professor but this post is wasting your talents! You should be appointed as a Deputy Premier Minister in the State Council in charge of the whole economy!"

"I am not keen on being an official. One official in my family is enough!" Dan Dan smiled.

Everybody laughed.

Zhang Feng said to Wang Hai,

"Dan Dan's suggestion is useful but we need the support from the Mechanical Ministry, especially to get the funding needed to import foreign equipment. You work out a plan and then we can go to Beijing and hopefully, get agreement from the Mechanical Ministry."

Wang Hai agreed.

A week later, Zhang Feng, Wang Hai and Lin Jianguo travelled to Beijing together. They gave a report to a Deputy Director in the Motor Vehicle Management Department of the Mechanical Ministry. They explained that their proposal was mainly to apply for funding to import equipment to make cars and minibuses from Germany. At the same time, they wanted to have the right to expand their market inland and abroad and the right to set the price for their products.

The Deputy Director listened to them very politely as the Jili Motor Vehicle Factory was the biggest in China at that time. Central Government usually helped them. The Deputy Director said he would send their report to the leaders in the Ministry and ask them to discuss the proposal, so it would take a few days to get a decision. Zhang Feng and Wang Hai were worried about the result and they were not in the mood to go sightseeing in the capital.

Two days later, they were back at the Mechanical Ministry to see the same Deputy Director. He asked them to sit down and gave them some tea. Seeing the expression on his face, Zhang Feng guessed they would not be hearing good news. As expected, the Deputy Director apologized to them and said there was a shortage of funding at the moment because a lot of other big state enterprises also wanted to improve their equipment. However, the ministers quite liked their proposal. There was a possible way to resolve this problem which was to form a joint-venture with foreign companies but, according to some top leaders, this would be against the principle of a socialist economy. They worried it would enable capitalist private ownership to affect public ownership. In Shen Zhen, there was already a special economic zone with a trial to set up a joint-venture as an experiment, but it could not be expanded to other regions. Zhang Feng and Wang Hai implored the Deputy Director to ask the other leaders to reconsider as the Jili Motor Vehicle Factory was the biggest in the country.

"My honorable director, please help us," begged Wang Hai. "I will give you a Red Flag car if you can persuade the top leaders in the Ministry to help us."

The Director smiled and said,

"I would not dare to drive it!"

He thought for a while and added,

"Alright. I will discuss this issue with the ministers again."

After they had gone down to the main hall of the reception area, Wang Hai said he would like to have a cigarette. They all sat on the sofa and Zhang Feng thought about how to get their proposal approved. Suddenly, he saw a slim lady in red entering the hall. She wore a face mask as Beijing in March could suffer from sandstorms and many people wore face masks during this time.

Zhang Feng felt a bit strange that the figure of this lady seemed quite familiar to him. She walked to the reception desk to make some inquiry. Zhang Feng felt more and more restless. He had a strong feeling, like a vibration in an emotionally magnetic field that he used to feel in the past whenever he was with Yu Mei. He stood up and walked slowly to the reception but the lady had already got into the lift. Watching, disappointedly, as the lift moved up, he saw it stop on the eighth floor – the same floor as the Motor Vehicle Management Department. He could not wait for the lift to come back down again and ran up the stairs. He was gasping for breath as he reached floor eight but it was very quiet in the corridor and he could not see the lady. He could only gently pass each door and listen to the speech coming from inside but could not hear any female voices. He had to go back down by the lift.

Wang Hai asked him,

"Brother Feng, what's wrong? What happened?" Wang Hai suddenly remembered the lady in red.

"Brother Feng, you must miss her madly but I also think it looked like her."

"Who are you talking about?" asked Lin Jianguo.

"Director Lin, we are all old friends and you are Brother Feng's saviour. I can tell you this lady looked like his previous girlfriend, Yu Mei," Wang Hai explained.

"Yu Mei! Of course, I know her! She is the daughter of the late Secretary Li Jianguo. I saw her quite often when I worked as secretary for General Zhao Wu. Didn't she become a Taoist nun some years ago?"

"She came back to secular society a few years ago but we did not know where she went to. Brother Feng still misses her," Wang Hai said.

Seeing Zhang Feng bury his head in his arms, Wang Hai patted his shoulder.

"Do not be sad. Maybe it wasn't her after all. There are many beautiful, slim ladies in the capital who look like her."

Zhang Feng sighed and asked them, with an imploring look, "May we stay here for another 30, no, just 20 minutes?"

"No problem."

Zhang Feng kept watching the lift but the lady did not come down.

Zhang Feng finally said,

"Sorry, let's go."

Wang Hai murmured,

"Brother Feng is really a man with deep affection."

They left the building and walked away but, unknown to them, the lady in red was watching them from behind a huge stone pillar, wiping her eyes.

Two days later, they visited the Mechanical Ministry again. Surprisingly, with a smile, the Deputy Director told them their proposal had been approved. The Mechanical Ministry had agreed to give them a large sum of foreign currency to buy the equipment from Germany. If the output was good, they could repay 50% of the loan in five years' time. The Director said there was another option: if the Government allowed the joint-venture scheme to go ahead and if the German company was willing to join such a project, then they would not need to repay the loan which would become shares in the company. Also, the Ministry gave Wang Hai the right to expand their market and set the product prices. Wang Hai jumped up from the sofa happily and promised that if the Deputy Director ever wanted to buy a car one day, just contact him. The Deputy Director waved his hand and said they did not need to thank him. He said the reason why the Ministry had finally approved their proposal was because somebody in the State Council had given their support to it.

'The State Council?'

Zhang Feng felt confused as they did not have any association with the State Council. The Deputy Director added that the lady who passed on the decision from the State Council was a really beautiful, fairy-like woman.

'Fairy-like woman?' Zhang Feng thought. 'Could it be Yu Mei?' But Yu Mei did not have any connection with the State Council.

Leaving the Ministry, they were all very excited. Lin Jianguo said he would like to go to Tian An Men Square as he had not seen it for many years. He asked Zhang Feng to come with him. Wang Hai said he needed to go to Wang Fu Jing Street to buy some presents for Zhang Lin, so he would not go with them to the Square. They got out of the underground at Wang Fu Jing station and Wang Hai walked to the shopping street whilst Zhang Feng and Lin Jianguo walked to the Square.

On the way to the Square, passing a phone box, Lin Jianguo said he would like to make a phone call to a former buddy. Zhang Feng sat down under a tree and waited for him. After Lin had finished his phone call, they bought two bottles of soda water and sat on a bench to drink and talk. Zhang Feng asked Lin whether he had moved his family to Jili City. Lin replied that with Zhang Feng's help, he had got a house now and he would be able to move his family to the city next month. It seemed that Lin was not in a hurry to see the Square as he kept talking and on the way, he also kept asking about the functions of different buildings along Chang An Street.

Soon they saw the eastern side of the Square, enveloped in bright sunshine, with the trees forming rows of green screens. There were many tourists taking photos of the famous buildings and the scene brought back Zhang Feng's memories from twenty years ago, during the Cultural Revolution, on the Square for Chairman Mao's interview. Moving his gaze to a large tree in front of the Chinese Historical Museum, he recalled how just there, they had found a faint Yu Mei on the ground and Zhang Feng had taken her to the nearby hospital. Zhang Feng suddenly felt depressed. Where was Yu Mei? Why had she avoided him? She had sent a card for his wedding, sent flowers and bought his book during the Shakespeare Festival. She had even sent him letters to encourage him to become an official and supported his promotion. Why had she not tried to see him in person so he could thank her? He wondered what she was doing and whether she had found another man to love her. While thinking about these things, he saw a slim lady sitting on the bench under that very tree. He thought he was suffering from blurred vision but after rubbing his eyes, he still saw a lady in red sitting there.

At this moment, Lin said,

"Brother Feng, it seems there is a formal reception for some foreign guests in front of the Great Hall of the People. I am going there to have a look. You can meet me there in 30 minutes."

Hearing about this reception, Zhang Feng looked at the Great Hall of the People and could see the National Guard of Honour and hear the National Anthem. He wondered whether it was worth going as well. Lin Jianguo walked over but when he turned back to look at the bench, the lady in red had disappeared. He ran quickly to the bench and sat down. Oh, it was so strange! There was a pleasant smell like the face cream which Yu Mei used to use.

He stood up and searched around, hoping to find that lady in red but he could not see her. He was disappointed and sat down again. He thought he should wait for a while, and hopefully, she might come back but after waiting for over half an hour, she had still not shown up. He thought maybe he had missed her so much that he thought all slim ladies were Yu Mei. Fine, she must have her reasons not to meet him. He stood up and walked slowly to the Great Hall of the People but he did not realize that the lady in red kept watching him from behind a newspaper stand, wiping her eyes. At last, she became too sorrowful to stand any longer and sat down on the grass.

CHAPTER IV

On the Banks of the River Avon

After returning home from Beijing, Zhang Feng felt distracted, even though this Beijing trip had successfully laid the foundations for the long-term development of Wang Hai's factory. The city and provincial leaders all praised his capability. His colleagues also did not understand why he looked unhappy. Secretary Gong thought he must be tired after the intensive negotiations in Beijing and asked him to rest for a few days. Lin Jianguo guessed he felt stressed because he did not see Yu Mei in Beijing so he suggested he should have a holiday on the beach in the coastal city of Da Lian City. Dan Dan believed he must have found out something worrying about Yu Mei as he was never normally stressed by problems at work but she did not want to ask him directly.

It was just by chance that the leaders in the three provinces of Northeast China organized a delegation to visit the U.K. for the purposes of trading and culture. The members of the delegation included all the mayors in these three provinces. Everybody believed it would be a good opportunity for Zhang Feng to relax and rest. Zhang Feng also felt happy about it as for a long time, he had been keen to travel abroad to see the Western world and to learn from their experiences in developing their countries. After the Cultural Revolution, China gave up its old policy of shutting the door on the outside world. The Government started to send a lot of students to study in Europe, the USA, Canada and Australia, and sent officials, scholars and researchers to learn from these countries.

One day, in May, 1987, Zhang Feng and the other mayors travelled together to the U.K. by air. They landed at Gatwick Airport and officers from the Chinese Embassy met them at the airport and drove them to London by minibus. Driving on the motorway, Zhang Feng and his companions enjoyed the scenery outside: the green grass, dense woods, flowing rivers and attractive houses. When they reached London, they saw tall towers, Victorian buildings, museums and beautiful parks which amazed Zhang Feng because this was the first time he had seen the great capital described by Charles Dickens.

Arriving at the Chinese Embassy, they were received warmly and informed of the arrangements for their visit. They would attend seminars hosted by English commercial leaders, visit factories and farms and do lots of sightseeing in London. The most exciting thing for Zhang Feng was a planned visit to Stratford-upon-Avon, arranged by the British Council, and they would watch a Shakespeare play performed by the Royal Shakespeare Company. The Mayor of Shen Yang City knew Zhang Feng used to be a Shakespeare scholar so he said to the others,

"We should let Mayor Zhang tell us something about Shakespeare, shouldn't we?"

Everybody agreed because they were all young, well-educated officials who had been promoted recently by the Party and Government. They all knew something about Shakespeare.

They had one day's rest and the next day, they went to see Buckingham Palace, the Houses of Parliament, Big Ben, Tower Bridge and the British Museum. They were all amazed that the foggy, dirty London of Charles Dickens was actually a clean and beautiful metropolitan city. As they sat on a bench on the banks of the Thames, Zhang Feng saw that the river water was fairly clean, though everyone knew that the Thames had been quite dirty in the past. It seemed that the British had done a lot of work to improve their environment. Looking at the Thames, it made him think about the river in his own city where there were still some chemical factories draining their waste water into the river, polluting it. He thought he must do something about this issue when he returned. The economy could not be developed at the expense of the environment.

On the third day, an English businessman, who had business links with China, hosted a seminar about economic development in the U.K. A Hong Kong businessman in his fifties acted as an interpreter but his Mandarin was not very good, so sometimes, he found it difficult to translate exact meanings. Zhang Feng's English had been good when he worked in the university. As he had a very good memory, he could still understand the words of the English businessman. He tried to help the interpreter to translate. The other mayors all praised him. After the seminar, the English businessman asked Zhang Feng to stay behind for 20 minutes and they had an interesting talk about the economic reforms in China. Zhang Feng said, half-jokingly,

"To carry out the reforms needed for our state owned enterprises, we cannot mention privatization but I think, if we really want China to develop fully, we must introduce free markets and private ownership. When that happens, can we borrow your Mrs. Thatcher to help us privatize our inefficient state enterprises?"

The English businessman laughed, loudly.

"I am afraid it would be very difficult to do that as we have such different national conditions. Your several million workers might eat her alive."

In the next few days, Zhang Feng and his companions visited a range of factories, companies, shops, farms and even some residential areas, which gave them a rough idea of the social and political structure, economy, living conditions and some social issues in the U.K. The mayors said they were really impressed. During the Cultural Revolution, they had always been told that people in capitalist countries endured miserable lives and China should launch a world-wide revolution to liberate them. But now, they could see that the U.K. had a fairly harmonious society. People enjoyed a happy life, and earned much more than the Chinese. Their salary for one day was equal to one month's salary back home even though their cost of living was more. There was also a welfare system so that even poor people could have a fairly good life. There was a free education system and a free medical service. One mayor told Zhang Feng quietly that the U.K. was almost the perfect communist country as it had nearly abolished the three major distinctions: between town and country, between industry and agriculture and between physical and mental labour.

In the evening, one of the mayors who had a good relationship with Zhang Feng said they should re-think Marxist revolutionary theory. The theory stated that capitalist countries had to be replaced by socialism as Marx saw a collapsing Western world. But he did not realize that Western countries could develop further through self-adjustment, by resolving social class contradictions, establishing social welfare systems and taxing the rich to help the poor, not by killing the rich to help the poor which had happened in China. The others agreed with him. But which path should China follow? Privatization? What about political reform? Then they all had different opinions.

When they visited Stratford-upon-Avon, they watched Twelfth Night, performed by the Royal Shakespeare Company. It was Zhang Feng's favourite Shakespeare comedy so he really enjoyed himself. When he heard Olivia's lines in Scene I, Act III:

"A murderous guilt shows not itself more soon,

Than love that would seem hid: love's night is noon"

He almost had tears in his eyes as he thought of Yu Mei. He stood on the balcony outside the theatre during the break and had a drink. Watching the cheerful swans swimming on the clean River Avon, he felt it was one of the happiest moments in his life. He started to regret being a mayor with such a busy workload and so many unnecessary meetings and it was really difficult helping ordinary people. It might be better for him to return to his academic life and continue exploring Shakespeare's world. But the thought of the situation in China bothered him: people were still living in poverty and the political system was still not democratic. The country needed open-minded and capable leaders to strive for a better future so he felt he had to continue to swim hard in the sea of officialdom. He called to mind a poem written by the famous ancient Chinese politician Fan Zhongyan who was a typical follower of Confucius:

"Be the first to be concerned about your country and people,

But the last to enjoy the benefit of your achievement."

Mr. Fan achieved and suffered a lot in his political career. But he still firmly followed the faith of Confucius.

On the last morning in London, he visited Hyde Park where he enjoyed the green grass, trees and active pigeons and squirrels. Jogging for a while, he found a quiet area to practise his martial arts. He had not had time for his Kung Fu after he became Mayor, so his father-in-law, Hai Jing, reminded him to practise. He practised Pili Boxing seriously for 15 minutes and stopped to wipe the sweat from his face. Suddenly, he heard applause. Turning his head, he saw two Chinese men sitting under a big tree.

"You did that really well. What kind of boxing is that?" a short man asked, not very fluently, in Mandarin.

Just before Zhang Feng answered his question, he recognized this man. He was the Hong Kong businessman who had worked as the interpreter during the business seminar. He also recognized Zhang Feng and they shook hands, warmly. The Hong Kong businessman introduced the other man to Zhang Feng. He was his younger brother. His name was Liang Fu and his brother's was Liang Hua. Liang Hua was a professor at the London School of Economics and a famous economist. Liang Hua was taller and very polite and looked like a scholar. Liang Fu told his brother that Zhang Feng was a talented and capable mayor in Northeast China. Zhang Feng was pleased to know them as China had just started to bring in economic reforms and needed to learn from Hong Kong and other 'Economic Small Dragons' in Asia as their economies had developed very rapidly in the last two decades.

Zhang Feng said that in recent years, the Chinese Government had developed Shen Zhen City, just opposite Hong Kong, into a 'Special Economic Zone', following the economic pattern in Hong Kong. Liang Fu said his company had some factories in Shen Zhen and the business there was doing very well. He believed Shen Zhen was actually an experimental zone to explore the adoption of a capitalistic economy. Deng Xiaoping would expand this model to the whole country if it was successful. Zhang Feng said this was exactly what he expected. He told them about the economic reforms in his own city and how he needed to help some enterprises find overseas markets. The Liang brothers said his plan was very interesting and they invited Zhang Feng to a Chinese restaurant to have dinner where they continued to talk very congenially. Zhang Feng knew the LSE was a famous university, worldwide, so he consulted Liang Hua on many economic issues.

When they said farewell to each other, Zhang Feng invited them to visit his city to give them some advice and suggestions on how to improve the economy there. They accepted his invitation happily. Liang Fu also spoke, half-jokingly, to Zhang Feng that his brother was 40 years old now, but still single. He loved Chinese ladies, but it was difficult to find suitable Chinese women in the U.K. so he hoped Zhang Feng might help his brother to find a nice Chinese girl. Zhang Feng smiled and said that would be easy.

When Zhang Feng returned home, he sent out the invitation letters to the Liang brothers and they got their visas quite quickly. They told Zhang Feng that they would fly to Beijing in two weeks' time, and then transfer flights to Jili City. Zhang Feng was pleased and asked the Foreign Affairs Department to give them a good reception. His colleagues who supported reform movement were all happy about this event but those who insisted on the old ways did not approve. They included Director Shen and his assistant, Li Qiu. They believed co-operation with foreign businessmen would erode socialist systems. Zhang Feng hated them as well, as these rigid, left-wing leaders constantly created problems for the reform movement but the problem was, these guys also had 'behind the scenes' supporters in Central Government.

Zhang Feng and Secretary Gong welcomed the Liang brothers warmly at Jili City Airport. Seeing such cordial hospitality, the two brothers were really surprised as they had not realized their visit would cause such a reaction. Qing Lian travelled to the airport and took a great many photos and wrote a news report in her newspaper about the visit of the Liang brothers. She commented on the need to carry out reforms and learn from the positive experiences of other countries. Shen Zhen was a good example of foreign investment and market competition.

Zhang Feng arranged the best rooms for them in the River City Guest House and entertained them warmly. The two brothers felt extremely flattered and they started their business tour straight away. Accompanied by Zhang Feng and other city leaders, they visited more than ten state enterprises in just a few days. Liang Fu was the CEO of a large Hong Kong company, with broad experience in investment, sales and management, so he gave advice and made various suggestions to the directors of these factories and companies. Liang Hua also took this tour seriously as he was writing a book on the economy in Asia. He made a lot of notes and collected materials from these enterprises. To help them investigate, the Provincial Foreign Trade Bureau also sent a Deputy Head and a female assistant. Zhang Feng recognized the assistant. She was Wang Li, the student in the Foreign Languages

Department of Jili University who had played Ophelia in 'Hamlet' in the Shakespeare Festival before she graduated.

Seeing the surprised face of Zhang Feng, she laughed,

"How do you do, comrade Hamlet. You do not recognize Ophelia now?"

Zhang Feng shook hands with her.

"Hamlet was saved by Chinese herbs, and in gratitude to China, he comes here to become a mayor, rather than a king in Denmark."

Everyone was amused by their conversation.

Wang Li asked him, quietly,

"Can Ophelia still see Hamlet from time to time?"

"No problem, welcome to my palace," Zhang Feng said.

Wang Li patted him, coyly.

Near the end of the visit, the two brothers said they had gained a lot and Liang Fu said he believed Jili City had great potential. As long as the enterprises in the city followed market rules, replaced old for new equipment and designed more original products, they would be very close to entering the international markets. He said he would help them to find overseas markets, at least for the motor vehicle products, in Hong Kong and other Asian countries because both the quality and price of Wang Hai's products made them quite competitive. Hearing about this, Wang Hai was very pleased.

Liang Fu said he would also help to find a market for the chemical products. The brothers also gave their opinions about the problems with these enterprises. In a discussion, they indicated that the product contract plan was good in the short term but might result in problems, longer term. If China really wanted to develop its economy, she should firstly allow the private enterprises to do business, and secondly, resolve the ownership issues for state enterprises, adopting something like the shared system in the West. Nobody dared to agree with their opinions as these ideas were still against the socialist principles in China at that time.

Zhang Feng arranged a private party a few days before the brothers left. He used his own money to have a Cantonese style banquet in the Jili Hotel. Only Dan Dan, Wang Hai and Wang Li came. He invited Wang Li, supposedly to help Liang Hua understand Mandarin as she had done during their business tour of the city, but his real intension was to introduce her to Liang Hua as a possible girlfriend. Liang Hua had said he would like to marry an educated Chinese girl and Zhang Feng thought Wang Li was a good candidate; so did Dan Dan. Even though Wang Li was over ten years younger than Liang Hua, in the 1980s, Chinese girls did not care too much about such age differences. A lot of women preferred to marry Westerners because they knew life would be better in the West.

Dan Dan had specially arranged for Wang Li to sit next to Liang Hua at the meal so they could talk. She herself sat on the other side of Liang Hua in order to balance the atmosphere. The two brothers were very relaxed as they had enjoyed a good trip. After a few toasts, Zhang Feng, Wang Hai and Liang Fu talked together and Wang Li, Liang Hua and Dan Dan talked with each other. Liang Hua spoke to Wang Li in English politely for five minutes, and then turned to Dan Dan to chat with her. Both were economists so they had a lot in common but Dan Dan suddenly remembered they wanted to introduce Wang Li to Liang Hua. She quickly changed the topic. Wang Li knew more about foreign trade in Jili Province but after a few minutes, Liang Hua turned back to Dan Dan once again to talk to her. Wang Li then joined in with Zhang Feng's conversation.

After the dinner, Zhang Feng asked Liang Hua what his impression was of Wang Li. Liang Hua said he was too old for her. Zhang Feng said what if she did not mind this because, unlike their parents, girls nowadays did not care too much about the age difference. Liang Hua wanted to think about it. His brother Liang Fu had said Wang Li was a good girl. Zhang Feng suggested they could communicate with each other by letter and he gave him Wang Li's address.

Back at home, Zhang Feng asked Dan Dan what Wang Li had thought about Liang Hua. Dan Dan said it seemed that Wang Li did not like to reveal her true feelings and had only said that Liang Hua looked like a pedant. Zhang Feng thought girls were usually shy and reserved so the best way was to let them get to know each other more via letters.

The next day, after the two brothers had left for the airport and Zhang Feng had returned to his office, Wang Li knocked on his door.

"What did you think about the Prince of Norway?" asked Zhang Feng.

Sitting on the sofa, Wang Li replied angrily,

"Mayor Hamlet, how could you sell Ophelia so easily to somebody else?"

"The Prince of Norway is a good man, although a little older than you but he is polite, with the manners of a scholar. You will have a lot in common if you get together."

"But he was born in Hong Kong and grew up in England so he is totally English, with very bad Mandarin," replied Wang Li.

"In that case, he is an English gentleman! You graduated in English Language and Literature so you are half an English lady! Ok, this is his address in the U.K. You can exchange letters to get to know more about each other."

Wang Li reluctantly took the note with the address and left the office. As she walked to the door, she murmured to herself,

'I will not marry anyone except Hamlet.'

But Zhang Feng did not hear it.

PART IV

The Dream Lover

Comes out of His Dream

CHAPTER I

The New Deputy Secretary

Soon after returning to Hong Kong, Liang Fu helped Wang Hai find some overseas markets, mainly in South-East Asia. Wang Hai sold his cars and minibuses to Thailand, Malaysia and Vietnam, with prices 30% higher than those in mainland China. At the end of the year, workers and staff in the factory received an unbelievably large bonus.

Wang Hai bought an upmarket, commercial, three bed apartment. His relatives and friends all said that the product contract scheme had worked really well because it normally took between four and six years for people to get a basic council apartment. More money had really resolved some problems.

On the removal day, Wang Hai held a party in his new home and his friends and relatives all came to congratulate him.

Wang Hai said to Zhang Feng,

"Brother Feng, I really must thank you for this lovely apartment. I would never have had the money needed to buy this home if you had not introduced that Hong Kong businessman to me."

"Do not be happy too soon as the market keeps changing!" replied Zhang Feng. "If there are more motor vehicle factories in the market, you will have more competitors."

"You are right, my brother-in-law. I am already planning to reduce the cost, improve the quality, and design new products."

Wang Hai also told Zhang Feng that those young workers who had left the factory regretted their laziness and the fact that they had quit. They tried to find a 'back door' way to return. Zhang Feng suggested Wang Hai could give them some training and a trial period and those who performed well could be reinstated in the factory. Wang Hai said this was a good idea.

During the party, Zhang Lin asked Dan Dan if there was any progress in the relationship between Wang Li and the professor in London. Dan Dan explained that they were writing to each other but were more like ordinary friends. Dan Dan said that the professor had written to her quite often, asking about the progress of economic reform in China.

Zhang Lin said, quietly,

"Sister-in law, maybe he is fond of you. Wang Hai told me that the expression in his eyes when he watched you was different from his expression when he watched Wang Li."

Dan Dan gave Zhang Lin a nudge.

"Nonsense, he is just a pedant. He is more keen on research than on finding a girlfriend."

Zhang Lin covered her mouth and laughed, secretively.

"Do not worry, sister-in-law. I will not tell my brother. But if I was that Professor Liang Hua, I would love you too. He likes scholars and loves beautiful ladies but it is rare to find a beautiful female scholar like you!"

Dan Dan pinched Zhang Lin to stop her.

Zhang Feng's father, Zhang Wenbo had not been feeling well recently. Maybe it was because he was old now, nearly 70. He was having headaches and suffered from insomnia. Family and friends suggested that he should see a doctor of Chinese Medicine. Zhang Feng took him to the Provincial Hospital of Chinese Medicine to see Li He. Li He was the Director of the Department of Internal Medicine and a very experienced doctor. He warmly received them and checked Zhang Wenbo's tongue and pulse and asked about his symptoms. Then he prescribed some herbal medicine and also advised him to do Qi Gong and wash his feet with hot water before going to sleep.

When a nurse took Zhang Wenbo to the pharmacy, Zhang Feng asked Li He how he was getting along with Qing Lian. Li He lowered his head and sighed. He said they had quarreled with each other quite often recently. Normally, he gave up but sometimes, she behaved like the Red Guard she used to be. There was actually nothing major to bother her but she still seemed unhappy and looked down on him. She once even mentioned his betrayal of Zhang Feng during the Cultural Revolution and said he was not a real man because he was not loyal to his friends. Zhang Feng said this had all happened in the past and did not need to be recalled. In the end, Li He said they were living separately now. She had moved to the dormitory in the newspaper offices. Zhang Feng remembered that Qing Lian had almost walked away on their wedding day.

He wondered whether Qing Lian might constantly be comparing him with Li He and that was why she looked down on her husband. Seeing Li He in such a low mood, Zhang

Feng tried to comfort him and said he would ask Dan Dan to persuade Qing Lian to change her mind.

Back home with his father, Zhang Feng remembered Qing Lian came to him quite often about things which sometimes, had nothing to do with work. Her visits often made Lin Jianguo and Chen Tao look at her with curious eyes.

'No, I need to stop her doing this,' Zhang Feng thought.

He just regarded her as his younger sister and saviour but he had Dan Dan and a fine son now so continuing to love him was pointless.

In the evening, he told Dan Dan about the problems between Qing Lian and Li He and asked Dan Dan to persuade Qing Lian to change her mind. After a few days, Dan Dan told Zhang Feng the result of her intervention. Qing Lian had told her she was fine about Li He before they married but after, she was worried about housework and relatives. Li He was a bit fussy which she did not like. Qing Lian said she now fully understood why people said marriage could be the 'tomb of love'. She said she would wait to see what would happen after a period of separation. Zhang Feng said they would all have to wait and see.

One day, after a few weeks, when Zhang Feng and his assistants were discussing how to further business reforms, Zhang Feng received a phone call from the Provincial Organization Department, asking him and Secretary Gong to visit. Zhang Feng thought that maybe the party committee had appointed new officials for the city council.

Arriving there, the director of the department told them that the Central Party Committee had decided to disarm one million officers and soldiers which meant that a lot of high ranking army officers would need civil posts. Jili Province needed to take over ten of them. After some discussion, the Provincial Party

Committee appointed a previous commander of a division as a Deputy Party Secretary of Jili City to work together with Secretary Gong and Zhang Feng. Zhang Feng liked officers with army backgrounds, like Lin Jianguo, as they were normally courageous and resolute but he also worried that some carders might be conservative and rigid if they had not suffered during the Cultural Revolution.

The next day, Zhang Feng got to his office half an hour late as his son had not been feeling well. In the corridor, he could hear loud laughter and talking. He felt curious. Opening the door, he saw a man in army uniform talking with Lin Jianguo and Chen Tao. Seeing Zhang Feng, he stood up and gave Zhang Feng a standard army salute.

"How do you do, Mayor Zhang."

Zhang Feng tried to shake hands with him but he suddenly felt the face of this person looked very familiar. After gazing at him carefully, he recognized him and said,

"Chang Zheng, it is you!"

This tall and straight army officer was actually his previous rival and friend and Yu Mei's former classmate and neighbour. His family and Yu Mei's family knew each other well because his father, General Zhao Wu, had been a comrade-in-arms of Yu Mei's father, Li Jianguo, the late First Secretary of the Provincial Party Committee. He had once regarded Yu Mei as his girlfriend automatically and had not liked Zhang Feng's relationship with Yu Mei but after Yu Mei's father was persecuted by the Red Guards, he grew away from her and found another girlfriend. During the civil strife, he and Zhang Feng were in conflict with each other a few times but Zhang Feng had never wanted to hurt him. Afterwards, Chang Zhang started to admire Zhang Feng for his loyalty to his friends and helped him when his sworn enemy, Cai Wenge, plotted against him. Since then, they had become friends.

Chang Zheng patted Zhang Feng's shoulder.

"What do you think about my prediction eight years ago? It has come true now. Do you still remember what I said during the funeral of Yu Mei's father, Li Jianguo?"

Zhang Feng suddenly remembered and said,

"Yes, I remember! You were a commander of a regiment at that time and you persuaded me to become an official. You said we might be political partners, one a mayor and the other, a city party secretary. I thought you were joking as I was keen to follow my father and become an academic at that time. I did not realize that, one day, your prediction would come true. It is really mystical!"

They had not seen each other for eight years and so they had endless things to talk about. Zhang Feng said it would be good to have dinner at his house with some family members and close friends. Chang Zheng said his family was still in Shen Yang and would be moving here in the next few weeks. Zhang Feng said he should just come himself along with Lin Jianguo, who used to be his father's secretary.

On Saturday morning, Zhang Feng and Dan Dan cooked quite a lot of dishes which were all popular Northeast cuisine. Zhang Feng bought some famous Mao Tai spirit and Harbin beer for the guests. Nearer lunch time, Chang Zheng and Lin Jianguo arrived. Chang Zheng greeted Dan Dan warmly and said she was still young and beautiful. Dan Dan said she did not realize that army officers were also good at flattering women. Lin Jianguo immediately said he told the truth. Everybody laughed. Wang Hai and Li He came later and Chang Zheng also greeted them warmly.

When all the guests had sat down, somebody knocked at the door. It was Qing Lian, dressed very smartly. Wang Hai tried to seat her next to Li He, but she sat next to Chang Zheng instead and said to Wang Hai and Li He,

"I belonged to the Second Headquarters with Chang Zheng during the Cultural Revolution but you belonged to the Commune Faction!"

Actually, she just wanted to find an excuse not to sit next to Li He.

Chang Zheng smiled and said,

"Yes, our Second Headquarters did…"

He was going to say the Second Headquarters won the battle during the civil strife but he suddenly remembered that it was a bloody battle which almost killed Wang Hai. Luckily, he had been saved by Zhang Feng.

Instead, he said, immediately,

"No, no, we were all fooled by that terrible revolution which was a nightmare in modern Chinese history."

"Waking up from this nightmare, our Party learned a historical lesson which has brought about today's achievements and all the political and economic reforms," Zhang Feng said.

"Yes! Nowadays, people can eat delicious food every day which they could only have once a year in the past, and they can have colourful and fashionable clothes as well," Li He said.

"In the past, the most valuable things a family owned were bicycle, watches, sewing machines and radios," Wang Hai added.

"But now, most families have a colour TV, washing machine, fridge freezer and tape recorder," Lin Jianguo said.

"Brother Lin reminded me that I have some watermelon in the fridge freezer to cool ourselves in this hot weather after our meal," Dan Dan said.

Then she said to Qing Lian,

"The washing machine really liberated our women from hard housework. In the past, it took me half a day to do the washing at the weekend. Now, it only takes one hour and we have time to go out or visit friends."

Everyone agreed that reform had given ordinary people happier, more relaxed and enjoyable lives.

Dan Dan put ten different dishes and one type of soup on the table and all the guests praised her cooking skills.

"Today, Mayor Zhang is in a good mood, so he cooked half of the dishes, like the Lion Head meat balls, braised pork with soy sauce, steamed chop pork and Gong Bao chicken," Dan Dan said. All the guests cheered.

Wang Hai picked up a bottle of Mao Tai and said,

"Today, we must get drunk before we finish."

He gave some Mao Tai to every man in the room and Dan Dan gave some beer to Qing Lian, but she said,

"I also want some Mao Tai."

"She still has the manners of a member of the standing committee in the rebellious faction," Chang Zheng said.

They all laughed as they knew Chang Zheng was talking about Qing Lian's past as an active Red Guard. Li He worried that Qing Lian might want to drown her sorrows but he dared not try to stop her.

Half way through the lunch, Chang Zheng said he would like to smoke and asked Zhang Feng to go outside with him.

Zhang Feng guessed he wanted to talk about something private and after they'd had a cigarette, Chang Zheng quietly asked Zhang Feng,

"Do you still have any contact with her?"

Zhang Feng knew he meant Yu Mei.

"She left the Taoist temple a few years ago, but I do not know where she is now. Sometimes, she sends me cards or short letters but she has never given her contact details. Last year, when I performed in the Beijing Shakespeare Festival, she sent me flowers and bought my book. This year, when Wang Hai and I were in Beijing to apply for funding, she helped us as well. I saw her on Tian An Men Square, but she hid herself quickly. It feels like she is just next to me as she knows everything I do but the problem is, she dare not face me."

Chang Zhang tapped his head and said,

"I can understand her. She is really a woman who feels love deeply and she is completely infatuated with you. It looks like she has not found another man to love so she still misses you all the time. But she does not want to disrupt your family, especially now you have a happy family with a beautiful wife and fine son. I can imagine how she must suffer as you are life-death lovers. She also knows you cannot forget her. Ah, all this misfortune was caused by that evil Cai Wenge who cheated her and ruined her with a false marriage. Is Cai still in jail?" Zhang Feng said,

"He was sentenced to twelve years in prison and he still has four years to go."

Chang Zheng had a smoke and said,

"I guess Yu Mei will see you soon as no woman could bear such emotional pain for so long. She will at least see you once and reveal her innermost feelings to you. She will not have high expectations and might just want to be your close friend and see you sometimes, if both of you agreed."

"Is it possible for this to happen?" Zhang Feng asked.

"My predictions are normally fairly accurate. Just like the one I made eight years ago about us being official partners."

Zhang Feng wanted this to happen although he did not realize that Chang Zheng's prediction about Yu Mei would come true so soon.

CHAPTER II

The Secret Head of the Department

In a flash, 1987 arrived. The co-operation between Zhang Feng and Chang Zheng carried on smoothly and they did a lot of work to push forward the process of reform, especially in helping self-employed vendors, village-township enterprises and state enterprises to boost their businesses. In a meeting, they were told that in Shen Zhen and other areas in Southern China, people had started to invite foreign companies to invest in factories and infrastructure and to run tourist businesses as well. Zhang Feng and his colleagues were very excited about this information.

Zhang Feng told Chang Zheng, Lin Jianguo and Chen Tao that his impression of his trip to the U.K. was that if a country intended to develop itself, it must have a free exchange of funding and technology with other countries, otherwise, it would be a poor, closed shop, like China during the Cultural Revolution. Chang Zheng said he had heard there were some leaders in the Central Party Committee who were opposed to the new policy of openness and believed this would be an invasion of capitalism. However, Deng Xiaoping believed a cat would still be a good cat if it could catch a mouse, no matter what colour it was. Any effective way should be used to develop the economy and it was ridiculous to say the country had been betrayed by using foreign investment.

A few days later, Zhang Feng received a phone call from Wang Li in the Foreign Trading Department. She said there would be a business delegation from Taiwan visiting the three provinces in Northeast China. If Zhang Feng was interested in the visit, she could arrange for the delegation to visit Jili City. Zhang Feng was very pleased to know this and said yes straight away. He said the city would welcome the delegation warmly and he asked her to make a date for the visit.

Before they finished this telephone conversation, Wang Li said jokily,

"Will the Prince of Denmark give Ophelia a kiss?"

"Yes, if the Taiwan businessmen agree to invest in our city!" Zhang Feng laughed.

"Remember! You must keep your promise!" Wang Li said. Zhang Feng put down the phone and said to himself,

"A naughty girl."

The date for the visit was set and Zhang Feng wanted to meet the delegation at the airport but a Deputy Governor of the province and Director Shen warned them that the reception must be kept low profile. The members of the delegation must not feel they were distinguished guests as the Chinese Communist Party defeated the National Party and drove them away to Taiwan 40 years ago. They could not be allowed to feel they had won this time and could now proudly 'counter attack' the mainland. Receiving this warning, Zhang Feng was angry.

He said to Lin Jianguo and Chen Tao,

"We must look forwards and not back to history if we want to develop our country. Yes, we used to be the enemy, but now, we should be co-operative partners as Taiwan has changed greatly, politically and economically."

He decided that Lin Jianguo and Chen Tao should meet the delegation at the airport first and then he would meet them later. He asked Chang Zheng not to go. If they were blamed by the higher authorities afterwards, he would take all the responsibility, but Chang Zheng insisted on going because he did not care about those rigid, left-wing leaders.

One week later, the delegation arrived and Lin Jianguo and Chen Tao warmly welcomed the members on behalf of the River City. The Head of the delegation, Mr. Du Shan, was a businessman in his fifties and the Director and CEO of the Taiwan International Tourist Company. He said his company was very keen to invest in and build five star, luxury hotels in mainland China as there were more and more tourists visiting China from Taiwan, Japan and South Korea. There was a shortage of luxury, five star rated hotels in China and if they could help to build international standard hotels, this would increase tourism. Lin Jianguo and Chen Tao told Mr. Du Shan, their city welcomed the visit and investment from their compatriots in Taiwan. A couple of children presented flowers to the delegation and Mr. Du was very happy. He picked up a little girl, who presented flowers to him, in his arms and kissed her. The journalists took a lot of photos of this reception.

Afterwards, Lin Jianguo and Chen Tao led them into the waiting room for distinguished guests. Zhang Feng and Chang

Zheng stood up and greeted the delegation. Mr. Du Shan was confused as the reception was already very welcoming so who were these two men? Lin introduced Zhang Feng and Chang Zheng to the delegation.

"This is our City Mayor and this is our City Deputy Secretary."

Du Shan and his colleagues were surprised that such high ranking officials would meet them. Zhang Feng and Chang Zheng shook hands with each member of the delegation and said they really welcomed the visit by the delegation and the potential investment. Mr. Du told Zhang Feng that it was a Head of the Shen Zhen Foreign Investment Department who had recommended that they should visit Jili City. This Head had told him that Jili City was also called the River City and had beautiful scenery, making it a perfect tourist destination. Mr. Du said the company had asked them to visit a few cities in Northeast China and submit a report to the Board. Then the Board would decide where to invest the funding. Zhang Feng did not pay much attention to Mr. Du's mention of the Head of the Foreign Investment Department in Shen Zhen as in recent years, so many people, including university graduates, businessmen and officers had moved to work there. They had all settled there well as Shen Zhen was a very dynamic city where capable and intelligent people were able to get important jobs.

Mr. Du noticed Chang Zheng wore an old army uniform and so he knew Chang Zheng used to serve in the Army. He told Chang Zheng and Zhang Feng that his father used to be a Commander in the National Party's 45th Division and fought against the Japanese during the Second World War together with the Communist Party's Eight Route Army. However, during the Civil War, he did not want to fight against the Communist

Party's Army so he quit and moved to Taiwan. He was nearly 70 years old now.

Chang Zheng said,

"Just by chance, my father also used to be a Commander in the Eight Route Army. He actually mentioned your father to me when he told us his experiences during the war. He has now retired from his post of Commander of a great military area."

Mr. Du said,

"That is great! My father and many veterans are keen to return to the mainland to visit their hometowns now that relations between the two sides are so much more peaceful and relaxed. We are all Chinese anyway."

Zhang Feng and Chang Zhang said they would welcome Du's father.

On the second day, Zhang Feng and his colleagues accompanied the delegation to visit the city. They went to the North Mountain, the banks of the Song Hua River and Song Hua Lake. Du Shan was especially interested in the scenery along the river and he took a lot of photos there. He told Zhang Feng that a city with a river flowing through it could be a beautiful and great city, like London, Paris, Moscow and some other cities in China such as Shanghai, Nanjing and Wuhan. He felt Jili City was really beautiful with a blue sky, flowing river, weeping willows, and green mountains. It looked like an enchanting picture. So if they built a multi-storey, five star hotel on the banks of the river, the tourists could enjoy the beautiful scenery from their windows. That would be wonderful and, they could look at different scenery in different seasons. In many other cities, winter scenery would not attract tourists, but here, they could see crystal ice rime on the trees and snow covered mountains. They could visit skating rinks and enjoy skiing holidays in the nearby mountains. He was in high spirits and the people around him could already visualize this great hotel, standing on the river bank, in front of their very eyes.

The delegation's business investigation finished in a few days. Mr. Du Shan and his assistants were quite satisfied about the investment potential in this River City and he told Zhang Feng that they would go to a few other cities to investigate as well, then he would send a report to the Company Board and they would decide where to invest and build the luxury hotel. He believed Jili City had the best chance of getting the funding. He also asked Zhang Feng to pass on his proposal to the authorities in the city and province to get their approval. At the same time, he also wanted to get some preferential terms and conditions for leasing and taxation. Zhang Feng knew the local authorities in China would normally give favourable business terms to the foreign investors as they needed to make a profit; that was the reason they made investments. He told Mr. Du that there would be no problem with good terms.

After the delegation had left, Zhang Feng held a meeting to discuss this project. Most officials in the City Council supported this project because it would improve tourist facilities and attract more foreign tourists, foreign business and international conferences because summer in Jili City was not as hot as in Southern China. This would attract academic or business conferences to Northeast China. As for the terms and conditions, they would review the experiences in the South. They proposed giving the Taiwan Company a cheap land lease for twenty years, which could be extended, and which would be duty-free for the initial two years. In the end, they felt very confident about handing in the report to the Provincial Party Committee for ratification. Zhang Feng thought it would be easily approved as it was a very beneficial project for the city even though Secretary Liu was in Beijing for a meeting. Yet, bad news came after a few days.

The decision from the provincial authority was that this five star hotel project would attract too much attention and invite trouble. To build such a big luxury hotel symbolized a capitalist flag being planted on socialist land. Some leaders with neutral attitudes suggested delaying for a period of time but the sharpest criticism again came from Director Shen. He said the younger generation of the Chinese National Party building such a hotel meant the return of old political enemies.

Hearing this, Zhang Feng and his friends were very angry. Why were there always so many obstacles to reform set by the hardliners? Zhang Feng clearly knew that the key point for this resistance was these men were worried about losing their power and privilege if Chinese society became more democratic and private ownership and free markets replaced state ownership and the centrally controlled economy. They always used the party leadership and socialist principles to resist reform.

Unexpectedly, there was more bad news. His secretary received a letter from Mr. Du Shan. In his letter, Mr. Du said the Directors on the Board had different opinions about his report. Some of them supported his suggestion to build the hotel in Jili City, but others wanted to build it in Harbin which was also a big river city in Northeast China. They were still discussing the report. He himself firmly wanted to build the hotel in Jili City. He said he was happy that the Head of the Shen Zhen Foreign Investment Bureau strongly supported his proposal and was trying to persuade the other Directors to change their minds.

Zhang Feng wrote a letter to Mr. Du to thank him for his efforts and also, to thank the Head of the SZFI bureau for his help. He told Mr. Du that the City Council had agreed to give favourable terms and condition to the Taiwanese company but he also frankly told Mr. Du about the opposition from some leaders in the provincial authority. He would try his best to get this proposal approved. Having foreign investment was a very important step towards developing the economy in China.

This bad news made Zhang Feng feel huge stress. He became sick after being exposed to strong winds when he was sweaty after exercise. He went to bed for a few days and Dan Dan looked after him, carefully. Chang Zheng, Lin Jianguo, Chen Tao and other colleagues visited him and hoped he could recover quickly but the left-wing hardliners took pleasure in his misfortunes. They said those who damaged socialist practice would come to a bad end.

Wang Hai and Li He visited him as well. Li He brought some Chinese herbs to treat his cold and stress. Zhang Feng tried to persuade Li He to work on his relationship with Qing Lian but Li sighed and said he would always wait for her but he did not know her mind. By chance, Qing Lian arrived at this moment but she hid herself until Wang Hai and Li He had left. Knowing there was nobody else in the house, she walked quietly into Zhang Feng's bedroom and put a package of fruit on the table.

Looking at Zhang Feng's wan and sallow face, she felt a heartache and said to him,

"Brother Feng, it is a great pity you are suffering. I know you are always strong and never get sick. It is just because those evil leaders did not approve your proposal."

She suddenly grabbed hold of his hand and started to cry. Zhang Feng withdrew his hand and patted her shoulder to comfort her and said he would recover soon, and also, he would not give up his efforts to get the proposal approved. After a while, he persuaded her to keep her marriage to Li He going. She frowned and said she preferred to live alone rather than to live with a man she did not love.

She then murmured to herself,

"It is enough to see Brother Feng sometimes."

But Zhang Feng did not hear what she had said.

The next day, Zhang Feng still lay on his bed, restlessly, reading an economics book Dan Dan had given him. Suddenly, he heard an astonished shout from Dan Dan. He thought there must be some important figure coming. He sat up and was very surprised to see the man he had missed day and night these last few days. Yes, it was Secretary Liu, his supporter and the most powerful leader in the province. Secretary Liu put two bags of Beijing dry fruit on the table and said, with a smile,

"Xiao Zhang, I know you are sick through anxiety. You feel anxious as your proposal to build the five star hotel using the investment from Taiwan was turned down. Now I can give you some good medicine! I have just returned from a meeting in Beijing to discuss investment from abroad. The outcome is to the immense satisfaction of those who want to go further to carry out economic reform. Deng Xiaoping gave his instruction that we should extend the policy of inviting foreign investment by using foreign funding and technology to speed up our economic development. We also welcome investment from Taiwan because of the improved relations with them. We are not enemies any more. The co-operation should be easy and smooth as we share the same language and cultural background. Yesterday, I delivered the main points from the meeting to the Provincial Party Committee and discussed your proposal. The result is your proposal has been fully approved and we have even agreed to give them better terms and conditions."

After listening to Secretary Liu, Zhang Feng jumped up from his bed and said,

"Wonderful! Secretary Liu, you are my saviour! I will go downstairs to make a phone call."

He ran down in his pyjamas and Dan Dan gave him a coat. He excitedly rang Lin Jianguo and told him this good news. He asked Lin to send a telegram to Mr. Du and tell him that the project had been fully approved by the authorities and that he would receive better terms and conditions. He hoped that the other Directors in Du's company could also be persuaded to support this proposal.

After walking back up to his bedroom, Secretary Liu said,

"Do not hurry back. Recover fully from your illness first."

"Thank you for your very effective medicine! I am ok now, and I will be at work tomorrow," Zhang Feng replied, happily.

Both Secretary Liu and Dan Dan laughed.

Zhang Feng went to work the next day. Seeing him, his colleagues were very happy and Zhang Feng told them that the good news Secretary Liu had brought him yesterday had almost cured him. Chen Tao said,

"If we get more good news today, will you recover fully?"

Everybody understood what Chen Tao meant.

What really surprised Zhang Feng and his colleagues was, after they had finished their lunch in the City Council dining hall, Lin Jianguo rushed into Zhang Feng's office, waving a piece of paper in his hand and shouted,

"Good things come in pairs! This is the telegram with more good news from Mr. Du!"

Zhang Feng took the telegram and read:

'Our board has ratified your proposal to build the five star hotel in your city. I will arrive in Jili City on 6th May to sign the contract. The Head of Shen Zhen Foreign Investment Bureau will also be with me.'

Zhang Feng was so pleased he almost jumped up from his chair. His colleagues were delighted and Zhang Feng was pleased that he could, at last, see this Head and express his heartfelt thanks.

On the morning of 6th May, Zhang Feng and his assistants drove to the airport. It seemed that the airplane had landed earlier than scheduled as they saw Mr. Du and his party waiting in the arrival hall. Zhang Feng shook hands warmly with Mr. Du and his colleagues but he did not see any unfamiliar faces. He asked Mr. Du where that Head of Bureau was and Mr. Du said probably in the distinguished guests' room but they could not find anybody there. Du said maybe the Head had been picked up by some friends or relatives in the city but Zhang Feng would see this Head when they signed contracts. Zhang Feng would be able to express his thanks then.

At 10.00 am on the 8th May, in the big conference hall of the City Council, a grand signing ceremony was held between Jili City and the Taiwan International Tourist Company. Both sides agreed to name the hotel as 'The Song Jiang Hotel'. Those at the ceremony included city and provincial leaders, business leaders, journalists from TV, radio, newspapers and magazines. Qing Lian arrived quite early to get a good seat. Wang Li also sat in the hall with her colleagues, but her eyes always followed Zhang Feng.

Near to the start of the ceremony, the Head from Shen Zhen had still not arrived and Zhang Feng asked Mr. Du when the Head would be arriving. Du said his assistant had just received a phone call saying the Head had some urgent issue to deal with and could not come to the ceremony. Mr. Du said the Head was not needed to sign the deal so they could start the ceremony on time. Zhang Feng said that was fine as he still had time to meet this Head later on.

On behalf of the River City, Zhang Feng firstly expressed his heartfelt thanks to Mr. Du Shan's company for investing in and building this great hotel which marked a milestone for co-operation between mainland China and the Taiwan people, and also, a big step for economic reform in the city and province. Mr. Du also delivered a speech in a Taiwanese accent. He thanked the city for accepting this big project. He said that the hotel would be the first international, five star hotel in Northeast China and would attract more foreign tourists, businessmen and conferences. His speech created loud applause. Then Zhang Feng and Mr. Du signed their copies of the contract under the flashing cameras and to warm applause.

After the ceremony, on behalf of the City Council, Zhang Feng invited Du and his party to lunch in the Jili Hotel. Because of the success of the joint venture, both sides felt very happy and relaxed. Du enjoyed Northeast cuisine and drank a lot of the famous Jili spirit: Yu Shu Liquor. He said his father liked Yu Shu Liquor so Zhang Feng asked a waiter to get two bottles for Mr. Du to pass on to his father. Zhang Feng also invited Du's father to attend the foundation stone laying ceremony. Du said his father would definitely like to come. Mr. Du was a heavy drinker so Zhang Feng tried to keep up with him and they talked about how to organize the construction team and import special materials.

Du suddenly said,

"Mayor Zhang, do you know, the Head of the Shen Zhen Foreign Investment Bureau played a very important role in this deal. It is great that this Head not only has superb skill in public relations, but is also a devastating beauty."

Zhang Feng was feeling a bit dizzy because of the alcohol and he did not hear clearly what Mr. Du had said so he asked Du to repeat his words.

After hearing Du's words once again, Zhang Feng was surprised.

"Devastating beauty? So this Head is a woman?"

"Yes," Du answered, then he patted his head and said, "Sorry, I forgot that in Mandarin, we read 'he' and 'she' in the same way as 'ta'. So I should have explained to you earlier that this Head was a woman. It seems that she is familiar with you because she told me several times that Mayor Zhang is a capable and responsible man."

Zhang Feng's head was clearing. He thought, 'What? A beautiful lady who knows me. Yu Mei? No, she seems to live in Beijing and she is not good at public relations. Then who is this lady? Anyway I must see her.'

He asked Mr. Du how he could see this female Head. Du said she would be staying with her female secretary in a hotel called the North Mountain Guest House for a few days.

The next day, after sending Mr. Du and his party to the airport, Zhang Feng, Lin Jianguo and Chen Tao went to the North Mountain Guest House. Zhang Feng asked at the reception whether the two ladies from Shen Zhen were still there. The receptionist checked the register.

"Sorry. They checked out an hour ago." Zhang Feng was quite disappointed and sat on the stairs outside the guest house.

He said to Lin and Chen,

"This is really a strange and very secretive lady. Why does she keep avoiding us?"

Lin Jianguo smiled and said,

"I think she is mainly trying to avoid you!"

"We should see her anyway because we need to thank her for her help," said Zhang Feng. "Also, we might need her help in the future as we will have a lot of business links to Shen Zhen as the first market experiment zone in our country."

Lin Jianguo replied,

"Leave it to me. I will arrange for you to see her tomorrow."

"Why are you so confident?" Zhang Feng asked.

"Have you forgotten? I used to be a scout in the army!"

CHAPTER III

I Thought I Would Never See You Again

As expected, on the next day, Lin Jianguo told Zhang Feng that he had found this female Head. She and her female secretary were staying in the Jiang Nan Guest House now but would be leaving at 12.00 noon. He suggested Zhang Feng should get there at 11.30 to catch her. Zhang Feng was very pleased as at last he would see this secretive lady. Lin said he would stay in the office to deal with a citizen's work issue.

Jiang Nan Guest House was quite near the officials' accommodation. Learning from yesterday, Zhang Feng got to the guest house early and went to the reception where he saw a young woman checking out. He walked straight up to the counter and prepared to talk to the receptionist who recognized him and greeted him,

"My honourable Mayor Zhang, welcome!"

Hearing her words, the woman who was checking out turned her head to look at Zhang Feng and looked frightened. Zhang Feng asked the receptionist,

"The two ladies from Shen Zhen – are they still here?"

The receptionist looked at the woman checking out.

"This lady is the Head's Secretary and she is checking out now. If you had come five minutes later, you would have missed them."

Zhang Feng was very pleased that he could, at last, see the secretive lady today.

"Hi, I am the Mayor of the City. I would like to see your boss to thank her for her help making this deal."

The young woman was too surprised to say anything and stammered,

"Oh! Oh! May I… go to … ask my boss…"

Zhang Feng did not want to miss this good opportunity of catching her so he said,

"I will go with you."

The young woman gingerly led Zhang Feng to the first floor and Zhang Feng asked her the room number to which she hesitantly replied,

"2…2…206."

Zhang Feng quickly walked to the room which was not locked. The door was slightly open. Zhang Feng was very eager so he gently pushed the door fully open and walked right in. He suddenly had an unusual feeling which he only ever got when he was with Yu Mei. Because they were life-death lovers, there was a magnetic attraction between them which they both felt when they were close to each other. The further he walked into the room, the stronger the feeling became. There was nobody in the sitting room, but when he looked into the main bedroom, he saw a woman in white who stood up from the sofa and walked to the window. She was holding the curtain with a trembling hand.

At this moment, Zhang Feng was 100% sure this was Yu Mei.

He felt his heart beating wildly but he tried to control his emotions and said quietly,

"Yu Mei… is it you?"

She turned around and said, in a shaking voice,

"Brother Feng… is it you?"

Zhang Feng felt as if his heart would jump out from his body. His dream lover, whom he had missed day and night, was just standing in front of him. She was still delicate and lovely, with her fairy-like face but now, with the additional charms of a mature woman. She looked so young and not at all like a woman in her late thirties. With tears in her eyes, she walked slowly towards him. Both of them raised their arms at the same time to embrace each other but seeing the young secretary outside the bedroom, they stopped. The secretary realized that they had an unusually close relationship so she closed the door.

Yu Mei was more in control now and asked Zheng Feng to sit down. She gave him a cup of tea. Each of them had so much to ask but did not know how or where to start. In the end, they said, at the same time,

"How are you?"

Having calmed down for a few minutes, Zhang Feng asked,

"Yu Mei, I have missed you for so many years. Where did you go after you left the temple? Are you well and happy with your life in Shen Zhen?"

Wiping away her tears, she said,

"To cut a long story short, a few years after being in the temple, I started to look on the bright side of things. I decided to leave there and forget my sad experience. I travelled to the

South and did a Master's degree in Zhong Shan University where both of our fathers studied before the liberation. Then I went to Shen Zhen City because it is such a dynamic city. I worked in the Foreign Investment Bureau and built up more experience to deal with businessmen from Southeast Asia. I was promoted to the Head of a Department in the bureau because I worked hard and did well. I used to visit Beijing quite often to get instructions and ratifications."

"That is why you were able to send me flowers and bought my books during the Shakespeare festival, and helped Wang Hai get funding," said Zhang Feng.

"Sorry, I know I should not disrupt your life like this but I cannot control myself. Although I know we can only be dream lovers, you are the other half of my spirit. If my spirit can be together with yours, then I am satisfied even if I cannot have you physically."

Zhang Feng was too deeply moved to say anything else. After a while, he asked, carefully,

"Have you found a good man to stay by your side for the rest of your life?"

Yu Mei shook her head sadly.

"I will never fall in love with another man after my life-death love experience with you. This is my punishment for my weakness and gullibility."

Zhang Feng said quickly,

"Yu Mei, it's not your fault. That evil Cai Wenge plotted to frame us."

Yu Mei continued,

"There are quite a lot of rich businessmen and high ranking officials who would like to woo me but I just ignore them. Many women think that being a rich wife will bring them happiness. I do not want material comforts without a deep love. That is not my goal in life."

Zhang Feng changed to a topic which he longed to know about.

"Why did you avoid me in Beijing last time?"

"Brother Feng, this is my painful dilemma. I was keen to meet you, but at the same time, I did not want to bring you more stress and sorrow. I know that even though you have Dan Dan now, you still miss me. She is a good wife and loves you deeply. I like her as well and regard her as my sister. But love is selfish. We cannot share you like in the past when China allowed polygyny." She paused. "I would be happy if I could just meet you and be a good friend from time to time."

"Shen Zhen is a long way from here so how come you know everything which has happened to me?" Zhang Feng asked.

"I have an 'informer' here and old relations as well," Yu Mei smiled.

Zhang Feng suddenly recalled the weird reaction of Lin Jianguo in Beijing.

"Is Lin Jianguo your spy?"

Yu Mei laughed and said,

"Do not call him that! You are not a drug dealer! Yes, I begged him to protect and care for you. When I found out from General Zhao Wu that Lin would leave the Army and work in Jili City, I gave him this 'task'."

"I was lucky to have his help," Zhang Feng said. "When we tried to rescue He Hua, he helped me to fight against a group of bad militia."

Yu Mei smiled and said,

"I knew you were a powerful martial arts master when you rescued me from that hooligan, Tei Tou."

Somebody knocked at the door gently. They knew it was the secretary, reminding them of the time. Looking at the clock, they realized that they had talked for over two hours. After talking to her secretary, Yu Mei said she would stay a few more days to see some old friends. Zhang Feng suggested having a meal with Secretary Liu, Chang Zheng and Lin Jianguo but not Wang Hai, Li He and Qing Lian. Also, he decided he would not tell Dan Dan about his meeting with Yu Mei. Yu Mei asked him not to tell the others she was still single. She wanted him to say she had married an overseas Chinese man with a PhD.

Before they said goodbye to each other, Yu Mei asked,

"Brother Feng, I would like to see the big poplar tree on the river bank once more. Would you like to go with me? Meet me there at 4.00 this afternoon."

Zhang Feng agreed, happily.

Zhang Feng telephoned Lin Jianguo and told him he had seen the Head.

"Jianguo, you did very well as her spy! Why did you not tell me earlier it was Yu Mei? You let me worry for so long. Alright, because you saved my life, I will forgive you anything!"

Lin Jianguo laughed and told Zhang Feng to take more time with Yu Mei as he did not need to get back to his office. Zhang Feng rang Dan Dan and said he had something to do this evening and would return later that night. He had some dumplings in a small restaurant and then walked slowly to the river bank.

He could see that huge poplar where he had pledged his love to Yu Mei over twenty years ago. He walked to the tree and touched the huge trunk of it and thought that time had passed so rapidly. Looking at his watch, it was only 2.00 pm. Why was time passing so slowly today?

Leaning on the tree and enjoying the beautiful scenery, he waited for Yu Mei. Because he had gone to bed very late last night, he was lulled by the gentle caress of the soft wind and fell asleep. In his dream, he saw a lady sitting in the guest house. Sometimes, she was Yu Mei and sometimes, she became another woman. When he walked towards her, she looked like Yu Mei but she suddenly waved her hands at him and, with tears in her eyes, jumped out of the window.

Zhang Feng ran to her anxiously and shouted,

"Yu Mei! Yu Mei! Do not take your own life!"

Suddenly, somebody was shaking his shoulder and shouting to him,

"Brother Feng! Wake up! Wake up!"

Opening his eyes, he saw Yu Mei next to him. He was embarrassed and explained,

"Sorry! I fell asleep and had a nightmare."

Yu Mei comforted him.

"Do not worry, everything in a dream is the opposite to reality."

She was happy that she had heard him call her name which meant he was thinking of her.

Looking at her, Zhang Feng was really surprised as she was wearing a blue track suit and had changed her hair into braids which made her look exactly like she did twenty years ago when they had first met here. Seeing Zhang Feng's expression, Yu Mei asked, with emotion,

"What has happened? Don't you recognize me?"

Zhang Feng rubbed his eyes and gazed at her again.

"Yu Mei, have we travelled back in time and returned to the year we were dating?"

"I really wish we could travel back to that time, even if we had to suffer the ordeals of the Cultural Revolution again. If we did, I could avoid the mistake I made back then and marry you." Yu Mei replied,

Zhang Feng did not want to hurt her and quickly changed the subject.

"Yu Mei, your face and figure have not changed at all! You still look like a beautiful little fairy."

Yu Mei was happy to hear this praise and sat next to Zhang Feng, shyly.

"Brother, you still look tall, sturdy and handsome. Do you remember, in the morning on that day, you sat here, drawing. I saw you drew my figure in your picture. I was pleased as I knew you were thinking about me. Then we explained the misunderstanding between us. I told you Chang Zheng was not my boyfriend, and you told me Dan Dan was not your girlfriend. Then we fell in love with each other."

Zhang Feng said, with emotion,

"Yes, Yu Mei, I have not forgotten. Every minute with you in the past is engraved on my memory."

Enjoying the beautiful scenery, they were immersed in their happy memories. They kept talking and did not notice it was getting darker. A tranquillity surrounded them and they could only hear the sounds of waves and the rustling leaves.

Yu Mei suddenly sighed and said,

"Brother Feng, we cannot live in our memories. We have to face reality. I am afraid we can only ever be dream lovers."

Seeing that nobody was around, Zhang Feng could not control himself. He raised his arms to embrace her.

"Yu Mei, may I…?"

Without answering, she threw herself into his arms straight away.

"Brother Feng, I have longed for this moment for so many years."

She then enjoyed the warmth of his wide and powerful chest, whilst she trembled and quietly cried.

"Brother Feng, I really wish time would stand still right now! It would be worth it, even if I died the next second!"

Zhang Feng caressed her hair and said,

"Do not say this. The dream lover has at last woken from my dream. We can meet each other again from now on."

"Even though I cannot be your wife, I can be your friend, or your 'sister'. Dan Dan used to be your 'sister' and I am happy to exchange positions with her."

Looking at her ivory-like, beautiful face and the crystal tears in her eyes, Zhang Feng recalled all the loving scenes between them and he could not help wanting to kiss her. But thinking of Dan Dan, he hesitated. Yu Mei noticed his dilemma and she suddenly took hold of his head and kissed him. Zhang Feng forgot everything and returned her kiss warmly. Their bodies and minds were transformed into flames of love. The world ceased to exist.

A night breeze blew over and they woke from their passionate love. Zhang Feng thought of Dan Dan's tender and beautiful face, 'Oh, my God, I should not betray her.' He released Yu Mei from his arms.

"I am so sorry, Yu Mei, I was too excited."

Yu Mei sighed gently and said,

"No, Brother Feng, it is my fault. I should say sorry to you and Dan Dan. I will control myself in future."

The moonlight was shining on the river. Yu Mei said she needed to return to the guest house and Zhang Feng walked with her, arm in arm. Feeling the cool wind, Zhang Feng put his coat around Yu Mei.

Leaning on his shoulder, Yu Mei said,

"Brother Feng, I really envy Dan Dan. She has a good husband in you but she deserves your love. She looked after you carefully for so many years as a 'sister', although she loved you secretly during all that time."

Zhang Feng said,

"Yu Mei, I must tell you my inner feelings for you and Dan Dan. I love both of you but the love for you is in my spirit, which is like the turbulent waves on the sea. My love for Dan Dan is the love for a wife which is like peaceful water on a lake."

Yu Mei smiled.

"Brother, it is safer to swim in a lake! It is more risky to swim in the sea."

She looked at her watch.

"It is already 7.00 pm! Go back quickly to your 'lake'!"

"Do not worry, I called her and said I would be back quite late tonight."

Walking closer to the guesthouse, Zhang Feng asked Yu Mei whether her young secretary would suspect their relationship. Yu Mei said this young woman was a very simple, country girl. She was very loyal and would not care about her private life.

Entering her room, they found the secretary had already gone to bed. Yu Mei asked Zhang Feng to sit down and gave him a cup of tea. Zhang Feng knew they had not seen each other for many years and this was Yu Mei's way of making him stay longer. They talked about her work and life in Shen Zhen and the progress of reform there. They also discussed how to meet Secretary Liu and Chang Zheng. The room got warmer and warmer, Yu Mei took off her track suit which showed off her attractive figure. Zhang Feng noticed she was plumper than before. She used to be slim, but now she had the charm of a mature lady.

Seeing Zhang Feng staring at her intently, she asked with a smile,

"What's wrong? Am I not as slim as I used to be?"

"No, Yu Mei, no man could resist the charms of your mature body."

Yu Mei flushed and asked,

"Can my charms be compared with those of Dan Dan? Are you excited? Do you want to swim in the sea?"

"Please turn back, Yu Mei. I dare not look at you again."

Yu Mei flushed scarlet and she said quietly,

"Do not worry, Brother, there are only two of us in the room."

Yu Mei was actually hinting that they could make love. Zhang Feng could feel the passion burning in his body but he had to control himself and not let Dan Dan down.

He lowered his head and said to her,

"Sorry, I have to go."

He could hear Yu Mei's disappointed sighing. After a few minutes, she said,

"Brother Feng, I will not force you to do anything but please will you embrace me before you go?"

They hugged each other tightly: her plump breasts pressed against his wide chest. She shut her eyes and enjoyed this warm moment.

"Brother, can we do it… Just once."

Zhang Feng could feel his passion was almost beyond his control and he was shaking.

"Yu Mei, I, I, I really want to…"

He wanted to take her to bed but if he did, he would go beyond the moral limits of a married man and he would betray his wife and son. At last, he released Yu Mei and sat on the sofa to calm himself down. Yu Mei also sat down on the bed, disappointed. The room was very quiet and their breathing could be heard.

Zhang Feng said,

"Sorry, Yu Mei, I would like to…but I could not…"

Wiping her eyes, Yu Mei said,

"Brother, it is my fault. I will only be your sister from now on."

Zhang Feng left the guest house and walked back home. He was in a bad mood and recalled how once, during the Cultural Revolution, when they were staying in a relative's flat, Yu Mei had wanted to make love but he had politely declined. As a responsible man, he could not offer her a better life at that time. The opportunity had been lost forever. Now, here was another opportunity but he was unable to do it as he was a married man. Just bad luck. He sighed.

Before Yu Mei left for Shen Zhen, Zhang Feng arranged to have dinner with her in a restaurant, with Yu Mei, Secretary Liu and Chang Zheng. Both Secretary Liu and Chang Zheng praised Yu Mei's unchanged beauty. Secretary Liu recalled the holiday in Feng Man, Song Hua Lake with Yu Mei and Zhang Feng, just before the Cultural Revolution. Knowing Yu Mei had a husband now, Chang Zheng started to make a joke. He said in the past, both he and Zhang Feng had loved Yu Mei. They hated each other as rivals but in the end, neither of them had won Yu Mei. He did not forgot to curse the evil Cai Wenge who cheated her and abandoned her and ruined her future.

Seeing the sad expression on Yu Mei's face, Zhang Feng quickly changed the topic and asked Chang Zheng whether he wanted to invite his father, General Zhao Wu, to attend the foundation stone laying ceremony of the five star hotel since the father of Mr. Du Shan would be coming for the ceremony from Taiwan. It would be a historical meeting. Chang Zheng said it should not be a problem as his father was still healthy. Zhang Feng said that was good as he had missed Uncle Zhao who had also helped to save him during the Cultural Revolution.

CHAPTER IV

The Foundation Stone Laying Ceremony

Zhang Feng and his colleagues were very busy with the preparations for the foundation stone laying ceremony. They cleared and tidied the site, compensated the households which needed to be moved, arranged the best building teams and tried to import special materials, such as marbles from Italy. Because this was a five star hotel, the outside and inside decoration would be magnificent.

One day, Wang Li came to Zhang Feng's office to tell him about the progress of these imports. After listening to her words, Zhang Feng said she could have just telephoned him; she did not need to come in person for tiny things like this.

"Comrade Hamlet, will you keep your promise?" she smiled.

"What promise?"

"Somebody promised that if the proposal to build the hotel was approved, he would give me a kiss!"

Zhang Feng suddenly remembered that he did say this to her, casually.

"I… I was just joking…"

Wang Li suddenly lowered her head and kissed his cheek and then ran away, laughing.

Zhang Feng shouted after her,

"Contact Professor Liang Hua and tell him…"

He hoped she would rekindle her relationship with Jiang Hua and not bother him again.

Dan Dan noticed that her husband was in a very good mood these days as he sang Russian and English folk songs and played the violin as well. Dan Dan thought he was happy because he had made good progress with all the reforms and the luxury hotel would be built very soon. But clever Dan Dan could feel there must be another reason for his happiness. Sometimes, she could hear he was making a phone call but quickly hung up when he caught sight of Dan Dan. At those moments, the expression in his eyes looked unnatural and he would treat her very warmly, bringing her slippers and tea in a very polite manner, as if she had just returned from a trip.

As his closest childhood friend, she could normally read his inner-most thoughts through his expressions. His explanation was that he had just received a phone call from the construction company about some urgent issue which had to be resolved. To account for his good mood, he said it was because he had made more contributions to society after he took the political post of Mayor, even though he'd had to fight against the rigid, left-wing officials from time to time. Yet Dan Dan still felt there was some other reason for his happy mood. Wang Li and Qing Lian? No, he would not be so interested in them. Something about Yu Mei? There was no new information about her. She would leave it. Anyway, he was a good husband and would never betray his wife.

The preparations for the ceremony were complete. The main leaders of the city and province would all attend the ceremony as this project, using foreign and outside investment, marked a mile stone for the country's economic reforms. The co-operation between mainland China and Taiwan also symbolized a new relationship between both sides, with important political significance. The Taiwan Company also paid great attention to this ceremony. Not only was the General Director of the Board coming but also, the Director of the Taiwan Trading Society. Also, Mr. Du's father, the previous General of the Chinese National Party, would attend. So this ceremony created a great deal of attention in the Chinese media and was given a high profile.

Even better for Zhang Feng, Yu Mei would attend on behalf of her bureau, which meant she would come officially, but not privately, because Shen Zhen City wanted to establish business relations with cities in Northeast China, like Jili City.

One day before the ceremony, Dan Dan said she would also like to attend the ceremony but Zhang Feng quickly persuaded her not to go. His reason was because the other leaders would not be bringing their wives to the event. His real reason of course was in case Dan Dan saw Yu Mei which would cause unnecessary suspicion and envy between them. Zhang Feng thought all the photos of the ceremony would be focused on both parties in the deal and Yu Mei would not be involved. Even if Dan Dan watched the TV reports and read the newspapers, she would not see Yu Mei. This would allow him to meet her without being prevented by Dan Dan.

One day, in the middle of June, in the meeting hall of the provincial guest house, the ceremony took place with a great many people from both sides. The guests included Secretary Liu and other provincial leaders, Secretary Gong, Zhang Feng, Chang Zheng, Lin Jianguo, Chen Tao and leaders from different departments of the city. But the hardline leaders, like Director Shen and Li Qiu, refused to attend the event. Mr. Du, the General Director of his company's board, and the Director of the Taiwan Trading Society were there. An old man in a wheelchair, with grey hair, was in the crowd. He was the father of Mr. Du, the previous General in the Army of the National Party. Chang Zheng was talking to him and told him his own father, Zhao Wu, would soon arrive. In five minutes, a car approached and people saw a straight-backed, old man, in army uniform, walking into the hall.

Chang Zheng shouted to him,

"Father! Commander Du is here!"

General Zhao Wu walked towards the wheelchair. General Du made an effort to stand up and said,

"General Zhao, is it you?"

"General Du?"

The two old men saluted each other and then embraced. Zhao Wu sat next to Commander Du and they talked about the fighting they took part in during the Anti-Japanese War. The people around them listened to them, with great interest. Commander Du said,

"It is very good that we have a peaceful relationship between mainland China and Taiwan now and we can return to the mainland to visit our hometowns and friends. Mainland China has changed quite a lot."

Zhan Wu replied,

"We were delayed by the Cultural Revolution for ten years. But now, under the leadership of Deng Xiaoping, we can concentrate on building a new, modern China. We will make more and more progress. Look! Taiwan businessmen are also joining us and they bring funding and technology. We are members of the same family!"

People around them all laughed.

While Zhang Wu and Du Ming talked, Zhang Feng saw the slim and graceful Yu Mei in the crowd. She wore a red suit and looked especially beautiful. Facing a group of high ranking officials and businessmen, she looked graceful and poised, and she spoke with confidence and assurance, like an astute director of public relations, not a shy and tender-hearted, fairy-like girl. Zhang Feng was very surprised with her different manner today. As she came out of the wash room, Zhang Feng appeared from behind a pillar and said to her, pretending to be formal,

"How do you do, Head Yu Mei."

"How do you do, Mayor Zhang."

Yu Mei answered him in the same tone which sent an emotional shiver down his spine.

"You take these men by storm!" Zhang Feng said.

"That is another side of me."

"I miss you," he confessed.

"I miss you too," she replied.

"Let's meet when we get time."

"One meeting is not enough," said Yu Mei.

After Zhao Wu and Du Ming had finished their talk, Zhang Feng walked up to Zhao Wu and said to him,

"How are you, Uncle Zhao?"

"Xiao Feng! You are still so handsome. You are Mayor of Jili City now. That's wonderful!" Zhao Wu turned to him and said.

"Uncle, I could not have achieved anything if you had not saved me during the Cultural Revolution."

"Oh, that's all in the past now. How is your father?" Zhao Wu asked.

"He is fine. He has just retired but is still busy with his research."

"I will visit him in the next few days," Zhao Wu said.

Chang Zheng and Yu Mei came up to them. Looking at Yu Mei, Zhao Wu said,

"Is this Yu Mei? Chang Zheng told me you are doing well in Shen Zhen."

"Uncle Zhao, you still look young!" replied Yu Mei.

Remembering that Zhao Wu was her father's old comrade-in-arms and that her father died many years ago, Yu Mei's eyes looked red.

Zhang Feng noticed this and said to Zhao Wu,

"Uncle Zhao, it is not easy to get the children from our three families together at one time. Let's have a photo taken."

At noon, on a spacious site on the river bank, the deafening sound of gongs and drums could be heard and colourful banners could be seen fluttering in the wind. Many excavators, trucks and several hundred construction workers lined up, along with journalists and photographers and the teams from both sides of the project. Everybody was in high spirits.

On behalf of the River City, Zhang Feng expressed heartfelt thanks to the Taiwan International Tourist Company for helping to build this grand, international standard, five star hotel in his city. He said this was a huge project with both economic and political significance. Jili City Council would try its best to co-operate with the Taiwan Company to ensure the project was finished on time and to a high standard. His speech drew loud applause from the audience.

Then Mr. Du delivered his speech. He said he was very pleased to participate in this project with his mainland countrymen after forty years of separation between mainland China and Taiwan. The Taiwan Company would try its best to finish this great project on time. His speech also drew loud applause from the audience.

The ceremony began. In the bright flash of cameras and the sounds of shutters clicking, Zhang Feng and Du Shan brandished shovels to lay the foundation stone and then shook hands warmly. A group photo was taken to mark the occasion. On the left of the stone were Secretary Liu, Secretary Gong, Zhang Feng, Chang Zheng and other officials. On the right were the Director of the Taiwan Trading Society, the General Director of the Taiwan International Tourist Company, Mr. Du Shan and others. In the middle, the photographer cleverly arranged Zhao Wu and Du Ming, those two old generals, who shook their hands to symbolize the beginning of a new era between mainland China and Taiwan. There was thunderous applause from the audience.

But just before the photographer clicked the shutter, Mr. Du drew Yu Mei next to him. Yu Mei tried to decline but it was too late and the photo was taken. So the beautiful figure of Yu Mei featured in this freeze-frame with all those wealthy and powerful men but Zhang Feng did not see her at the time.

Qing Lian saw Yu Mei just at the moment when the photo was being taken because Yu Mei tried to hide herself behind the others; she did not like to show herself to the local people.

Seeing that Yu Mei was still exceedingly beautiful, Qing Lian became nervous. 'She has come back! Has she been with Zhang Feng?' She wanted to know why Yu Mei had returned and what her position was. Ignoring her assistant's call, she tried to find Yu Mei in the crowds.

During the Cultural Revolution, of the three women around Zhang Feng, Yu Mei was the one with the closest relationship as his girlfriend. Dan Dan was the second closest; she had looked after him as a 'sister' before the secret of her age was revealed. But Qing Lian could only watch him from a distance as she was an active Red Guard and his enemy. After being saved by him, she was transformed back into a normal woman and could get closer to him as a 'servant' or a normal friend. But after the Cultural Revolution had ended, Yu Mei went to the Taoist temple as a nun and Dan Dan became Zhang Feng's girlfriend, then Qing Lian was promoted to his 'sister'. Yet, if Yu Mei had returned to Zhang Feng, Qing Lian would be downgraded to 'servant' again. Qing Lian was quite anxious to know the intention and background of Yu Mei's return.

After a nervous search, Qing Lian found Yu Mei on a bench under a big tree. Yu Mei recognized her straight away and asked her, politely, to sit down. Qing Lian asked Yu Mei about her experience after leaving the temple and the reason for her visit here again. Yu Mei knew Qing Lian loved Zhang Feng secretly but he treated her only as a friend. So she quietly told her that after leaving the temple, she had travelled to the South and completed a Master's degree and then worked for the Shen Zhen Foreign Investment Bureau. On this occasion, she had accompanied the Taiwan Company to the ceremony and she would return to Shen Zhen tomorrow.

Listening to Yu Mei, Qing Lian felt more relaxed and asked carefully,

"Have you met Brother Feng?"

"Yes. He has a happy life with Dan Dan and they have a lovely baby son."

"Have you got a partner?" Qing Lian asked.

"I married an overseas Chinese man with a PhD. He loves me," Yu Mei answered.

"That's good." Qing Lian felt relieved.

"I heard you married Li He. He is an honest man. Are you enjoying your married life?" asked Yu Mei.

"Just so, so," Qing Lian answered, coldly. She knew for sure that after their separation, they would definitely get divorced.

After the ceremony had finished, the City Council entertained the Taiwan guests with a rich banquet so it was quite late when Zhang Feng returned home. Seeing the dishes on the table, he realized that he had forgotten to tell Dan Dan he would not be having dinner with her this evening at home.

"I am so sorry, darling, I forgot to tell you I would be having dinner with the Taiwan guests this evening."

Dan Dan put down the book she was reading and looked at him.

"You are pleased because your wish to build this luxury hotel has been realized."

He sat down and said,

"Yes, I am really happy."

"Is there something else making you feel even happier? Have you met some old friends?"

"Yes. I met General Zhao Wu, my saviour," answered Zhang Feng.

"Have you met anybody you have not seen for many years?"

Zhang Feng looked confused and said quietly,

"Oh, nobody in particular."

Dan Dan stood up suddenly and passed him the evening newspaper.

"Look here. There is a friend you have always missed."

Zhang Feng took the newspaper and read the headline about the ceremony and saw the group photo. He was surprised to see Yu Mei standing next to Mr. Du and became nervous and started to sweat. He did not realize that Yu Mei was in the photo.

"Oh… well… she is married now. She went to the ceremony with Mr. Du and will be returning to Shen Zhen tomorrow."

Watching his embarrassed reaction, Dan Dan knew for certain that he did not want her to know anything about Yu Mei coming back to the city. Dan Dan was an open-minded and magnanimous woman and not at all jealous. She smiled and, like the sister she used to be, said,

"Xiao Feng, why you are so nervous and why were you so quick to tell me she is married? Do you think I will be jealous? No. Yu Mei is also my good friend. She helped me to look after you and save you during the Revolution. I have sympathy for her suffering and ordeal. Have a cup of tea to help you sober up and tell me all about what happened to her after she left the temple."

Zhang Feng wiped away his sweat and told her about Yu Mei's experience during the last three years but he did not mention that Yu Mei had secretly tried to help him in various ways, and he did not talk about her marriage in detail. After listening to him, Dan Dan looked much happier and said she was pleased that Yu Mei had returned to society and now had a career and a partner. Zhang Feng relaxed and thought his embarrassment was over but he suddenly heard Dan Dan's request.

"Why not ask her to stay a few more days in her hometown? I really miss her and I would love to meet her again because I not only sympathise with her; I also like her as my sister. Invite her to come over for dinner. Don't tell me you haven't got her phone number."

Zhang Feng felt very awkward and was worried that, if Yu Mei came to the house, her single status might be exposed. But if he refused to invite Yu Mei, Dan Dan would suspect their relationship even more so he said he would invite her. Dan Dan deliberately went off into the kitchen when he made the call and five minutes later, when she heard Zhang Feng had finished, she walked out and asked him whether Yu Mei would be coming or not. Zhang Feng looked relieved and told Dan Dan that Yu Mei had accepted the invitation and said she would like to see their son as well, as she loved children.

The next day was Sunday. Dan Dan woke up quite early to do all the shopping. She still remembered what dishes Yu Mei liked, so she bought all the ingredients. Zhang Feng was busy in the kitchen all morning, helping Dan Dan to cook. He remembered Yu Mei liked to drink Chang Bai Mountain wine so he made sure they had some to offer her.

At lunch time, Yu Mei arrived. She wore a very simple dress which did not hide her beauty and slim figure. Dan Dan shook hands with her warmly but Zhang Feng was constrained. Dan Dan knew if she had not been there, they would have embraced each other at the very least. Dan Dan would not have been jealous as she knew they were life-death lovers. Zhang Feng should have been Yu Mei's husband if it had not been because of the suffering and pain caused by the Cultural Revolution. Yu Mei gave Dan Dan a fashionable Hong Kong scarf and gave their son some toys. She picked him up and kissed him. He was so cute and would be a handsome man like his father when he grew up.

They all sat around the table and Dan Dan said she was very pleased that Yu Mei had been able to come to their home for lunch. She felt happy to see Yu Mei was still beautiful and confident despite the pain and nightmare of suffering she had experienced during the Cultural Revolution. She hoped Yu Mei would visit their home often in the future. Yu Mei smiled and said she would come again. Dan Dan had been her 'sister' since they had met in the Beijing hospital during the revolutionary tour. Seeing the table was full of dishes, Yu Mei said,

"I have given you too much trouble. All these dishes are my favourites as in Shen Zhen, I can only eat Cantonese style cuisine."

Dan Dan said,

"Brother Feng cooked some dishes you specially like."

Zhang Feng opened the special bottle of wine and gave a glass to Dan Dan first, then Yu Mei.

"You should have served the wine to our guest first!" exclaimed Dan Dan. "You should know this as the Mayor!"

Yu Mei knew Zhang Feng had done this deliberately as he did not want to show his close relationship with Yu Mei.

"It is alright. Serve the hostess first and then the sister."

They all laughed. During the eating and drinking, the two ladies became more relaxed and intimate, like real sisters, but Yu Mei talked about her partner very little, which worried Zhang Feng. Dan Dan thought Yu Mei did not like to compare her husband to Zhang Feng, so she stopped asking her for more details.

Watching the two women he loved most in the world, Zhang Feng's mind was restless. One was his beautiful, kind and devoted wife who gave him the happiness and peace of a tranquil lake. But the other, was his life-death lover who gave him the excitement and turbulent emotions of surging waves on the sea. As a man, he would like to have both of them, but in reality, he could only have one of them.

Zhang Feng and Yu Mei were very polite with each other but Dan Dan knew the affectionate feelings which existed between them. Dan Dan understood and sympathized with Yu Mei: she liked her. But the problem was, she could not share Zhang Feng with her. Anyway, Yu Mei had her own husband who might not be as perfect as Zhang Feng but all women needed at least one man to love them. Dan Dan did not think about how she would cope with the knowledge that Yu Mei was really single. How would she manage this complex love triangle?

Seeing Zhang Feng and Dan Dan had such a happy family, Yu Mei felt guilty. She knew she should not do anything to hurt them but her love for Zhang Feng stubbornly stayed in her spirit, like a rock. She sighed deeply in her mind and thought she would be satisfied if, from time to time, she could see him, talk to him, help him and even have a brief kiss or embrace from him, like a sister.

The lunch continued until 4.00 pm. Yu Mei said goodbye to them because she would be going back to Shen Zhen tomorrow for work. Dan Dan knew Zhang Feng and Yu Mei would be reluctant to part from each other, so she turned back to look after her son but Zhang Feng and Yu Mei only waved to each other, meaningfully.

Dan Dan embraced Yu Mei and said, warmly,

"My dear sister, come to see us again soon."

"Sister Dan Dan, I will miss you," Yu Mei said.

She deliberately did not say: I will miss both of you.

PART V

You Can Marry Her Now

Chapter I

I Want to See the Outside World

At the end of the eighties, there was a trend for going abroad. Young people wanted to study in Europe and the USA to learn advanced science and technology. The Central Government selected many excellent students and sent them to study in Western countries. Rich families and those who had foreign relatives abroad also sent their children to study there privately. University scholars and research fellows in research institutions went abroad to carry out investigations, take part in exchanges and co-operate internationally to improve their knowledge and skills.

Dan Dan specialized in economics so it was important for her to have the opportunity of studying abroad but there was a limited quota for each university and long waiting lists. Dan Dan thought of Processor Liang Hua in the London School of Economics. He wrote to her quite often to discuss economic issues, especially, the new economic reforms in China. It would be excellent if Liang Hua invited her for an academic visit.

Dan Dan explained her idea to Zhang Feng who said it was worth trying. He supported his wife and wanted her to see the Western world as he felt his trip to the UK had been very beneficial even though it was so short. Professor Liang Hua was a typically kind and straightforward scholar. His brother, Liang Fu, had helped Wang Hai to promote Chinese products abroad. With the support of her husband, Dan Dan happily wrote to Liang Hua to explain her proposal but she was not confident; she did not know the regulations for inviting foreign scholars to the UK, especially Chinese scholars.

Unexpectedly, Liang Hua wrote back directly. He said it would be an honour to invite Dan Dan to visit his University. He could apply to the University for a Funding Grant to support a research programme on Chinese economic reform as the West was quite interested in a changing China and its potentially vast market. If he got this funding, it would support her visit financially. After reading this letter, Dan Dan was very pleased and she told Zhang Feng who was also happy with this opportunity for his wife.

Liang Hua soon sent another letter saying his application had been approved. The University not only approved the funding, but also wanted to establish an academic link with Jili University so they asked Liang Hua to visit Jili University on an exchange for both sides. He would give some seminars there and also discuss the details of the research project with Dan Dan. After this trip, he would send an invitation to Dan Dan and apply for a visa.

Showing Liang's letter to Zhang Feng, Dan Dan said, excitedly,

"This is great! At last I have an opportunity to see the outside world!"

One week later, Liang Hua made an international phone call to Dan Dan and told her that he would start his trip the following week. He would fly to Hong Kong first to see his brother, then he would fly to Beijing and would transfer there to Jili City. He asked Dan Dan not to meet him at the airport as he was not sure of the exact time and date of his arrival but he remembered the way to Jili University. Dan Dan was happy to know this and she contacted her department to arrange the seminars for Liang Hua and planned her research scheme. She was too busy to tell Zhang Feng about the dates of Liang's trip.

Liang Hua stayed in his brother's home in Hong Kong for a few days. His brother, Liang Fu, asked him about his relationship with Wang Li. He said he was going to meet her on this visit but he preferred more mature women, like Dan Dan. Liang Fu reminded him that Dan Dan was a married woman and she was quite traditional; he shouldn't waste his time on her.

After arriving at Beijing, Liang Hua stayed in a hotel in the centre of the city. He quite liked Beijing as it was a great capital with both an ancient history and modern architecture. He went to the Wang Fujing shopping area the next day to buy some souvenirs for friends and he noticed that the shoppers wore very fashionable clothes now, not the simple blue and yellow outfits of Mao's time.

Suddenly, he saw an attractive couple in front of him. The man was tall and sturdy and the lady was slim. People around them seemed to gaze at them as they passed by. Liang Hua was curious and he wanted to see the faces and figures of this couple. They stopped at a soft drinks stand and bought some soda water. Liang Hua passed them and turned sideways to look at them. He was surprised to see the tall and handsome man was Dan Dan's husband, Zhang Feng, and the lady was an exceedingly beautiful lady who Liang Hua did not recognize. He was almost about to greet Zhang Feng but he suddenly realized that maybe, he should not bother them as he did not know their relationship. Growing up in England, Liang Hua had a more reserved character, like the English, and he was not concerned with other people's private affairs. He passed them in order to do his shopping.

Later on, he began to feel hungry and wanted to eat something so he explored a small lane with a lot of food stands and restaurants. He bought some barbecue lamb and then he thought he should try a few genuine Beijing snacks. He walked into a small restaurant which served quick-boiled tripe and, as he was looking for a seat, he suddenly saw Zhang Feng eating, with that beautiful lady, at a corner table. Zhang Feng picked up a piece of tripe and put it into her mouth and Liang Hua also noticed that Zhang Feng's other hand was holding her hand. Liang Hua quickly left the restaurant as he did not want to bother them. It seemed that they had a very intimate relationship. Liang Hua felt strange because Zhang Feng looked like a loyal husband and not the type to have affairs with other women.

Near Qian Men Street, next to Tian An Men Square, Liang Hua saw a very long queue outside the first Kentucky Fried Chicken restaurant in China. He was curious and asked a young man why people were waiting in such long queues to get fried chicken. The young man told him that, after China opened its doors to the outside world, people were keen to try everything from abroad in the same way that Coca-Cola had only become very popular recently.

Liang Hua arrived at Jili City where Dan Dan had arranged a seminar for him in her department, with the title: 'The Development of the Economy in the UK after the Second World War'. His seminar was well received by the teachers and students and many students from other departments also attended. Because the lecture hall was very full, some students stood in the corridor listening to his speech. There was a warm reaction to the point that China could learn from the experience of the changes in privatization and nationalization in the UK economy. Liang Hua's Mandarin Chinese was better than before, but sometimes, he got stuck with some expressions. At these moments, Dan Dan would help him. He explained to her in English, then she translated into Chinese. The Directors of the University and the department awarded him the post of 'Visiting Professor' which made him very happy.

Dan Dan did not forget about the connection between him and Wang Li. She bought cinema tickets for them both and asked them to see a film together. The film was a comedy about life but Liang Hua did not understand why the audience laughed so much as he did not live in China so Wang Li explained the jokes to him. Wang Li invited him for dinner after the cinema. They treated each other very politely, like friends, but neither of them felt their pulses racing.

The arrangements for Dan Dan's academic visit to the UK went smoothly. Both Jili University and her own department fully supported her visit. The date to leave was fixed and visa issues were resolved. Dan Dan was pleased and invited Liang Hua to her home for a meal. He asked whether Zhang Feng was at home and Dan Dan told him that her husband was just back from a Beijing trip – something about the building of the five star hotel. Liang Hua did not tell her that he had seen Zhang Feng with a beautiful woman on the street in Beijing as he thought it was a private matter.

Entering their house, Zhang Feng shook hands warmly with him and told him about the great project of the luxury hotel since inviting foreign investment was Liang Hua's research field. They talked very congenially as Zhang Feng used to be a scholar and Zhang Feng regarded him as a good friend. He was confident Liang Hua would look after Dan Dan on her UK trip. He also asked Liang Hua about his relationship with Wang Li and hoped that they would soon become attached. Liang Hua said he needed to wait and see what happened in the near future. Zhang Feng asked about the arrangements for Dan Dan's accommodation and study in London. Liang said his department had arranged everything for her for one year, after that, they were able to arrange a possible extension if she wanted to do a PhD. Dan Dan said she would miss her son if she stayed abroad for so long as he was so young but she was looking forward to the one year visiting programme. She would decide what to do after that.

In spring, 1988, Dan Dan left home and flew to London. The airplane landed at Gatwick Airport and at the exit, she saw Liang Hua holding a card with her name on it. He took her luggage and asked her about her flight. He drove along the motorway. Watching the green fields and traditional English houses go by, Dan Dan felt very comfortable. In London, Liang Hua brought her to a lovely, one bed apartment in a Victorian building with a spacious kitchen, bathroom and old style furniture. Dan Dan said,

"Is it very expensive to rent this nice apartment?"

"No problem! You have enough funds to stay here."

He opened the fridge-freezer and showed her the food already inside: meat, vegetables and fruit. He also told her how to use the cooker and control the heating.

"Thank you very much, Professor Liang, you have spent so much time and money making me feel welcome here."

"It is my duty. We need help from friends when we are in an alien country," he said. "Please feel at home. Just call me Liang Hua, as we are not only colleagues but also friends."

Dan Dan felt Liang was a very kind man, a typical English gentleman: polite, humorous and considerate. Not a lot of Chinese men were like that.

After one day's rest, Liang Hua took Dan Dan to the LSE. Dan Dan was amazed by this internationally famous University which had produced twelve Nobel Prize winners. Dan Dan visited the library, reading rooms, computer studio and lecture halls, and saw students of all nationalities from all over the world. Liang Hua took her to the Department of Oriental Economy and helped her to register and introduced her to his colleagues. In a small office, specially arranged for her, there were two tables, with a Chinese woman in her thirties sitting at one table. Liang introduced them to each other. The woman was called Chen Mei, a lecturer from Zhong Shan University in Guang Dong Province. She had just finished her one year visiting programme and started her PhD. The two ladies shook hands politely. Chen Mei said she could help Dan Dan if she had any problems in the UK.

At the weekend, Liang Hua invited Dan Dan to his upmarket, three bed apartment in a good area of London. Dan Dan saw his apartment was very clean and said she did not realize a man's accommodation could be so clean. He said he might be obsessively clean. He cooked some Cantonese style dishes and said he had learned his cooking skills from his parents who had lived in England for many years. After his father died, his mother and brother moved back to Hong Kong.

Dan Dan asked why he did not have a partner, considering he was already in his forties and Liang said he liked Chinese ladies but there were not many of them in England. She asked about Wang Li. Wang Li was a good girl, he told her, but she was too young and uninformed; he liked more mature ladies. He suddenly flushed and stammered, and said if only he could find someone like Dan Dan – mature, beautiful and intelligent. It was no wonder only a handsome and talented man like Zhang Feng could get her. Dan Dan smiled and said it took her twenty years to get him.

Thinking Liang was a good friend, Dan Dan told him about the complex love triangle between her, Zhang Feng and Yu Mei. Liang was moved and said that this was really a moving love story. He asked more about Yu Mei because Dan Dan had described her as a fairy-like, beautiful lady, and he recalled the lady he saw in Beijing with Zhang Feng. She had also been a fairy-like woman. He thought it might have been Yu Mei but he said nothing to Dan Dan.

During the next few weekends, Liang Hua took Dan Dan to some of the attractions in London, such as Buckingham Palace, Westminster, Tower Bridge and Hyde Park. Dan Dan liked London very much and she had a strong feeling of being at home. This was not only because she liked Western culture, but also, because she liked a natural, tranquil and relaxing environment. She also found most English people were polite, quiet, respected privacy, observed public order and had fairly uncomplicated relationships between themselves. She was amazed that even when English people had their meals, they still seemed quiet and polite compared to the noisy habits of Chinese people.

With the help of Liang Hua, she learned how to use forks and knives to eat. Sometimes, she noticed the adoring expression in his eyes when he looked at her but she knew she was a married woman and could not have an intimate relationship with him although she knew Western people tended to have a more open-minded attitude towards sex and love. Women here were not very conservative when it came to affairs. The more men who loved them, the more attractive they felt. Thus, Dan Dan did not pay too much attention to the emotions shown by Liang Hua, and anyway, it was normal for men to love beautiful women.

Dan Dan felt quite happy in the first few months in England with her research with Liang Hua and her comfortable life going smoothly. She wrote to Zhang Feng every one or two weeks and asked how he and their son were getting on. International phone calls were very expensive. Over the weeks, she started to miss her son more and more and wanted to travel back to see them. Liang Hua considerately arranged a trip for her to collect data in China. She was anxious to return so she did not tell Zhang Feng about her trip. She wanted to give them a surprise.

It was about 5.00 pm when she arrived back home from the airport. She thought that Zhang Feng might not be back from his work yet, so she opened the door with her key and entered the house quietly. But suddenly, she heard voices coming from the sitting room. She listened carefully and realized it was Zhang Feng and Yu Mei talking. Dan Dan thought she would walk in, to talk to them, but she was worried that her sudden appearance might frighten them; they may be embracing. She felt her heart beating fast and did not know whether she should leave quietly or walk in and greet them. She heard Yu Mei saying,

"Brother Feng, I miss you every day in Shen Zhen and cannot concentrate on my work. Fortunately, Dan Dan is abroad and so I can come and see you often."

Dan Dan could hear the sound of kissing. Zhang Feng said, "I miss you as well and see you often in my dreams."

"Do you miss me more than Dan Dan?" Yu Mei asked.

"I miss you more, as Dan Dan is my wife and we can be together legally but you and I can only meet like secret agents. You used to be my dream lover but you have come out of my dreams. It is a pity we can still only meet secretly."

"Brother, can I stay here tonight…?"

"I would like you to… We have been life-death lovers for so many years but have never made love. Yet Dan Dan loves me deeply. I cannot betray her…"

Dan Dan could hear Yu Mei's gentle crying. She left the house quickly as she was almost crying herself. It seemed that they had to control their passion even though they loved each other desperately. Actually, Dan Dan could accept them making love as they were life-death lovers. She wondered whether they would really be able to control themselves tonight.

She stopped off at a small food stand very near her house for some soda water whilst watching the front door of her house. After half an hour, she saw Zhang Feng sending Yu Mei out of the house. He watched her walking into the distance and waved at her. Dan Dan thought that her husband had controlled himself in the end and had not let her down but she did not go to the house directly. Instead, she made a phone call to Zhang Feng saying she had just landed at the airport and would be back home in 40 minutes. She waited outside for the 40 minutes to pass and then entered the house. Zhang Feng rushed to her, embracing and kissing her and said he had really missed her.

Dan Dan thought, 'You are not really telling me the truth. You miss Yu Mei more.'

Zhang Feng made some tasty food for people who had just finished a long journey: porridge with preserved duck egg, pickled cucumber and minced, red bean buns. His care and attention still moved her. She knew he was still a good husband even if he missed Yu Mei desperately. That night, they made passionate love because they had been apart for so long but also, because Zhang Feng felt guilty.

Zhang Feng did not tell his wife about Yu Mei's visits and Dan Dan did not want to ask because Yu Mei had her own husband now. They had just missed each other and hadn't dared to have an affair.

After a few days at home, Dan Dan returned to the UK. In her office, Chen Mei warm-heartedly asked her about the situation in China as she had not returned to the country for over half a year. Talking about Shen Zhen, Chen Mei said that as a capitalist, economic experimental zone, the city had developed very rapidly and the model was worth expanding to the whole country. She said she knew a former university classmate who now worked in the Foreign Investment Bureau in Shen Zhen. Dan Dan could ask this friend of Chen Mei about the progress of reform in the city. Dan Dan suddenly remembered that Yu Mei also worked in this bureau, so she asked Chen Mei for her name.

"Her name is Yu Mei, an exceedingly beautiful woman. It is a pity she is still single because she suffered from such great emotional trauma in the past."

Yu Mei was still single! Dan Dan was shocked. She asked Chen Mei,

"But some of her old friends said she married an overseas Chinese man with a PhD!"

Chen Mei laughed.

"That is because so many men were courting her and she said that as an excuse to stop them."

Yu Mei was still single? Dan Dan did not sleep well for a few days. No wonder they had met so frequently. Yu Mei would not love Zhang Feng so desperately if she had a husband.

Noticing Dan Dan was in a low mood, Liang Hua started to worry about her. One day, he took her back to her apartment and seeing that she was reluctant to cook for herself, Liang Hua made her some noodles. She ate very little and sat on the sofa, wiping her eyes. Liang Hua asked her what had happened. Was she having trouble with her work or had something happened at home? Dan Dan was a strong woman and she had even been able to bear the suffering during the Cultural Revolution; she did not like to tell others about her worries. She was worried that single Yu Mei would try to meet Zhang Feng more often and bring trouble to her family. Do not forget, Yu Mei was even willing to die for her love for Zhang Feng.

Dan Dan felt she really needed to confide in somebody and talk about her pent-up feelings. Seeing the caring expression in Liang's eyes, Dan Dan thought he was a person she could trust. Wiping away her tears, she said if she told him about her private life, would he keep it a secret? He said definitely; he always respected other people's privacy and anyway, she was his good friend. Dan Dan then told him that she had just discovered Yu Mei was still single and she had met up with her husband more frequently recently. Liang suddenly remembered how he had seen Zhang Feng walking down the street in Beijing with a beautiful woman. He asked Dan Dan whether Yu Mei was fairy-like and beautiful and then revealed what he had seen in Beijing. Hearing his description, Dan Dan believed this proved Yu Mei was really still single otherwise she would not have been able to meet Zhang Feng in this way.

Dan Dan said she did not know how to deal with this difficult scenario. She could pretend she did not know about their intimate relationship but in China, this kind of amorous affair could be spread very quickly. She knew Zhang Feng would not divorce her but that would mean the three of them would live in stress and sorrow. She wondered if she should give her husband to Yu Mei, after all, they would have been a couple if the Cultural Revolution had never happened.

Seeing how upset Dan Dan was, Liang Hua patted her shoulder gently and said,

"You could persuade your husband to stop meeting Yu Mei although it will not be easy. If you really cannot bear this difficult situation and you have to divorce him, you do not need to worry. Many men love beautiful and mature ladies like you." He suddenly summoned up his courage and said to her,

"Dan Dan, to be honest, I fell in love with you when I met you the very first time even though I knew you were married. I continue to miss you and that is why I do not have any feelings for Wang Li. But I will not seize this opportunity to pursue you. If you can continue your relationship with your husband, I will bless you but if you decide to leave him, I would like to be the man by your side for the rest of your life. Of course, it is your choice. Maybe you think I am not a good candidate as I am not as handsome as Zhang Feng."

After hearing his words Dan Dan opened her eyes fully and looked at him, surprised. When she noticed the honest expression in his eyes, she said,

"No, Liang Hua. Brother Liang, you are an excellent man, like an English gentleman, the favourite choice for many Chinese women, with your intelligence, humour, and kindness. I quite like you and regard you as a trusted friend although I have never thought about going further with our relationship. You won't feel disappointed, will you?"

Liang Hua said,

"No, not at all. Whatever decision you take, I will always stand by you to support and help you."

That night, Dan Dan had a dream, in which Zhang Feng was fighting with Liang Hua. Liang Hua was beaten to the ground by Zhang Feng and was bleeding. Dan Dan had to call an ambulance. In the end, she was woken up, in a sweat, by the siren of an ambulance outside her window.

CHAPTER II

Let Me Still Be Your Sister

Dan Dan felt very depressed for a few weeks. She did not take Liang Hua's courting seriously as she needed to sort out this love triangle first. It seemed that there were two ways to resolve this problem: either, she sacrificed herself and gave Zhang Feng to Yu Mei, or, she asked Yu Mei to end her relationship with Zhang Feng, and not even remain as his 'sister'. If Yu Mei had a husband, she could be Zhang Feng's sister, but because she did not have a partner, she was a time bomb which could destroy Dan Dan's family at any point.

At last, Dan Dan decided to discuss the situation with Yu Mei directly and find out how she felt. Dan Dan guessed Yu Mei would promise not to break up her family, but there was still a potential danger if she did not make the effort to find another man. Dan Dan wrote to Yu Mei, saying she would be visiting

Shen Zhen for her research and would like to meet her there. Yu Mei made an international phone call to her and said she would welcome her visit. Dan Dan told Liang Hua about her decision. He said he would always support her, whatever she decided to do and he helped arrange her visit.

Arriving at Shen Zhen, Dan Dan marvelled at the great changes in the city. She remembered that the city had been a small fishing village only ten years ago, but now, it was a huge, modern metropolis with tall buildings, wide roads, beautiful urban areas and several million citizens. Dan Dan thought that if the Government decided to extend the economic policy of Shen Zhen to the whole country, China would soon become a modern, developed country. But she was not in the mood to go sight-seeing as she was worried.

She met Yu Mei in a secluded coffee bar. Yu Mei did not know the real intention behind Dan Dan's visit and just thought the investigation of Shen Zhen was part of Dan Dan's research programme. The two women warmly greeted each other. Seeing Yu Mei still looked so young and beautiful, Dan Dan began to understand why Zhang Feng could not give her up. In the last few years, Dan Dan had been busy with her family, her son and teaching and she never seemed to have the time for make-up and smart clothes. Maybe this was the reason her husband loved Yu Mei more? Although Liang Hua complimented her for her poise and beauty, perhaps he was just flattering her.

They chatted for a while. Dan Dan suddenly asked Yu Mei about her husband and said she would like to meet him some time to discuss his study experience abroad. Yu Mei looked a bit nervous and said her husband was in the USA at the moment, on a business trip. Dan Dan did not want to put it off any longer. She gazed at Yu Mei and asked,

"My dear sister, please tell me the truth. Do you really have a husband?"

Yu Mei flushed.

"I...I..." She did not know what to say.

Dan Dan understood completely that she was still single. Not wanting to make the atmosphere too tense, Dan Dan said,

"Yu Mei, I did not deliberately set out to question you. Just by chance, I know that you are still single from your former classmate. I also know that you have been meeting Brother Feng quite often. I am not a jealous woman and I trust Zhang Feng. Even I know his handsome appearance and manliness are quite attractive to women."

Yu Mei lowered her head.

"I am so sorry, Sister Dan Dan. I never intended to cheat you. I want to see Brother Feng but I do not want to break up your family and so I said I was married. Do not worry, Sister Dan Dan. I will not see him again."

Dan Dan said, magnanimously,

"Yu Mei, Sister, I do not regard you as the 'other' woman. Originally, Zhang Feng should have been yours, but the red storm of the Cultural Revolution separated you and I got him by luck. I have thought about this difficult situation for a long time now. If I insist on your separation, it would be painful for both of you. We should not be too selfish. I should give him to you as I have enjoyed a happy life with him for many years now."

Listening to Dan Dan's words, Yu Mei looked frightened.

"No, no, Sister Dan Dan! You cannot do this!"

"Listen to me," explained Dan Dan. "We cannot carry on like this. You can still be his sister and I do not care about your relationship as you are life-death lovers anyway. It would be alright in the West because men there seem to be able to have a wife and a lover. If they get along, people do not blame them. But China is different. Gossips will spread this affair widely and people will blame you and mock me. The worst is, it will damage the political future of Brother Feng. Do you know that it is very difficult to keep your relationship secret? My supervisor, Liang Hua, actually saw your meeting in Beijing but he did not tell anybody about it as the English way is to respect privacy. It was only when he saw I was depressed and wanted to resolve this problem that he told me about your meeting." Yu Mei replied, honestly,

"Sorry, Sister Dan Dan, I am wrong. I promise not to see him again. I would rather find another religious temple again in the South if I cannot bear the pain."

"No, Sister Yu Mei, I cannot let you live alone with only candle light and religious worship for company. I have an idea. My supervisor says he has fallen in love with me and he is keen to be with me for the rest of my life if I leave Brother Feng. He is a polite, intelligent and considerate gentleman and both of us are academics in the same research field, with a common language. He likes my son. I would be happy to live with him. Do you know Zhang Feng doesn't act like a scholar any longer? We disagree quite a lot now. Sister, I can even tell you some private things. He is no longer very interested in my body and sometimes, he seems reluctant to go to bed with me. Our relationship is becoming more like that between brother and sister. Another thing I need to tell you is he quite often calls out your name in his dreams so it would be very cruel if you are separated against your will."

Yu Mei was startled and did not know what to say. After a few minutes, she said,

"Sister Dan Dan, that will not work. He will not divorce you. He wants to keep your happy family, not destroy it. He is a responsible and loving man."

"People can be changed. I will try to persuade him," Dan Dan said.

Yu Mei wanted to tell Dan Dan that he had refused to make love to her several times which meant he could control himself not to betray his wife. It would be impossible to ask him to divorce Dan Dan. But she did not mention any of this to Dan Dan. It might offend her.

Seeing that they could not resolve the problem, Dan Dan said she would talk to Zhang Feng directly to see if their complex love triangle could be sorted out. When they said goodbye to each other, Yu Mei embraced Dan Dan.

"I am so sorry, dear sister. You can be sure that I will not contact him again."

"Thank you, dear sister. Wait for more news. I do not want you to continue living in this depression for the rest of your life."

The two women parted, both upset.

Back at home and seeing her adorable son, she kept kissing him over and over. Zhang Feng was busy cooking in the kitchen. Chinese people, who had been eating Western meals for a long time, would certainly have missed Chinese noodles with soybean sauce. Looking at his thin face, Dan Dan asked him whether he had been over-tired recently. He said it was not easy being Mayor as there was always resistance from the hard headed, left-wing group to any reforms. Looking at her happy family, Dan Dan was hesitant to talk about the situation.

She waited until the last day of her visit before she decided to discuss this matter with her husband. She sent her son to her parents and asked Zhang Feng to return home earlier and cooked some dishes he liked for dinner. Afterwards, she gave him a glass of orange juice and sat down on the sofa with him.

Zhang Feng noticed the serious expression on her face and the tense atmosphere in the room so he was a little bit nervous.

Dan Dan leaned back and said to him, in the tone of a 'sister',

"Xiao Feng, I am leaving tomorrow and I must discuss an important matter with you. How well have you been getting along with Yu Mei recently?"

Zhang Feng flushed and asked,

"What do you mean? She has just phoned me occasionally to ask about our family and your situation abroad."

"She is happy with her husband?" Dan Dan asked.

"I think so," he replied.

"Look in my eyes. Do not forget I have known whether you are lying or not from the expression on your face since our childhood."

He looked startled and said,

"She told me she has an overseas Chinese husband. Have they parted recently?"

Dan Dan looked a bit angry and said,

"You can even lie to your most intimate childhood friend and wife? I just met her in Chen Zhen, and she admitted to me that she is still single. You know this. Why do you still lie to me?"

Zhang Feng lowered his head and said, in a low voice,

"I am sorry, Dan Dan. We did not tell you the truth because we did not want to upset you."

"I know you do not want to hurt our family and only want to keep your relationship secret. If we lived in the West, there would not be such a problem. In England, men sometimes have a wife and a lover at the same time and if this does not cause a family problem, it is not condemned by the public. But in

China, such an affair would be a sensational scandal. Yu Mei would be blamed as the third woman and I would be mocked and humiliated. Even worse, your political career would be destroyed. The hard left-wing leaders could use this affair to make an accusation against you and dismiss you from your post. You might think you can do it secretly, but paper cannot hold fire and, sooner or later, it will be revealed. Even your recent meeting in Beijing was seen by somebody. Luckily, he did not speak about it to other people." Zhang Feng took hold of Dan Dan's hands and said,

"Darling, I will never see her again."

"Yu Mei also promised me that she would never meet you again. I trust both of you but the problem is you will both live in depression and emotional pain. No, actually, the three of us will live in sorrow and anxiety which will affect our careers and futures. Yu Mei might go back to a religious temple. I do not want to see these consequences."

She sipped her juice.

"Xiao Feng, there is a way to resolve this problem. I can take myself out of this triangle and give Yu Mei to you. She should have been yours anyway had the Cultural Revolution never happened. I have enjoyed your love and the happiness of our family life yet, I will not live alone for the rest of my life. To be honest, Liang Hua has fallen in love with me but he is not a man trying to steal a woman from her husband. After he found out about my dilemma, he said that if I decided to leave you, he would like to be my partner for the rest of my life. He said he liked mature women which is why he does not have any romantic feelings for Wang Li. He is just like an English gentleman and we have a common language. We will be happy together."

Listening to her speech, Zhang Feng suddenly took hold of her and choking with sobs he said,

"No, Dan Dan, I cannot live without you! In the past, you hid your age and looked after me as a 'sister'. You sacrificed so much for me. I cannot forget it was you who helped me when I was tortured by the Red Guards. You nearly drowned yourself in the river for your love of me when I was sent to be executed. No, no, I cannot leave you, and our son! Do not say you have found love with Professor Liang Hua. I know that is just an excuse for you to leave me."

Then he cried like a woman. Dan Dan was moved by his reaction. She was patting his shoulder to comfort him, like a child but she was a wise and reasonable woman. She knew when Zhang Feng thought about the moral principles involved, he would maintain his love for her and their son but when he became emotional, he could not resist Yu Mei's love for him because she was part of his spirit. Even if they left things as they were, it would be very hard for him not to contact her. In all those years when he did not know where Yu Mei was, he could only miss her quietly. But now, he knew where she was and he could stand not contacting her for the time being, but not in the long term. It was the same for Yu Mei. Dan Dan knew clearly that they would sacrifice anything, including their lives, for the sake of their love.

"Xiao Feng, let's be reasonable. We should all keep calm. I will go back to the UK. You and Yu Mei should think about this as well. I do not like the thought of both of you living in sadness. The Revolution is over now. We are the social elite and can control our own destinies and future. The worst is only that I will leave you and marry Liang Hua. If my happiness index with you is '1', it will be at least '0.5' with him! If you marry Yu

Mei, the total index for both of you should be '2', and the total index for the three of us will be '2.5'! But if we keep the existing situation, we will all be unhappy. The index would be '-1' for each of us and '-3' in total. So there is a big difference between 2.5 and -3."

Dan Dan had been a top student in mathematics from her childhood. She could even use mathematics to analyze emotional problems. Zhang Feng admired her wisdom even though he was deeply upset and thinking about the possible impact on their son. He still did not agree with her suggestion.

He embraced her the whole night long, as if she would be gone forever. Dan Dan was crying in her heart but she was a woman with strong willpower. She knew they had to resolve this emotional issue in a good way.

CHAPTER III

I Am Satisfied to Sleep with You Only Once

There was chaos in Zhang Feng's home after Dan Dan left. His parents-in-law could not look after his son because they were taking a long holiday that winter. Winter was very cold in Jili City, with temperatures of minus 20° to 30° at night time. In the late 1980s, a lot of retired people took holidays in Han Nan Island in Southern China, living in exclusive hotels or apartments, because the weather there was still warm. The white beaches, green palm trees, blue sea water and bright sunshine there attracted many tourists from Northern China.

In the past, from the 1950s to the beginning of the 1980s, Chinese people did not have a sense of 'holiday'. They stayed in their hometown all their lives because of household registration and the food coupon system. The economic and political reforms brought about movement in the population. Young people could leave their hometown and go to big cities to find better jobs because the food coupon system was abolished. They could then apply for citizenship registration after a few years working and living there. The better living conditions and increased income also boosted tourism, so more and more people started to take holidays.

Zhang Feng was happy that his parents-in-law were having a holiday after suffering such hardship and political persecution during the Cultural Revolution but unfortunately, his father had developed heart disease recently and he needed the care of his mother. Therefore, Zhang Feng had to look after his three year old son himself as well as working. He sent him to the city kindergarten in the morning and picked him up at 5.00 pm, after he finished work. He needed to cook two different meals as the boy could not have spicy food. After supper, he had to play with him and coax him to go to bed which made him very tired.

Lin Jianguo suggested he should find a nanny. Zhang Feng hired a young girl from Southern China, working as a nanny, but she was not very experienced and his son tended to cry when he saw her, probably because she was not very patient with him. Zhang Feng had to dismiss her. While he waited for a better nanny to come along, Dan Feng caught a cold because of the chilly weather and Zhang Feng had to take him to hospital which made him feel exhausted.

One day, Zhang Feng returned home a bit earlier with Dan Feng. The boy was better but he asked his father to play with him which meant there was no time to cook. Zhang Feng was feeling stressed when somebody knocked at the door. It was Qing Lian standing there, in a red coat, looking very smart. Looking inside, Qing Lian realized how difficult his situation had become so she took off her coat and picked up Dan Feng.

"Feng! Feng! Play with your aunt!"

Zhang Feng felt relieved and kept thanking her.

"Not at all. I heard from Lin Jianguo that you were having difficulties coping with your son as Dan Dan is still abroad and your parents cannot look after him so you have to function as both father and mother. But do not worry, leave Dan Feng to me. I can pick him up every day as my newspaper office is very close to the city kindergarten. You can still concentrate on your work and do not need to finish so early. I will not only look after the boy, I will also cook and clean the house. A free nanny! How great is that!" Zhang Feng shook his head and said,

"Thank you very much, Qing Lian, but it will just cause more problems as you have just separated from Li He and Dan Dan is abroad so a married man and a married woman in one house might cause gossip." Qing Lian smiled and said,

"It does not matter. I will divorce Li He soon because I do not want to waste his time. A lot of young female doctors and nurses in his hospital are waiting for his divorce to come through and want to marry him. I do not care about any gossip as you are my saviour and I am re-paying a debt of gratitude."

Thinking of his busy work and how hard it had been to find a reliable nanny, Zhang Feng agreed to her helping him for a while.

Over the next few days, Qing Lian picked up Dan Feng every evening and brought him home. She then played with him, cooked and did some cleaning at the same time. She was a very capable woman.

When Zhang Feng returned home, he saw the house was very clean with delicious food on the table and his son happily playing with a toy car Qing Lian had bought for him. Zhang Feng did not know how to thank her. She treated him like her own husband, taking off his over coat, giving him his slippers and asking him to sit down to eat. Interestingly, Dan Feng quite liked her and wanted to sit next to her to eat. Zhang Feng felt very relaxed and comfortable, just like he used to feel when Dan Dan was at home. Qing Lian also looked very happy, being the hostess in this family, although she knew this happiness was only temporary. She knew Zhang Feng would never put her before Dan Dan and Yu Mei. She would be happy if she could just be his sister.

Qing Lian noticed that Zhang Feng was stressed beyond his work. Had he disagreed with Dan Dan? He did not talk about her situation abroad. Was there a problem with Yu Mei? But Yu Mei had a husband now. Qing Lian tried to talk about something that might please him. He looked happier and said Qing Lian was still young and beautiful and he blamed Li He for his ignorance but she looked disinterested and asked Zhang Feng not to mention Li He. Qing Lian left the house quite late. Zhang Feng wanted to accompany her back home but she said she did not want to cause gossip and left by herself.

Zhang Feng was, indeed, feeling depressed as the two women he loved most deeply were treating him coldly. Dan Dan did not write to him as often and mainly just asked about their son. She did not respond when he asked her to change her mind. Yu Mei acted the same way. She did not telephone him after she promised Dan Dan that she would not contact him again and asked him not to contact her either.

Mr. Du Shan and his assistants had arrived in the city yesterday to monitor the progress of the Song Jiang Hotel. Seeing the tower had been built up to the eighth storey, he was very pleased and he praised the excellent efforts of the construction workers. He felt confident that the hotel would be finished by the end of the year. When Zhang Feng and Du Shan had lunch together, Du said this time, he had asked Yu Mei to come with him but she declined. In the past, she had always been impatient to come to Jili City. Du also said some staff in her bureau had told him that she was in a bad way, physically and emotionally. Hearing this, Zhang Feng felt very upset as he knew she was suffering because she had been forced to cut off her relationship with him.

When he returned home, he saw Qing Lian and his son were already back home and Qing Lian was cooking in the kitchen. Zhang Feng told her he was tired and would like to have a rest but Qing Lian noticed that he did not look well and thought he might be sick. She gave him a cup of tea and asked whether he needed some medication but he said it was nothing serious; he was just feeling worried and stressed. Qing Lian went out and bought a large, fresh carp from Song Hua Lake and braised it with soy sauce to please him.

After a few minutes, she heard he was on the phone and it seemed he was arguing with somebody.

"You cannot be my sister, but why not a friend? Why can we not meet occasionally? What? You say I have a new lady? No, she just helps me look after Dan Feng and does some house work, temporarily. How could I have anybody else in my heart except you and Dan Dan?"

The phone call ended, abruptly. It seemed they were not happy talking to each other. From the content of the call, Qing Lian guessed he was talking to Yu Mei and they had mentioned her as well. Yu Mei was probably jealous because Qing Lian was helping him.

During dinner time, Zhang Feng was still depressed even though he praised the carp she had cooked and said it was delicious. After his son went to bed, Zhang Feng took out a bottle of liquor and said he was going to drink well tonight, and he asked Qing Lian to drink with him. She knew he wanted to drown his sorrows but she started to worry when he drank one glass straight after another. Qing Lian could stand quite a lot of alcohol but she dared not drink too much as it would cause trouble.

Eventually, Zhang Feng was drunk and could not find the way to the bathroom. Qing Lian helped him and then put him on the bed, taking off his clothes and shoes and covering him with a blanket. She was bringing him a cup of tea to help him sober up when she heard his wild talk.

"Dan Dan, you cannot leave this family…and leave our son…! Do not say you want to marry Professor Liang…This is an excuse for you to sacrifice yourself for the benefit of me and Yu Mei…"

Hearing this, Qing Lian was surprised. It seemed that his stress was caused by the fact that Dan Dan wanted to marry a professor? Seeing Qing Lian, he suddenly said to her,

"Yu Mei, at last you have come… What do you want me to do?"

Qing Lian wore a white coat and trousers and looked quite slim with her hair and facial shape similar to Yu Mei's, Zhang Feng was confused and thought she really was Yu Mei. Qing Lian sat on the edge of the bed and helped him drink the tea and wiped the sweat from his face.

Zhang Feng suddenly grasped her hand and said,

"Yu Mei, you are part of my spirit and I… cannot live without you. I do not… want you only to be… my dream lover. I would be happy… if I can meet you …talk to you and embrace you sometimes."

Qing Lian said to him,

"Brother Feng, you are drunk! I am not Yu Mei. I am Qing Lian." In confusion, he rubbed his eyes and looked at her again and said,

"No, you are deceiving me! You are Yu Mei! You are worried you will be seen by Dan Dan…so you are pretending to be a different person."

He kept holding her hand. After a few minutes, she thought he had fallen asleep. Looking at his handsome face and recalling how she had loved him, secretly, for so many years, she could not help kissing him. Just as she lowered her head to kiss him, he woke up and grabbed hold of her, saying, excitedly,

"Yu Mei, stay here tonight! I didn't dare make love with you in the past because I did not want to betray Dan Dan. But now, I am waking up to reality so why must we control ourselves? We are life-death lovers, not people having an immoral affair. I will not let you feel so sad that you go back to the temple."

Then he took her in his arms and kissed her, warmly.

Qing Lian almost felt that she could not control herself but she still thought it best to get out from his arms.

She pretended to be Yu Mei and coaxed him,

"I will not go to the temple but I must get up to drink the tea."

Yet the passion started to burn in Zhang Feng and he started to undress her while kissing her. Qing Lian couldn't help but enjoy his caresses and her struggles became weaker and weaker. At last, they embraced each other with their naked bodies and enjoyed a trembling sexual climax. Then, they held each other tightly and fell asleep.

When Zhang Feng woke up the next morning, his head still felt heavy. He knew he had drunk too much the previous night but when he looked down at his bed, he was surprised to see a woman lying there, next to him. He thought Dan Dan had returned home but when he looked more carefully, he became scared. This woman was Qing Lian! He quickly jumped up and dressed himself. When he turned back, he saw Qing Lian had also woken and was covering her chest, shyly.

"I am so sorry, Qing Lian! What happened? I cannot remember as I got so drunk last night." Qing Lian replied, tenderly,

"Do not worry, Brother Feng, nothing happened."

She got dressed and walked to the kitchen to cook breakfast. She did not answer his questions so he followed her. Seeing the anxious expression on his face, she said to him, while cooking eggs,

"Brother, it does not matter. You were drunk last night and mistook me for Yu Mei. You held me in your arms and kissed me. I wanted to get away but you were too powerful, so we had…"

Zhang Feng broke into a sweat. This meant he had raped her.

Seeing his fear, she tried to comfort him,

"Do not worry, Brother Feng. I will not blame you because you were drunk and not conscious and also, you miss Yu Mei deeply. I knew from your drunken talk that your relationships with Dan Dan and Yu Mei have become strained which is making you so anxious."

She stopped cooking and watched him with deep feeling.

"Brother Feng, you know I have loved you secretly for so many years. I was reluctantly married to Li He because of you, and I will also divorce him because of you. Yet, I know for sure that you only regard me as your sister. Do not worry, brother, I will not ask you to take any responsibility for me. I will not fight for you against Dan Dan and Yu Mei. To be honest, I was willing to make love with you last night. I am lucky as many women dream of making love with you!"

Zhang Feng felt greatly relieved after listening to her explanation.

"Qing Lian, I will help you any time in the future, whatever difficulties you have." She smiled and said,

"Be calm, brother, I will not give you any trouble. I am very happy to be your sister forever."

Then she said his mother-in-law would return from the South the day after tomorrow which would be her last day helping him.

The next day, she cooked several dishes after picking up Dan Feng from the kindergarten. When Zhang Feng returned from work, they sat down together for a lovely dinner. He treated her very politely, with a guilty expression in his eyes. Qing Lian tried to coax him into feeling more relaxed.

When they said goodbye, Qing Lian held the boy in her arms and kissed him. Dan Feng loved this aunt very much. Zhang Feng gave her a jade bracelet saying it was a present given by his friend but he wanted to give it to her as thanks for her help. Qing Lian knew giving this valuable present to her was not only to show his thanks, but also, to comfort his guilty conscience. She put the bracelet on and said she liked it. Then she looked at him and said,

"Brother Feng, may I embrace you again?"

Zhang Feng hesitated but still raised his arms and held her. She enjoyed his caress and had tears in her eyes.

"I will miss you, brother, take care."

He saw her off and shut the door immediately. He sighed deeply and hoped she would not come back again. Two women had already given him a lot of headaches; three women would put him in a very sorry plight.

CHAPTER IV

At Last You Can Marry Each Other

Recent family issues were giving Zhang Feng a headache. The progress of reform was also being resisted by the rigid, left-wing group. They used the principles of public ownership and the centrally controlled economy to boycott private business and free marketing.

Lin Jianguo told Zhang Feng that a clever, self-employed businessman had opened a shop selling electrical appliances because he had done very well in the big trading markets. The City Business Management Department wanted to close his shop just because he employed a few more assistants. Zhang Feng wanted to investigate this case further and he went to the shop with Chang Zheng, Lin and Chen. Outside, Zhang Feng saw a group of officers from the CBMD rebuking a young man, the owner of the business.

"You employ workers and exploit them which is the way of capitalist business so we must shut down your shop." But the owner of the business argued,

"I pay my assistants! I do not ask them to work for free. I pay tax to the state from my profits. So what's wrong with my business?"

When Zhang Feng got closer, he saw the owner of the business was his former middle school classmate, Song Ping, who had started selling on the street first and then moved to the trading market which Zhang Feng had helped to build.

Seeing Zhang Feng, he felt that his saviour had arrived.

"Brother Feng! No, Mayor Zhang! Please judge this for me. Is the reason they want to shut down my shop right or wrong?"

Seeing the Mayor coming, the officers made way for him.

When Zhang Feng asked why they wanted to shut down this shop, the Head of the team said,

"Mayor Zhang, the regulations from my department state that the maximum number of workers to be hired is three, but he has hired five! It means he will gradually become a small, capitalist businessman."

Chang Zheng replied,

"What a ridiculous regulation! Hiring a few more assistants will lead to capitalism? If he needs more staff it means his business is thriving. His assistants get a salary, his customers get better goods and the state gets more tax. What is wrong with that?"

"This regulation is really dogmatic. Do not shut up his shop. The City Council will discuss it further," Zhang Feng ordered.

"Thank you very much, Mayor Zhang!" Song Ping applauded him.

After discussing this incident with the other leaders, the City Council increased the number allowed to be employed from three to seven. Actually, Zhang Feng thought there should be no limit to the number of workers allowed for employers to hire. Private enterprises should be totally legalized. Li Qiu reported Zhang Feng's policy to stubborn Director Shen who was quite angry about this. He believed Zhang Feng was pushing privatization further and further but he knew Zhang Feng always got support from Sectary Liu and so he had to suppress his anger.

Not only did self-employed businessmen like Song Ping find trouble, village and township enterprises were also being squeezed by local officers and state enterprises. He Hua had telephoned Zhang Feng yesterday and told him some local state companies were trying to squeeze their products out of the market. Some small cities did not even allow their products to enter the markets there. Zhang Feng was quite angry about this. A normal marketing operation should have fair competition but not a monopoly. He sent Lin Jianguo and Chen Tao to investigate and deal with this problem for He Hua.

Wang Hai also had problems with his production contract, mainly caused by ownership. The factory still belonged to the state and the contract holder just had management rights in the short term. Wang Hai told Zhang Feng that his contract term was for five years but after that, the contract quota would increase. If the factory had a new contract holder, Wang Hai would be wasting his money replacing new equipment. Zhang Feng believed that economic reform meant the relationship between ownership and rights of management should be resolved. The shareholding system in the West was a good way to sort out this problem but reform in China had not reached that stage. Zhang Feng told

Wang Hai to wait for a while until Central Government realized that they must resolve this problem.

One day, Wang Li came to Zhang Feng's office. Like his sister, she directly entered without making an appointment. She told him she would be travelling to England and other European countries with a business delegation. She would have the opportunity to see Dan Dan and Professor Liang. Zhang Feng did not say anything about Dan Dan's relationship with Liang Hua and instead, asked how she was getting on with Liang Hua. Wang Li said there was no hope. Liang Hua preferred mature ladies. She smiled and said to him,

"Be careful, Mayor Hamlet. Your wife is a beautiful and mature lady."

Zhang Feng shivered but he covered up his feelings. He said he would give her some dried food to pass on to Dan Dan. These were things Dan Dan liked but could not buy in England. Wang Li said that would be no problem.

"Mayor Hamlet really is a good husband!"

Dan Dan had been feeling upset recently. The research she and Liang Hua were doing still carried on smoothly but she did not know how to cope with this love triangle. She knew Zhang Feng was depressed because he did not want to damage their happy family but he also missed Yu Mei and worried about her emotional situation. Liang Hua still treated her carefully, as though he were her husband. Dan Dan was beginning to like him more and more but she didn't want to be seen as some other Chinese women who were only keen to marry Western men in order to have a better life abroad. Her colleague, Chen Mei, had divorced her husband in China recently and married her supervisor in the UK. She had even given up her daughter in China which Dan Dan thought was too much. But this was a personal choice as she herself was planning to give up her husband in the near future.

Chen Mei told Dan Dan that when she returned home for the divorce, she'd heard that Yu Mei was very ill because of emotional problems. Dan Dan was shocked because she knew Zhang Feng would be upset forever if anything happened to Yu Mei. She made a firm decision: she would divorce Zhang Feng and let him marry Yu Mei. She could bring Dan Feng to the UK where he could have an English education. Liang Hua said he could arrange for her to do a PhD and find a job afterwards. He would not put pressure on her privately. She could develop her relationship with him as she wished after the divorce and marry him if she liked, or they could just live together, or even, just be good friends. It would be entirely up to her. Dan Dan was moved by his reasonable and generous attitude and liked him even more. Yet, she still needed Zhang Feng to believe that she really loved Liang Hua and was not just sacrificing herself for his sake.

Wang Li was visiting London for a few days and contacted Dan Dan. She came to her apartment but felt a bit awkward as Liang Hua was there as well. Dan Dan said she had also invited him for a meal together. When Wang Li gave her the food Zhang Feng had sent, she did not show any delight or happiness. She said she now preferred Western food to Chinese food, which surprised Wang Li greatly. Dan Dan treated Liang Hua warmly, as if he was the main guest at the meal. She filled his plate from the dishes on the table, topped up his glass with wine and praised him for his English manners.

Wang Li felt quite uncomfortable and wondered why Dan Dan, who was loved so deeply by Zhang Feng, had become this different woman. It seemed she would throw herself into Liang

Hua's arms any second. Wang Li could not bear their intimate relationship and left quickly. It was strange that Dan Dan did not even open any presents from her husband and son. Would she soon abandon her happy family?

After returning home, Wang Li decided to tell Zhang Feng about the unusual relationship between Dan Dan and Liang Hua and warn him to keep an eye on this matter.

Visiting his office and seeing he was very busy, Wang Li said to him, seriously,

"Dear Mayor Hamlet, I must tell you something about your wife because I do not want to see you become a melancholy prince again. Do you remember, before my trip, I mentioned Liang Hua prefers older women, like Dan Dan? Well, I saw their intimate relationship when I visited them in London, and Dan Dan seemed to be enjoying it. In recent years, more and more Chinese women have been marrying foreigners and have even abandoned their children in China. If you want to keep your wife, you better do something straight away. Otherwise, it may be too late."

Her speech really shocked him. He thought that Dan Dan must really love Liang Hua and want to marry him after all. Perhaps it was not just an excuse. He asked Wang Li not to tell anybody else about this possible affair. She made a wry face and said,

"Do not worry, I will only tell Hamlet's father."

Dan Dan returned home two weeks later. She told Zhang Feng seriously that she would start her PhD soon and she would take Dan Feng with her so he could have an excellent English education. She would marry Liang Hua as she loved him. She said she loved her life in the UK not only because the living conditions were good, but also, because it was a free and democratic country. Their son would become a social elite with a Western education when he grew up. She had a deep gratitude to Zhang Feng for his love and care and she still wanted to be his sister or friend. He and Yu Mei could end their painful situation and marry each other. They would no longer just be dream lovers.

Zhang Feng still felt it would be difficult to accept her proposal and asked Dan Dan to reconsider. She would apply for a visa for Dan Feng and travel back to the UK in two weeks' time. During this waiting period, Zhang Feng treated Dan Dan more carefully. He wanted to move her through his deep love but she treated him politely, like an elder sister. She refused to sleep with him which made him feel she was very determined to leave him. He did not know that she cried herself to sleep each night.

The day arrived and Zhang Feng saw Dan Dan and Dan Feng off at the airport. After kissing their son, he wanted to embrace her, but she kept away from him, carrying her luggage and leading Dan Feng to the check in. Dan Feng waved his little hands at his father but Dan Dan did not turn back to say farewell to him which made him feel very sad. But if he could have seen the tears on her face, he would have firmly stopped her and asked her to change her mind.

After the airplane took off, Dan Dan watched the vast land pass by beneath the window, yet she felt very sad. The truth was, she had decided to sacrifice herself for the benefit of Zhang Feng and Yu Mei. She actually did not plan to marry Liang Hua and just felt they were friends. She had deliberately pretended to have an intimate relationship with Liang Hua when Wang Li visited them, knowing that she would tell Zhang Feng. Her plan was to let Zhang Feng and Yu Mei marry each other and have the happy life they deserved but for herself, having her son and career was enough for the time being. Marrying Liang Hua was not important.

Back home, Zhang Feng was feeling very depressed and saw a few papers on his desk. Picking them up, he realized they were divorce papers with Dan Dan's signature. She had left him another note:

'Xiao Feng, this is the divorce agreement. You just need to add your signature and visit the registration office for a seal. Then our marriage will end and you can marry Yu Mei. Bless your marriage which is ten years overdue.'

Zhang Feng did not feel happy at all. On the contrary, he felt deeply upset. Although he could now marry his dream lover, he had had to pay a heavy price for it. He had lost his dear wife and son, and maybe, he would be blamed as a traitor to his family. He did not contact Yu Mei immediately to tell her this 'good news'.

He decided to consult his family first for their opinions. He visited his parents-in-law first. Seeing him, they guessed why he had come. His mother-in-law, Wang Hui, asked him to sit down and offered him tea.

"Xiao Feng, we all know that Dan Dan wants to divorce you. We tried to persuade her to change her mind as you have such a happy family but she said your relationship has changed. She is an academic and you are an official, with no common ground. You cannot give up your leadership position to go abroad with her. Her supervisor loves her and she loves him too. She said this was a solution with a double benefit: she will marry her supervisor and you will marry your previous girlfriend, Yu Mei, which we think is a workable way to cope with this difficult situation."

His father-in-law, Hai Jing, added,

"Xiao Feng, do not feel depressed. I will remain your friend even though I am not your father-in-law."

"You are still my saviour," Wang Hui said.

Zhang Feng embraced them gratefully, and said they were always his parents-in-law, whatever happened.

Back at his parents' home, he saw his father in his study, writing his book, and his mother, cooking in the kitchen. They did not look happy. They asked him why his wife wanted to marry a foreigner, although they understood life in the West was better than in China. Zhang Feng did not tell them Dan Dan was sacrificing her own happiness. He just said they had parted peacefully. His parents said the only pity was, they would not see their grandson so easily but they realized that having a Western education would be good for his future.

Zhang Feng also consulted his good friends. Chang Zheng initially felt sorry for him and said he had not realized that the Western world was so attractive to Chinese women.

After Zhang Feng explained how it was possible that Dan Dan had sacrificed herself for him and Yu Mei, Chang Zheng joked,

"Oh, so at last you have taken my girlfriend!"

In the past, both he and Zhang Feng had loved Yu Mei and used to be bitter rivals. Lin Jianguo also felt happy that Zhang Feng and Yu Mei could at last marry each other, and he could finish his task as a secret agent.

After consulting family members and friends, Zhang Feng thought he was finally able to contact Yu Mei. In the evening, he made a phone call to her. He could hear her voice sounded stronger than before and she told him she felt better now.

"Brother Feng. I know why you have telephoned me as Dan Dan rang me as well. She said she has divorced you and taken her son to the UK. She asked me to marry you as soon as possible as our relationship has already been disrupted for many years by the Cultural Revolution. She has, at last, handed you back to me. She blessed us and our marriage. Brother, I should feel happy because we can live together legally and we do not need to meet secretly any longer but I cannot feel totally happy." Zhang Feng said,

"I feel the same. I know Dan Dan divorced me because she wanted us to be together. She is not the kind of woman who wants to marry a foreigner. It is possible our happiness will be based on her sacrifice and sorrow. It is a pity."

After a moment's silence, Yu Mei said,

"Brother, let me think about it for a few days, and then I will contact you."

Zhang Feng agreed and thought he also needed a short period of time to think about things clearly.

Yu Mei did not tell him the content of her letter to Dan Dan which was:

'Dear Sister Dan Dan. I know you have divorced Brother Feng for me. Bless you, if you decide to marry your supervisor and have a happy life. But if you cannot find true love in a few years, I will hand Brother Feng back to you.'

PART VI

Leaving Political Circles

Chapter I

A Ten Year Overdue Wedding

One day, in the summer of 1988, the River City was bathed in bright sunshine and the limpid river flowed quietly to the distance. On the river bank of weeping willows, a tall, white building, with sixteen storeys, towered in the blue sky: the new landmark of the River City. Citizens could hear the deafening sounds of gongs and drums and saw colourful banners fluttering in the wind. The ribbon-cutting, opening ceremony of Song Jiang Hotel was being held today.

Zhang Feng, and other city officials, were waiting for the Taiwan businessmen to arrive. The ceremony girls wore beautiful Mandarin gowns. Wang Li stood behind Zhang Feng. With his help, she had been appointed the Deputy General Manager of the hotel. The General Manager had been appointed by the Taiwan Company.

Near to midday, a line of cars stopped in front of the hotel. Mr. Du Shan and his assistants got out, followed by a handsome, middle-aged man who was the new General Manager. Zhang Feng and the other leaders greeted the Taiwan guests warmly. Mr. Du shook hands with Zhang Feng and pointed to the last car in the line, saying,

"Mayor Zhang, I have brought a distinguished guest to your opening event today."

Distinguished guest? Zhang Feng felt strange. Suddenly, an exceedingly beautiful lady in red got out of this car.

Yu Mei!

Zhang Feng cried out in alarm, in his mind, as he had not realized that Yu Mei would come to the ceremony. A few days ago, when he telephoned her, she had not decided whether she would marry him or not. If she did, she would come to this ceremony. She was dressed especially smartly and looked like a beautiful fairy. Her face was full of smiles today which meant she had left her sorrow and depression behind. She was the centre of attention and attracted admiring looks from all the men there. Mr. Du said to Zhang Feng,

"What do you think? Her appearance adds extra beauty to our ceremony."

Zhang Feng did not want to reveal their special relationship, so he just simply waved his hand at her. Chang Zheng and Lin Jianguo walked to her car and accompanied her. They knew her visit indicated she would be with Zhang Feng forever.

The ceremony went smoothly. Afterwards, Mr. Du took guests on a tour inside the hotel. Everybody was amazed by the luxurious interior decoration and they visited the grand reception hall, the imposing dining halls, bars, swimming pool, gym, cinema and the spacious meeting rooms. They all said this tour was a real eye-opener as they did not know what a five star hotel looked like. During the tour, Zhang Feng turned back to see Yu Mei from time to time and she noticed this, and responded with a smile.

When they entered the cinema, Mr. Du said he would like to show them a tourist video of Taiwan, in which they would see all the main attractions. If they were interested, they would be welcome to have holidays in Taiwan. They all said it was very good to watch and it might encourage Jili City to make its own promotional video. Yu Mei had seen this video before and told Mr. Du she would take a nap in the nearby rest room because she had not slept well last night.

Entering the rest room and lying on the sofa, she felt quite comfortable and she soon fell asleep. In her dreams, she and Zhang Feng walked together in a wood and saw a deer. Zhang Feng chased the deer but she could not follow him and fell down on the ground. Suddenly, the deer found her and lowered its head to scent her. The deer then started to kiss her. She tried to avoid its lips but at the same time, she also enjoyed the kissing. The deer held her arms which frightened her and she tried to struggle to get away when suddenly, she woke up and saw that it was Zhang Feng kissing her. She was very worried about being seen by other people so she sat up and said,

"No! No, Brother! It will be embarrassing if other people see us!" He looked at the shut door and said with smile,

"It does not matter! You will be my wife soon."

"Nonsense! I have not made up my mind to marry you yet." She pretended to be unhappy.

"Why have you come if you won't marry me then?" asked Zhang Feng.

"Because I want to see whether this hotel is truly a luxury hotel or not," she replied.

"Or to see whether I am still handsome or not?" he smiled. "Why are you not watching the video?" asked Yu Mei.

"I cannot concentrate on it while a beautiful lady in red is close by. Yu Mei, it seems that you have recovered from your illness but I worry about you all the time." Pausing a moment, he added, "I think we have to sort out this dilemma. Dan Dan and I have divorced. Half of my love towards her is more like the emotional attachment for a family member so it would be better if I learn to think of her as my sister."

He did not want to delay this matter anymore. Facing Yu Mei, he suddenly went down on one knee and took a ring from his pocket and held it up to her.

"Marry me, Yu Mei!"

This new way to propose had become fashionable in China recently but Yu Mei had not realized that Zhang Feng would be so formal. Thinking of all the joys and sorrows she had experienced with him in the past 20 years, she could not help covering her face and crying heartily.

At this moment, they heard warm applause behind them. Turning back, they saw a group of people watching and clapping, including Chang Zheng, Lin Jianguo, Mr. Du, the General Manager, Huang Li, and Wang Li. They were all so pleased that these two life-death lovers could at last marry each other. Wang Li felt a bit disappointed but she still admired their enduring love as she knew their unusual love story. Seeing Yu Mei take the ring, shyly, Mr. Du said,

"The wedding will be held in our hotel in three days! It is a lucky day! Huang Li and Wang Li, you must prepare for the wedding."

Huang and Wang said there would be no problem with that.

Three days later, the wedding was held in a small banqueting hall. Both Zhang Feng and Yu Mei preferred a simple wedding because both of them were marrying for the second time. Zhang Feng did not invite his subordinates as he did not want them to buy presents. They just invited family members, good friends and their closest colleagues. Zhang Feng's parents arrived first. They knew Yu Mei very well because during the Cultural Revolution, they had regarded her as Zhang Feng's girlfriend.

Unexpectedly, Yu Mei saw Dan Dan's parents. She made a deep bow to them and said shyly,

"I am sorry, Uncle and Aunt."

They said to her, kindly,

"Do not worry, Yu Mei. It was Dan Dan's choice to leave Xiao Feng and nothing to do with you. We all survived the red storm, and we regard you as our own daughter." Yu Mei said, gratefully,

"Yes. Aunt gave me a lot of help in the past and Uncle saved me with that special herb."

Hai Jing said,

"That is all in the past now. The storm has passed. Let's enjoy our happy life."

Wang Hai and Zhang Lin arrived next. Wang Hai said loudly to Yu Mei,

"Good morning, my new sister-in law!"

Zhang Lin gave him a nudge and Wang Hai said quietly to Zhang Feng,

"If I had known you were going to marry Yu Mei in the end, I would have courted Dan Dan more seriously during the red storm."

Wang Hai used to love Dan Dan. Zhang Feng punched him gently.

"Nonsense!"

Li He arrived. Zhang Feng carefully asked him about Qing Lian, but Li said he did not have any new information about her since their divorce. He had been told she had moved to Da Lian City and still worked for a newspaper. Li also said he would be marrying a young lady doctor soon and Zhang Feng and Wang Hai congratulated him warmly. Chang Zheng, Secretary Gong, Lin Jianguo, Chen Tao were also guests.

Just before the wedding ceremony started, somebody said loudly, outside the door,

"You will start the wedding without the chief witness?"

It was Secretary Liu, smiling and walking into the room. Zhang Feng and Yu Mei welcomed him immediately. Secretary Liu said,

"I was the first person to witness their relationship twenty years ago in the Feng Man holiday resort. Am I not qualified to be the chief witness?"

Everybody agreed that he was.

The wedding went smoothly. The guests all said Zhang Feng looked very handsome in his Western suit and Yu Mei, dressed in a red, Mandarin gown, was extremely fairy-like and beautiful. They were really the perfect couple. Chang Zheng joked,

"If I had known Yu Mei wanted a ring, I would have given her one a long time ago!"

"Nonsense. You'd better look after your wife, Lin Hong," Yu Mei replied.

Mr. Du arranged for a luxury room in the hotel to become the bridal suite. Walking into the room, arm in arm, Yu Mei snuggled up to Zhang Feng. They gazed at the moonlit scenery outside their window and felt so happy and content.

Yu Mei suddenly pointed to a large tree on the river bank and asked him,

"Brother, do you remember this tree?"

Zhang Feng looked at the tree and said,

"In the past, we had so many walks along the river bank, but I cannot remember any special meaning connected with this tree."

Yu Mei sighed and said,

"On the day you were sent to the execution ground, I saw you standing in the prison truck, under this tree. I shouted to you, asking you to wait for me and then collapsed under the same tree."

Yu Mei's memory made Zhang Feng's blood boil.

"Yu Mei, I only understood after the incident that you actually asked me to wait for you in the heaven because you would like to die with me. You tried to commit suicide by swallowing a poisonous chemical but fortunately, Hai Jing found the special herb on Chang Bai Mountain and saved you. And I was also saved at the last second, just as the firing squad opened fire, by Lin Jianguo. We nearly became Romeo and Juliet!"

Yu Mei had tears in her eyes. She held him tightly and sighed,

"Brother, we will never be apart again."

Zhang Feng carried her to the bed and they were immersed in their passionate love-making.

A few days later, Yu Mei received a card from Dan Dan. She congratulated them and asked them to enjoy their marriage, which was ten years overdue. Interestingly, Qing Lian also sent her a card. She also congratulated their hard-earned marriage. Her card was posted from Da Lian, a beautiful city on the Bo Hai Sea. Yu Mei knew Qing Lian had loved Zhang Feng secretly in the past. Yu Mei thought it was as if they had all gone back to their roles at the end of the Cultural Revolution. She was Zhang Feng's wife, Dan Dan was his 'sister' and Qing Lian, his servant. Yu Mei did not show these cards to Zhang Feng because she thought they might disturb him emotionally and affect their perfect little world.

A few weeks later, Yu Mei was transferred to Jili City and appointed as the Head of the Provincial Foreign Trading Bureau where she could use her experience in inviting foreign investment to promote the province's economy.

Their peaceful existence together did not last too long. It was disrupted by the economic, political and social issues which occurred during the reform movement. Firstly, in 1988, there was panic buying all over the country, which was caused by the 'double-track' price system. The Government intended to reform the price system to gradually fix prices according to the market. But in a transitional period of time the prices of part of products were fixed by the Government and the prices of other part of products were fixed by manufactures and commercial sectors. The prices fixed by the government prices were cheaper, but those fixed by the manufactures and commercial sectors were higher. Because at that time, manufacturers were not yet competitive, therefore prices did not come down. So the public worried about the possible inflation. All of this caused the public to panic buy.

One day, Zhang Lin rushed to Yu Mei's home and said to her,

"Sister-in-law, why haven't you started your shopping? The price of things will rise soon."

"What should I buy?" Yu Mei asked.

"Anything! Let's go shopping. You will see people are panic buying everything. It's almost like everything is free!"

Taking some money, Yu Mei went to the Fifth Department Store with Zhang Lin. They were shocked by the scene in front of their eyes: it was so crowded inside the shop. People shouted to the shop assistants for goods on the shelves. Sweating profusely, people bought valuable things like TV sets, washing machines and fridge-freezers. Even ordinary, daily necessities, such as towels, soap and toothpaste, were being bought in the panic. With no time to talk to Yu Mei, Zhang Lin rushed to the clothes department to buy something.

Yu Mei could not remember what she needed so she bought some knitting wool and a few shirts for Zhang Feng. Seeing many shoppers buying jewellery, she bought a golden necklace and a valuable watch for her husband. She was also persuaded to buy a sewing machine by Zhang Lin.

When she returned home, Zhang Feng was just back from his work. Seeing she carried many boxes, he quickly came up to help her, and asked with a smile,

"You also did some panic buying?"

"No way to avoid it. People have bought everything. They think that the end of the world is coming."

Sighing, and sitting down on the sofa, Zhang Feng said,

"It is very difficult to change from the centrally controlled economy to a free market economy. The price system needs to be changed as well but you cannot change it too quickly. The best way is probably to change it gradually. Shen Zhen had the same problem a few years ago but after there were more joint ventures and private companies, the competition brought down prices and we saw a stabilized market. The progress of introducing free marketing is slow because some left-wing leaders are still stuck in the old system. We have to wait until the private companies are legalized and that will push the state enterprises to operate by free marketing rules. Then the goods will be made in quantity and high quality and the price will be adjusted by the market."

He added that the City Council would make an announcement tomorrow, asking the citizens not to panic buy as the state would adjust the prices so they did not rise. Yu Mei asked him if there was a new policy and he said there would be one, very soon, as Central Government did not like to see this kind of panic purchasing. Yu Mei said it was just as well as she did not want to see such chaos again.

The problem with the double-track system also caused trouble in the production sector with corruption. Some people, with 'special' social connections, especially the children of high ranking officials, could get some products from the centrally controlled system and sell them on to factories, making huge profits. People called them speculators.

One day, Wang Hai came to Zhang Feng and complained to him that he needed more steel products to increase his production but the planned supply from the state was not enough; he would have to buy the extra from the black market, paying double the usual price. He found out later that the speculator was called Shen and was actually the son of the evil Director Shen who had always created trouble for Zhang Feng. He was now the Deputy Governor of the province as he was very good at flattering the higher authorities.

What made Zhang Feng really annoyed was in official circles, those who did not do practical things, and only talked, would be promoted quickly but officials who dared to think and dared to act, like him, would be criticized. Secretary Liu was an open-minded leader and supporter of Zhang Feng but sometimes, he was also swayed by the old leaders in the central party and government. This Deputy Governor Shen looked like an honest and incorruptible official, but behind the scenes, he would allow his son to scalp the controlled state product materials.

Zhang Feng asked Wang Hai to collect evidence of corruption by Shen's son in case they could expose him when the opportunity occurred. He told Wang Hai that the double-track system should be a temporary method for a transitional period of time. Along with the progress of free marketing, it would be removed although it was causing a lot of problems right now.

Zhang Feng was worried that political reform was happening much slower than in the economy although the lifelong leadership system had been removed and officials had to retire when they reached the age limit. The functions of party and government were also separated. The party officials controlled everything in the past. The new, younger officials, like Zhang Feng, were mostly educated professionals now. The main problem was caused by the struggle between the two political groups inside the party.

One group of open-minded leaders, headed by Secretary Hu Yaobang and Prime Minister Zhao Ziyang, intended to make China a more free, democratic and harmonious society. But the other group, with hard headed, left-wing leaders, still stuck to the rigid Stalinism and wrong policy of Chairman Mao. They used the Four Principles (Maxims and Mao Zedong Thought; Leadership of the Communist Party; Socialism and People's Democratic Dictatorship) to suppress the people's ideology and control their social practices. They regarded ideology liberation as 'bourgeois' and supported some policies very similar to those of the Cultural Revolution. The struggles between these two political groups caused quite a lot of political turmoil.

Recently, there had been student-led democratic protests in some regions of China and this happened in Jili City one day.

Just as Zhang Feng entered his office, Lin Jianguo rushed in and cried,

"Something just happened! There was a protest, organized by Jili University and other universities this morning which blocked the traffic at the Jiang Nan Bridge."

Zhang Feng always supported the democratic rights of students, but as the Mayor of the City, he also had responsibility to maintain the smooth running of traffic. He rang the Head of the City Traffic Bureau and asked him to maintain order there with the traffic police.

He and Lin Jianguo and Chen Tao drove to the bridge and were shocked by the scene which confronted them. The traffic was totally blocked by the student demonstration. All the buses, cars and trucks were stopped on the bridge which was blocked by several thousand students. Zhang Feng and his colleagues could hear slogans being shouted and the sound of singing. They could see the fluttering banners and posters.

Zhang Feng, Lin and Chen got out of their car and walked along the bridge from the other end. Approaching the students, Zhang Feng could see a few leaders at the front, one of whom was the Student Union President of Jili University, Chai Li, who had spoken with him before when Zhang Feng had attended the alumni gathering at the university. Confronting the students were the Head of the City Security Bureau and the Head of the City Traffic Bureau, with over one hundred policemen who carried batons and guns. Seeing Zhang Feng, the Head of the City Security Bureau said to him,

"Mayor Zhang, the situation is quite urgent. The students refuse to retreat. We will have to disperse them by force or arrest their leaders."

Zhang Feng replied,

"No, no! We cannot use force because their actions are based on political enthusiasm. We cannot treat them harshly. Ask your men to retreat a distance!"

The Head of the City Security Bureau hesitated but he had to obey an order from the Mayor so he ordered the policemen to retreat 20 to 30 metres.

Zhang Feng said to him,

"Look after the crowd. I will negotiate with their leaders."

"You cannot do that. They might keep you as a hostage!"

"Do not worry. They are reasonable young people, not gangsters," Zhang Feng replied and then he walked up to the students in full view of the thousands of citizens all around.

Seeing Zhang Feng approaching them, the student leaders felt a bit nervous, apart from Chai Li.

Chai Li said to the other leaders,

"Mayor Zhang is an alumnus of my university and is kind and open-minded. He will not make things difficult for us."

As he expected, Zhang Feng greeted them kindly and patted Chai Li's shoulder. Then he asked why they were holding this demonstration today.

"Mayor Zhang, we are very concerned about national affairs. We want to make our society more open and democratic but the leaders of the universities and local officials just ignore our requests and do not even allow us to hold basic elections. Also, recently, there has been some bad social practice. Some greedy people have bribed officers and scalped limited, national resources for the black market which is disruptive to the normal economic process and creates obstacles to reform. Do you think our demands are nonsense?" asked Chai Li.

Zhang Feng shook his head.

"I support your demands completely but as the Mayor of

the City, I also have responsibility for maintaining good order. Could you please persuade your student colleagues to change to a different route to demonstrate which would not affect the traffic?"

Seeing the embarrassed expressions of these leaders, Zhang Feng added,

"Let me talk to the students."

Then he picked up the loudspeaker from the Head of the Security Bureau, stood on top of a police car, and spoke to the students.

"Dear students, I am the Mayor of the City. I understand why you are demonstrating. I was also a university student and I used to be the President of Jili University's Student Union so I fully understand your patriotic enthusiasm and political appeals. I fully support your demands for democracy and your fight against corruption which is also the task of our party leadership."

The students thought Zhang Feng would blame them and did not realize that he would support them instead, so they all applauded his speech.

Zhang Feng continued,

"But our demands should not affect the normal lives of our citizens and disrupt the traffic. You will win more support from the public if you can change your route or go back to your campus to hold a rally. Thank you!"

It seemed his speech was working, with a lot of students agreeing.

Chai Li shouted,

"What Mayor Zhang says is very reasonable. Please turn back to campus by the road next to the Jiang Nan Park."

In the end, in just a few minutes, the crowd of several thousand students had left the bridge and the traffic started to move smoothly once again. The citizens all applauded Zhang Feng's swift action. The Head of the City Security Bureau said, with admiration,

"That was great, Mayor Zhang! It is no surprise that you have an academic background! Your speech was very reasonable and convincing."

Yet, Zhang Feng had not seen his former classmate, Li Qiu, hiding in the crowd and recording his speech. He would later hand it to Governor Shen, Zhang Feng's sworn political enemy, as part of their plan to put barriers in the way of Zhang Feng's promotion and to remove him from office.

CHAPTER II

A Political Event Which Shocked the World

When Zhang Feng returned home in the evening, Yu Mei walked out from the living room and embraced him. Choking with sobs, she said,

"I was worried about you all day, Brother Feng! You finally resolved the students' demonstration but it was not easy. Sometimes, I think it would be better to leave local government. Like my father said to me before he died, it is ruthless and treacherous in the official circles although it has been better since the Cultural Revolution ended. You don't face persecution and jail as easily but there are still some wicked officials keeping a close watch on you and trying to dismiss you."

Zhang Feng helped Yu Mei to the sofa.

"Yu Mei, I was very ambitious when I first joined and I really wanted to contribute to the reform movement, to build a more democratic and prosperous China but I have realized how difficult it is to make changes. Whatever I plan to do, some top official will not allow it, saying it is against the Four Principles of Communism. Even the General Secretary of the Central Party Committee, Hu Yao Bang, was dismissed from his post by the old leaders and the inflexible left-wing group. They said he was involved with bourgeois liberation and the radical student movement. These old leaders and officials still miss the rigid Stalinism of the past and the wrong policies of Mao. The key point is, they do not really want to give people more freedom and democracy and they want to keep their own privileges and perks."

Yu Mei gave him a bowl of green bean paste to reduce the heat in his body, caused by his stress.

"The conflict between reformers and left-wingers will get worse, do you think?" Zhang Feng replied,

"Yes, but I am confident that the impetus for Chinese people to move towards freedom and democracy is irresistible. There will be more serious, political consequences in the future."

Unexpectedly, only six months later, in the spring of 1989, just such a world-shocking, political event happened on Tian An Men Square, Beijing. On 15th April, Hu Yaobang, the previous General Secretary of the Party, who had been removed two years ago, died of a heart attack. His death triggered large scale mourning in Beijing and nationwide. Initially, 500 students from the Beijing Politics and Law University laid a wreath on Tian An Men Square in honour of Hu Yaobang. Then, 4,000 students from the two best universities in China, Beijing University and Qing Hua University, went to the Square to mourn him. After that, thousands and thousands of students rushed to the Square with banners and slogans.

While mourning Hu, the students demanded a series of political requests, including: a re-evaluation of Hu's contribution to the reform movement; the rehabilitation of the people who had been denounced in the Anti-Bourgeois Liberation Movement; the end of corruption and punishment of the corrupt officials; giving the public freedom to produce newspapers and finally, that Party and Government officials and their children must declare their properties. Their requests were supported by people all over the country because they represented national opinion.

Under pressure from the students, the Party and Government gave Hu a state funeral, yet the students did not retreat from the Square. They wanted to continue to have a dialogue with the authorities and hopefully, have their political requests met.

How to treat the student demonstrations divided the Party Central Committee in two. One group, headed by General Secretary, Zhao Ziyang, wanted to talk with the students and listen to their political appeals. The other group, headed by Prime Minister, Li Peng, advocated harsher treatment for the students. They insisted that some people were deliberately trying to make trouble for the Communist Party and were trying to topple the Party's leadership, which made the students angry towards Li Peng. During this confrontation, other students and ordinary people across China held demonstrations to support the students on the Square.

One day, at the end of April, Zhang Feng received a phone call from the City Security Bureau, telling him there was a large scale, student demonstration taking place in the city centre. Zhang Feng asked them not to stop the students. He and Lin Jianguo and Chen Tao went to the city centre straight away.

When they arrived, they saw huge crowds gathered there, with banners and posters, showing their support for the students in Beijing. Drawing lessons from their last demonstration, they did not block the traffic so it was a totally peaceful demonstration. Zhang Feng saw Chai Li, the President of the Students' Union at Jili University and they waved to each other. Zhang Feng also made a 'thumbs up' gesture to show his support. A lot of citizens had also joined the students' protest.

Zhang Feng said to Lin and Chen,

"The students' demands are totally reasonable. They did not act to overturn the leadership of the Communist Party. They only made suggestions to improve the democratic process and combat the corruption which can only benefit the Party and the country."

Both Lin and Chen agreed with him.

Zhang Feng was keen to go to Beijing to see the situation on the Square for himself. It just so happened that there was a seminar there for the mayors in different cities to discuss the foreign investment situation. The cities could also send staff from the provincial or city's Foreign Trade Departments. The Head of the department suggested that Yu Mei was the perfect candidate to attend as she had extensive experience in foreign investment.

In the end, Zhang Feng and Yu Mei travelled together to Beijing.

On the train, they recalled their experience of the 1966, Revolutionary Tour to Beijing, held during the Cultural Revolution. They were parted at that time because they belonged to different political categories: the Black and the Red. But their unexpected meeting on the train was ruined by Zhang Feng's rival, Chang Zheng. They sighed with feeling at the rapid passing of time.

At the seminar in Beijing, they noticed that most of the delegates were not fully concentrating. The host of the seminar noticed the mood of these mayors and said,

"Look how absent-minded you are! I will give you a break this afternoon. Go around the capital and come back to the seminar tomorrow."

All the mayors and their assistants cheered up.

In the afternoon, Zhang Feng and Yu Mei went to Tian An Men Square. They were shocked by the scene there. Over a hundred thousand students and citizens were gathered on this vast Square, with banners and posters, singing and shouting political slogans. Some student leaders were delivering speeches and kind citizens were giving food and drink to the protestors. A lot of students were living in temporary tents which were dotted around the Square. No violence or damage had taken place and it was really a very peaceful demonstration. People could see the pickets were on patrol duty to prevent any violent activity. Zhang Feng said to Yu Mei, with emotion,

"Time has changed the world! What we saw 23 years ago here were fanatical Red Guards who had been brainwashed. They were a violent force, intent on damaging and destroying society without any judgement or independent thought. But 12 years after the Cultural Revolution, look what is happening! Knowing what is going on in the outside world has given young people their own political views and independent thought, and they want to strive for a brighter future for their country! This is a very positive action and in no way a protest designed to defy the Party's authority."

Yu Mei said,

"Before his death, my father said we must draw lessons from the anti-rightist movement of the '50s and from the Cultural Revolution. We should not treat people as slaves and idiots but rather, give them the right to care about state affairs in their own country."

Zhang Feng suddenly saw a banner with the name of Jili University on it. He walked over with Yu Mei and, as expected, he saw Chai Li organizing his team.

Seeing Zhang Feng approaching, Chai Li said to him, with a smile,

"Mayor Zhang, are you coming to arrest us or support us?"

"What do you think? How am I going to arrest you without policemen?"

The students from Jili University all crowded round Zhang Feng and Yu Mei. Gazing at Yu Mei, one of them said,

"Is this fairy-like, beautiful lady the wife of Mayor Zhang? Mayor Zhang, you really are lucky in love!"

Zhang Feng told them,

"23 years ago, during the Cultural Revolution, my wife and I were on this Square to attend Chairman Mao's speech but I was not a Red Guard. I was a child of the Five Black Categories."

The students were interested in his story and asked him to give the details of that day's events. After hearing his story, they sighed with emotion and said young people at that time were really fanatical, political followers but in the end, they became the victims. Zhang Feng suddenly realized that he should do something to help the students. He told Chai Li he would buy some food for them, and left with Yu Mei.

After one hour, he returned with Yu Mei and brought back a whole tricycle load of food such as milk, bread, sausages, cans of pork, and soda water which he handed to Chai Li who was grateful, but also worried.

"Mayor Zhang, you have given us such great help but if we fail in our appeal, those hard headed leaders might punish you and dismiss you from your post."

Zhang Feng replied,

"I do not mind. Even the late General Party Secretary, Hu Yaobang, dared to support the students' movement and I am only an insignificant mayor! I will go back to my teaching post at the University if I am dismissed."

The students all praised him for his courage and said there was a shortage of young officials like him who cared more about the people and less about their own positions.

When they said goodbye, Zhang Feng asked them to take care of themselves. He said he hoped the Party and Government would respond to the students' appeals but of course, he and the students also worried that the hardline leaders might suppress the protests by force.

Leaving the students, Zhang Feng and Yu Mei sat on the bench under the large tree where Yu Mei had fainted during the speech by Mao in 1966. They recalled how Zhang Feng had carried her to the hospital and they hoped for a few peaceful days together, which unfortunately, they did not get. Zhang Feng suddenly remembered that two years ago, when he came to Beijing with Wang Hai, he had seen a lady in red here, trying to avoid him. She was embarrassed and said,

"Yes, it was me. I wanted to meet you but gave up because I did not want to upset you."

Holding her hands, Zhang Feng said to her, with emotion,

"My dear little fairy, you have really suffered too much."

Seeing there was nobody nearby, she leaned on his shoulder and said sweetly,

"At last, I can live with you. I do not have any regrets in my life now."

Back in Jili City, Zhang Feng and Yu Mei watched the daily reports on the demonstrations in Beijing on the Chinese Central TV Station. In a change to their normal attitude, the main media reported on these events very objectively, even showing sympathy for the students.

One day, Lin Jianguo passed on a national newspaper, 'The People's Daily' to Zhang Feng. There was an editorial inside with the title: 'We must have a clear-cut stand to oppose this social upheaval'. Zhang Feng's first reaction was that this must be bad news! The hardliners had got the upper hand now. The editorial said there were some people who had ulterior motives and were using these student protests to create turmoil. This meant that the students' movement was not patriotic but was rather, a political attempt to topple the Party and the Government. This editorial obviously tried to whip up opinion to suppress the protests.

In the end, it only aroused the anger of the students and they demanded that this accusation be withdrawn. To show their protest, a lot of students started hunger strikes and more students moved into the Square, more than three hundred thousand. At the same time, in about 400 cities across China, students and citizens held huge demonstrations to support those on the Square. There was a large scale demonstration in the city centre of Jili City. From the City Council building, Zhang Feng could see the rally taking place on the crowded square. He sighed with emotion and said to his colleagues,

"This is the will of the people. Those left-wing leaders should listen to public opinion and not regard it as an attempt to topple the Party. The students and public are actually willing to make our society fairer and more democratic and do not want to make trouble for our leadership."

Zhang Feng wanted to go to the square to attend the Jili demonstration, but Chang Zheng stopped him.

"Be careful! Although the Cultural Revolution is over, there are still informers and villains all around us. They might put your name on their black list. I think that the hardliners will get the upper hand and they will treat the students harshly."

Thinking of the evil Deputy Governor Shen, Zhang Feng gave up his intention to go.

Unexpectedly, Dan Dan rang that evening from the UK. Yu Mei took the phone call. She was a bit nervous hearing Dan Dan's voice and thought she might be calling to complain about her situation but Dan Dan said,

"Yu Mei, it is not a private matter. I am calling about the events on Tian An Men Square. Please ask Brother Feng to come to the phone."

Dan Dan told him the demonstration on the Square had drawn much attention from the international community. Yesterday, there were over one million overseas Chinese holding demonstrations to support the students in Beijing. She had attended the one in London herself, with over ten thousand overseas Chinese students. She felt so excited because at last, it seemed that Chinese people were standing up for themselves. In the past, their voices were ignored by the Party and Government, but now, it was the other way round. Democracy was, at last, appearing in China. Zhang Feng was very pleased to tell Dan Dan about the progress of events in China.

Worrying about the expense of international phone calls, Zhang Feng quickly asked her how she and their son were getting on. She just said they were fine. She did not forget to urge him and Yu Mei to enjoy their marriage. After she hung up, Yu Mei was relieved as she felt that she owed Dan Dan a great deal.

To shock the people supporting the students, General Secretary Zhao Ziyang, who sympathized with the students, was discharged from his post. The hardliners, headed by the Prime Minister, Li Peng, declared a curfew in Beijing and sent 30 army divisions to occupy the capital. They thought this would be enough to frighten the students and make them retreat from the Square. Yet on the opposite side, the Beijing citizens tried to block the roads to stop the army from entering the city.

On television, Zhang Feng could see how the Beijing citizens talked to the soldiers and persuaded them not to suppress the students. Because of the hot weather, citizens gave water and food to the soldiers. The army officers also did not want to offend the citizens so the troops were stuck on the streets for a few days.

This situation infuriated the hardliners. On the evening of the 4th June, fierce shooting could be heard on the streets near the Square. The authorities sent in more troops from other regions and told the soldiers that some counter-revolutionary elements intended to bring down the Party and the Government. They were told to occupy the Square at any cost. Some citizens were killed when they tried to block the troops. Initially, they could not believe the army would shoot at its own people until they actually saw bloody, dead bodies lying in the street. The soldiers had no rubber bullets at that time so they used real bullets.

At last, they occupied the Square. In order to reduce the casualty numbers, the student leaders negotiated with the soldiers and asked them to give safe passage for the students to retreat from the Square. After one and a half month's occupation by the students, the Square was empty at last. This world-shocking political protest had been suppressed with much bloodshed.

Zhang Feng could not sleep that night as he felt so angry: why did the authorities not listen to the students and appease them, like General Secretary Zhao Ziyang had done?

The next day, Chang Zheng took Zhang Feng to a quiet office and told him some further details about the suppression last night. He said that although his father, General Zhao Wu, had retired, he still had connections with his previous subordinates. Zhao Wu also sympathized with the students and had asked his former colleagues not to injure the students. In the end, one of his previous commanders was sent to suppress the students but he refused to give the order to his soldiers to shoot the students and civilians. He was dismissed instantly from his post. He said he would rather leave his position than have students' blood on his hands.

This bloody suppression did not frighten the Chinese people. On the next day, in many cities, there were large scale demonstrations. Railways and roads were blocked in some cities and the authorities sent in further troops to suppress these protests. This also happened in Jili City. Some students and citizens lay on the railway tracks to stop the trains. Zhang Feng had to deal with this problem, even though he supported the protestors. He asked the Railway Management Bureau to cancel the trains. Then he walked up to the students and citizens on the railway tracks and talked to them with a loudspeaker.

"Dear students and citizen friends, I am Zhang Feng, the Mayor of Jili City. I understand your action completely. I also mourn the dead students and citizens in Beijing but blocking the railway will not resolve the confrontation between the public and the Government. It will only affect the transport and normal life of the people in our city. I can guarantee that we will not use police or soldiers to suppress you. I hope you will look after yourselves and finish this blockade."

Then he gave the students and citizens on the tracks some spring water.

His persuasive speech moved the students and citizens. The protest leaders felt that Mayor Zhang always supported reforms so they decided not to make more trouble for him. Then they stood up from the tracks and walked away, through the space the police had made for them under instructions from Zhang Feng. Zhang Feng asked them to go home and rest which really moved them. The trains started to run once again and the Head of the Railway Management Bureau smiled and thanked Zhang Feng profusely but Zhang Feng still had a very heavy heart.

CHAPTER III

The Retrogression of the Reform Movement

To punish the students and people who had dared to defy the authority of the Party and Government, a nationwide arrest, suppression and investigation process began. The hardliners declared a black list, naming over twenty student leaders, a few leaders of workers' organizations and seven intellectuals who had openly criticized them. Some escaped abroad, luckily, but some were arrested and jailed. Over twenty thousand Party or Government officials who had supported the students' movement were disciplined. Most of them were active reformers.

Journalists who had supported the students were also punished. Zhang Feng unexpectedly read a report in the Northeast Daily about the disciplinary action taken against Qing Lian, the Head of the news section of the Da Lian Daily. He was sorry for her. Thinking she had left Jili because of their 'accidental' love-making, he still felt guilty. But at the same time, she had changed from being a fanatical Red Guard to an active journalist with a liberal, political standpoint, so he was also pleased. Zhang Feng knew he could not avoid a punishment from the left-wing leaders who would take this opportunity to give him a hard time.

Dan Dan was very anxious when she saw the tanks and soldiers rushing into the Square on TV. The overseas Chinese were angry about the bloody suppression on the Square and also sympathized with General Secretary Zhao Ziyang and the officials of reform who had supported the students.

Dan Dan did not marry Liang Hua after she took her son to the UK and said she still needed to think about it. Yet Liang Hua carefully arranged their life and study together. He found a nearby primary school for the boy and arranged the PhD programme for her. He also sympathized with the students' movement in Beijing.

A few days later, Liang Hua told Dan Dan that his brother in Hong Kong was sending a friend from mainland China to the UK and he would pick him up from the airport. In the evening, Liang Hua brought a young man to Dan Dan's apartment and she was very surprised to see that it was Chai Li, the President of the Students' Union in Jili University. She used to be his lecturer as his subject was business management.

Seeing her, Chai Li said, politely,

"How do you do, Lecturer Dan Dan."

Dan Dan asked him to take a seat and gave him a cup of tea. She thought his visit must have something to do with the student protests because he was quite interested in politics. Chai Li said he had actually escaped from the Square despite the fact that his name was on the wanted list. Luckily, he had travelled to Hong Kong with the help of some kind Beijing citizens. He had the address of Mr. Liang Fu who had given him his contact details when Chai Li attended his seminar some time ago.

Dan Dan listened to his description of this bloody event which he gave with tears in his eyes. He also told her that Zhang Feng had visited them on the Square and brought food. He also said Zhang Feng was a committed reformer and the students and citizens all liked him. He was worried for him because the overseas media were saying that the officials who had supported the students would be punished politically this time.

He suddenly asked,

"Who was that beautiful woman who came with him to the Square? My friends called her the wife of Mayor Zhang and she did not deny it. Aren't you his wife?"

"She is his new wife as we divorced recently," Dan Dan replied. She did not want to give a bad impression of Zhang Feng so she added,

"It was my fault. I wanted to divorce him."

Chai Li guessed she might be in love with her supervisor, Liang Hua, but Liang Hua had not indicated that Dan Dan was his wife or girlfriend. He decided not to ask them. Dan Dan told Chai Li to relax because the overseas Chinese would help him to settle here. Western countries tended to sympathize with the students and would grant them political asylum. Liang Hua would help him to find a course for a Master's degree in a university here. Chai Li said he was very grateful for their help but he loved his country and would not give up his efforts for a more free, democratic and prosperous China.

As Zhang Feng expected, two weeks after the event, the 'June the Fourth' investigation team asked to see him. Entering the room, he could feel a stern and cold atmosphere. Deputy

Governor Shen, his sworn enemy, was sitting in the middle of a long table with other team members on both sides. Zhang Feng knew them well because of his work. Most of them were officials belonging to the left-wing group or those with neutral standpoints.

The Head of the Provincial Security Bureau said to him,

"Mayor Zhang, the purpose of asking you to come today is for you to explain your recent speech and actions, supporting the student protests. You know the Party's policy is: Lenience for those who confess their crime and severity for those who refuse."

Zhang Feng replied, without fear,

"Of course I know. I have recited it often when I was denounced during the Cultural Revolution."

His reply pricked the memories of some around the table who had experienced the Cultural Revolution. In people's minds now, the whole period was more like a tragedy and also a farce so some of the team could not help laughing. Shen was angry.

"Zhang Feng! You must take this investigation seriously. Your situation is very grave. After you accepted your political post, you continued to spread bourgeois ideology, promote capitalist economy and incite the student rebellions in order to bring down the leadership of the Communist Party."

"Really?" Zhang Feng replied. "If you think carrying out reforms, giving up the class struggle and creating a free, political atmosphere means following the capitalist road, then I am guilty."

Shen was angry at Zhang Feng's reply.

"How do you explain the fact that you went to Tian An Men Square and engaged with the students?"

"I am the Mayor of Jili City and have a responsibility to look after my citizens," Zhang Feng replied. "I had a meeting in

Beijing and I heard there were some students of Jili University on the Square and that some of them were on hunger strike. So I persuaded them to give up their hunger strike and think about their health and well-being. This was my duty as the Mayor. Even our Prime Minister, Li Peng, went to the Square to try and negotiate with the students. Are you going to investigate him? Also, Li Peng admitted that the request from the students to combat corruption was a patriotic action which is very important to maintain the reputation of our Party and Government. Unfortunately, in our city, the children of some high ranking officials are allowed to scalp national resources like steel."

His words hinted that Shen's son was one of these speculators. Shen flushed and was very angry. He was worried Zhang Feng might expose his disgraceful affairs so he stood up and banged the table,

"Zhang Feng! You are too aggressive! On behalf of the provincial authorities, I will make an announcement! You are dismissed from your mayoral post and you must do a self-examination! You must wait for further investigations."

Then he left the room, angrily. Zhang Feng also left the room, without fear.

With no work to do, he returned home in the early afternoon. Yu Mei rushed to him, embracing him and crying. Patting her shoulder, he said,

"Yu Mei, do not worry. We survived the Red Storm of the Cultural Revolution. I have even endured the tiger bench and possible execution! What else can they do to me? We don't need to worry because I did not attend the movement directly and I did not openly deliver a supportive speech. At the most, they might discipline me because I sympathized with the students. I do not mind going back to my university teaching and research. Then we could have a peaceful life – which is what you want."

Wiping her eyes, she said,

"Brother, I just feel this is not fair. You have worked so hard for the cause of reform in order to boost our economy and make our country more democratic and prosperous. But you have not had a proper reward. On the contrary, you will be punished!" Zhang Feng held her close and sat on the sofa with her.

"Yu Mei, I predicted quite early on that the left-wing leaders would use this event to attack the reformers because if the political system becomes democratic, they will lose all their power. If the economy is changed and becomes a free marketing system, they will lose out. But I am confident that reform cannot be resisted, even though it will not be plain sailing."

"Brother, I trust your vision. I will cook a delicious meal for you this evening. Think of this as a holiday from work," Yu Mei smiled.

In the evening, Yu Mei cooked Zhang Feng's favourite dish of braised pork with preserved vegetables. She normally did not make it as she worried it might give him high cholesterol. Just as they were enjoying the meal together, somebody knocked at the door. It was Secretary Liu. Zhang Feng knew immediately why he had come as he was also being pushed out by the left-wing.

Sitting down with a serious expression, he said to them,

"Xiao Feng, I am unable to protect you this time. The left-wing hardliners think I am too right-wing and that I have been too supportive of reforms. They have forced me to retire earlier than I should which is a disguised punishment to get rid of me and replace me with their own followers."

Zhang Feng tried to comfort him.

"Uncle Liu, do not worry. The enthusiasm for change is irresistible. This is a low point for the reform movement but the pressure of our increasing population and the rapid development of other countries will push the top authorities to carry on with reform again. If we do not, there will be a social crisis. I do not care about my personal loss. I can still teach at the university but I will never give up my political ambitions for my country and my people. I will never forget the deathbed injunction of Secretary Li, Yu Mei's father."

Secretary Liu and Yu Mei were moved by his words. Secretary Liu said he would continue to monitor the political situation and take an interest in the future of Zhang Feng and Yu Mei. They were very grateful for his support.

The next day, Zhang Feng received a phone call from Chang Zheng who told him he had also been asked to do a self-examination, although he had not been dismissed from his post. Lin Jianguo and Chen Tao were also requested to do self-examinations because the left-wingers hated reform so much. They wanted to stop the activities of this office totally.

Wang Li came to Zhang Feng's house in the afternoon. "Prince of Denmark, you have fallen prey to your uncle's plot. Ophelia has come to comfort you."

"Do not worry! I have prepared my sword of revenge!" he replied.

Yu Mei served tea to Wang Li. She quite liked this pretty and capable girl although she could tell that Wang Li loved Zhang Feng. She did not worry about this because of their age difference.

Wang Li said that what was happening now was more like the time of the Cultural Revolution. Everybody was nervous because they feared that their support for the students might be reported to the authorities. Anybody who had attended the demonstration to support the students was in danger. She herself also suffered from this. She had the opportunity to take a short course of hotel management in the USA but she had been refused on board by a security guard because somebody informed on her for her attendance at a demonstration. She said she knew it was a female colleague in the Foreign Investment Bureau who was jealous of Wang Li's promotion to Deputy Manager in the five star hotel.

Zhang Feng sighed and said,

"It is terrible that we seem to have returned to the time of the Cultural Revolution."

In the evening, at about 10.00 pm, when they were preparing to go to bed, the telephone rang. Zhang Feng picked up the phone and heard Dan Dan's voice. She was very worried and asked him whether he was under investigation because of his support for the students. She told him that Chai Li had escaped to the UK. From him, Dan Dan knew that Zhang Feng had visited the Square so she was worried he might be punished by the left-wing leaders. Zhang Feng told her that it was not too bad. He had just been suspended from his post. He would simply go back to the university. Zhang Feng could hear Dan Dan crying.

"Dan Dan, do not worry! This small incident does not matter! You must remember how we survived the horrors of the Cultural Revolution. I worry more about the damage to the progress of reform. What about you and our son?"

Dan Dan had no time to talk about her own problems and she asked to talk to Yu Mei.

Yu Mei took the phone with fear.

"Sister Yu Mei, how are you? I cannot be there to look after Brother Feng because I am abroad. Please take good care of him."

"Sister Dan Dan, do not worry. I will make great efforts to look after him. Take care of yourself and Dan Feng."

Hanging up, she started to cry.

Zhang Feng asked her what the matter was and she recalled the moment during the red storm when Zhang Feng was put in jail and faced the death penalty. She and Dan Dan made every effort to save him, like sisters. She said that she really regarded Dan Dan as her good sister and would even have shared Zhang Feng with her if China still allowed polygyny.

Zhang Feng wanted to please her. When he heard her secret desires, he explained that Dan Dan once had the same idea. But the problem was, this practice was illegal and immoral. He made a joke that they could be neighbours if Dan Dan ever came back and they could live in two apartments, next to each other. Dan Dan, as his ex-wife, living with his son in one apartment and he and Yu Mei, in the other. Then people would not be upset. Yu Mei thought a while and said it was actually a good idea but she would not let Dan Dan down. If it came to it, she would divorce him and let them re-marry. Zhang Feng quickly assured her that it was only a joke and suggested they should go to bed. He did not realize that this scenario would really come to pass, some years later.

Unexpectedly, Yu Mei travelled to Beijing a few days later. She said in her note to Zhang Feng that Dan Dan's talk had reminded her that she shouldn't just sit and wait at home: she should do something to help him. She planned to try to find some old friends of her late father in Central Government to see whether they could help. She said this time it was different from the situation during the Cultural Revolution when she had tried to save his life. This time, she was only trying to help him keep his post. If she could not do that, at least he could still teach.

Putting down her note, Zhang Feng thought how lucky he was to have such good sisters and life-death lovers.

Yu Mei returned after a few days. She happily told Zhang Feng that her father's old friends had promised to help as it wasn't a political mistake; he had just gone too far with economic reforms.

As they expected, at the end of 1989, the Provincial Personnel Bureau announced to Zhang Feng that he still held the same rank of mayor, with the same salary but he would have a new, temporary job as a high ranking investigator in the Reform Office. It meant he would not have any real power before the final outcome of his case but he could not return to his university work. He might be promoted once more because he was such a capable and intelligent official.

Zhang Feng felt this new post might work as he would not lose his party membership and would have time to investigate different sectors of the economy, building up more knowledge of management, finance, trading and marketing for the future. In the back of his mind, he had a plan to set up his own company when economic reforms had developed further and free marketing was introduced. He realized that the democratic system needed more middle class support. Free marketing would develop the economy more rapidly, improving living conditions and producing more middle class citizens. He knew the Chinese, like the Jewish people, had commercial talents which were suppressed by the rigid, socialist economic system. If their commercial talents were realized, there would be a huge boost in creative power and marketing drives. Added to which, the hard work, cheap labour and the rich, natural resources of the country could see the Chinese economy developing very rapidly.

One day, on the street, Zhang Feng bumped into his previous classmate, Song Ping, who looked quite upset. He told Zhang Feng his shop had once again, been closed by Li Qiu, Shen's lackey. The accusation was that his shop was a typical example of capitalism. Zhang Feng heard that Li Qiu had been promoted to Deputy Head of the Industrial and Commercial Department because of his success in the suppression of the student movement.

Zhang Feng thought this was really like floating and sinking on the sea of politics. Honest and hardworking officials lost their posts but political villains were promoted. How could China prosper if this situation continued? Because he no longer had any power, all he could do was comfort Song Ping and ask him to be patient for a while. He believed the need for reform could not be resisted. The plans of these evil, left-wing leaders would eventually, fall apart.

CHAPTER IV

Leaving Official Circles

After the 4th June protests, the political atmosphere became sterner. People were wary of talking about political reform. The country saw an economic depression which was partly due to international sanctions and partly, to the suppression of economic reform by the rigid, left-wing group. There was an editorial in the People's Daily, the major, national official newspaper, which said:

"The market economy is aimed at eliminating public ownership, denying the leadership of the Communist Party, removing socialism and furthering capitalism."

During Zhang Feng's work as an investigator, he saw many self-employed businesses, village and township enterprises and state enterprises, under production contracts, squeezed and pushed to the limit.

Once, he passed the free trading market which he had helped to build and he could see very few sellers renting the stands. He asked a few of them what had happened with their businesses and they told him the Commercial Management Department had put tighter controls on them. They were checked regularly for tax claims and smuggling, and had many more rules to observe. Zhang Feng knew Song Ping's shop had been closed by the unpleasant Li Qiu with the excuse that he had reduced the salary of his assistants. These sellers told him that if they could not prove the supply channels, their goods were regarded as smuggled products. Zhang Feng could only ask them to wait for possible improvements in the near future as he had lost his power to deal with these issues.

A few days later, Lin Jianguo rang him to say He Hua had called him as she did not know he had been punished politically. Hearing that Zhang Feng was no longer the Mayor because he had sympathized with the students had made her very angry. She could not believe such a good and capable official like Zhang Feng could be dismissed in this way. She told Lin that after the 4th June, her business, together with a lot of village and township enterprises, had got into trouble from local officers who felt that the development of these businesses had reduced their own power and interests. They used a lot of extra rules and regulations to bully these businesses. But she added that Zhang Feng and his colleagues did not need to worry about her. She would stand up to these difficult challenges. Zhang Feng was very angry about the harassment He Hua was receiving and he asked Lin to help her by contacting Secretary He in Hua Dan County. He might find a way to help her business.

The economic setback was also felt in state enterprises. Wang Hai came to Zhang Feng one day and told him he could not carry on with his contract scheme. After he had finished the first term, the higher authorities had increased the scheme's quota greatly because they thought his factory was making too much profit for itself. They also reduced the factory's self-management powers which affected the output of the factory. Who would dare to take the next contract scheme now?

Zhang Feng told Wang Hai that after the 4th June, the left-wing group had taken the upper hand and they hated any policy made by the reformers. This would damage the progress of economic reform in the country. The consequence would be economic depression, with low incomes, for people everywhere and employment problems which would take China back to the poverty and shortages of before, and during, the Cultural Revolution. Wang Hai said he would like to run his own company if private enterprises were legalized in the future.

Zhang Feng smiled.

"Great! It is good to want to be your own boss."

In the two years after the 4th June, Zhang Feng fully investigated different sectors of the economy and analyzed the potential progress of them, including heavy and light industries, transportation, energy and communication. He realized that real estate could be a very promising business in the future because of the huge demand for housing. With a population of over one billion, accommodation was always a big problem. In the cities, most people lived in very crowded and simple apartments and even state employees had to wait for many years to get a small apartment. A family of seven or eight had to squeeze into a tiny 30 or 40 square metre apartment without a sitting room and proper bathroom. The properties in poor areas were even worse.

The housing shortage was caused by the centrally controlled system. The state did not have enough money to build properties for the population. In recent years, some state-owned, real estate developers had built a few, residential properties but they were quite expensive and yet, in more developed countries, people with incomes could get mortgages to buy properties. Those who had little or no income could wait for council houses. The situation was much better in developed countries.

At the end of 1991, Zhang Feng received the final judgement on his political case. His case was a minor one and he would not receive any further political punishment although he would no longer hold the post of Mayor. His new job would be as Director of the City People's Congress, a sinecure post without real power. It seemed that the left-wing leaders did not want him to influence reform. Deputy Governor Shen said this was already very lenient but Zhang Feng was not at all pleased as he did not want to be a mediocre and unambitious official. If he could get directly involved in making society more democratic and prosperous, he would remain in office, otherwise he would rather quit. Shen thought he would be promoted to Governor of the province but Central Government appointed a new Governor which disappointed him. Chang Zheng kept his post as the Deputy Secretary of the City Party Committee. Lin Jianguo and Chen Tao were moved to other departments which made them very unhappy.

What to do next? Should he drift along aimlessly in political circles, or leave them? It was a turning point for Zhang Feng's career. He thought he should consult his family and friends first.

Yu Mei suggested it would be better to wait for the inevitable political changes to happen as the fighting between the two political groups was still going on. After the 4th June, the left-wing group seemed to get the upper hand but their retrogressive actions were boycotted by the international community which affected foreign investment and caused an economic recession. The anti-left-wing public faction encouraged the reformers to increase their politically cohesive influence. Even in the official media, people noticed the debate between the two groups about the political nature of free marketing: whether it was a socialist or capitalist thing.

In Dan Dan's letters, she said it would be a waste of time for Zhang Feng to stay in the political arena. She believed that, to build a new China, the development of the economy was more important. A richer country would produce more middle class citizens which was the foundation of a democratic nation.

Other family members and friends also suggested he should wait a while until the situation became more positive and then decide whether to leave or not. He could prepare for his own business venture in the meantime. His father thought that returning to an academic career was meaningless now. To publish more academic books would not contribute to the development of the country. China now desperately needed rapid economic growth to follow in the footsteps of Western countries. It could not be allowed to remain a poor country. This should be the main task for the social elite.

What about his Confucian faith? Yes, Confucius asked young educated people to serve their country by entering political circles. But in ancient times, this was the only way to contribute to society because China was a huge feudal kingdom. Now it is different. China needs to follow other developed countries in developing its economy to make the country prosperous. So entrepreneurship and making the country and people richer are equally ways to follow Confucianism. This mirrors the situation at the beginning of this century, when the last Queen Ci Xi and the Government of the First Republic encouraged people to develop industry and to do business to boost the economy. At that time, many educated people became 'Confucian businessmen'. So why should he not also follow them? In ancient China, when Confucian politicians suffered setbacks in officialdom, they would follow the Taoist way of withdrawing from society and living in solitude, becoming a hermit. 'But it is not yet time for me to follow Taoism' Zhang Feng thought. He would endeavor to follow Confucianism, serving his country through in the modern way as a Confucian businessman.

Zhang Feng contacted Mr. Du and discussed his idea to set up a real estate business. Unexpectedly, Mr. Du replied with great enthusiasm and said that real estate could be a very promising business considering China had a population of one billion. There would be a huge demand if every family wanted a good house to live in! He continued that he would like to be Zhang Feng's business partner and set up a company which could be called 'Song Jiang Real Estate Development'. Because he trusted Zhang Feng's capability, he would invest in the business himself. With other funds borrowed by Zhang Feng, they would have the money needed to launch such a promising business. Zhang Feng was very pleased with Mr. Du's response.

Zhang Feng waited and prepared as 1992 approached. It was a milestone year in the progress of China's economic reforms. In this year, the retired leader, Deng Xiaoping, was anxious to make China richer because he was an open-minded leader with experience of studying in Europe.

In order to give the green light to free marketing, he travelled to the South and Shen Zhen in particular, which was in the special economic zone. He saw the economy there was thriving because the city used foreign investment, joint ventures and had legalized private companies. In just ten years, the city, which used to be a small fishing village, had become a huge, modern metropolis with a population of several million, with tall buildings, wide streets and a beautiful urban landscape.

The success of the economic reforms in Shen Zhen and other Southern cities gave Deng the confidence to promote marketing reforms. He made a series of speeches to resurrect free marketing reforms politically and said a socialist country could still be socialist but also have free markets. It was just a waste of time to argue about whether free marketing was capitalist or socialist. As long as it could help to develop China's economy, it should be used. This reflected his popular theory that a cat is a good cat if it can catch a mouse, whatever colour it is.

His speech gave the green light to free marketing which exploded the restrictions of the centrally controlled economy like a bomb blast. His decision reinvigorated the reformers, leaving the left-wing leaders crestfallen. Before his speech, some businessmen who had secret, private, trading agreements, feared, every day, that the police might arrest them but after Deng's speech, they cried with happiness because this good news legalized their businesses. After Deng's speech was heard by the Central Government and the Central Committee of the Party, the leaders held a meeting immediately and announced the implementation of the socialist, free marketing policy.

This policy liberated the suppressed business enthusiasm and talent of the Chinese people and began a huge uptake of free marketing practices. By the end of 1992, there was a nationwide surge of new businesses. Almost everybody talked about doing business and every family prepared to set up their own companies. This was very different to the earlier stages of economic reform when most participants were poorly educated farmers and self-employed sellers. This time, most participants were members of the social elite like educated officials, institution researchers, university lecturers, scholars and students returning from abroad. These new businesses were more likely to succeed because of the excellent qualities of human resources. Hearing about and seeing this inspiring situation, Zhang Feng and Yu Mei embraced each other. Yu Mei said, excitedly,

"At last, the day we have waited for so long has come!"

Zhang Feng replied, happily,

"It is time to finish all the floating and sinking on the sea of officialdom and to begin swimming in the sea of commerce."

The telephone rang; it was Dan Dan. She said every condition was now favourable for Zhang Feng to start his own business which he should do immediately. Dan Dan said she would return home with their son when Zhang Feng had opened his own business as Dan Feng missed his father. She also talked to Yu Mei for a few minutes. To reassure Yu Mei, Dan Dan said she would return to the UK again, after Zhang Feng had set up his company.

After the call, Zhang Feng told Yu Mei that after Dan Dan had finished her PhD, she had started to work in a company in London, with experience in business management.

"We might persuade Dan Dan to stay and help us run the company. You will be the boss; Dan Dan could be in charge of the management; I will do the sales and public relations. Just find somebody in charge of construction!" declared Yu Mei.

"It sounds good! But how will you and Dan Dan get on?"

"There will be no problem; we are good sisters. I can give you back if she prefers to stay."

"No, no! We cannot suffer again from our love triangle!" cried Zhang Feng. "Anyway, she said she had married Professor Liang Hua. She could stay a few years with us and then still go back to the UK to visit Liang Hua from time to time."

Zhang Feng had started all the procedures to set up his company secretly as he did not want to alert the city and provincial authorities before everything was ready. He shared his plan with his close friends. Chang Zheng said he would fully support and help him. Lin Jianguo and Chen Tao said they would like to work in the business with him because they were fed up with being in politics. They believed running a business would make more of a contribution to society. Zhang Feng was very pleased as he needed to find a manager for the building construction work and wondered whether they would like to do this. They said that they would actually prefer to do anything he liked as they trusted him. They believed he was a capable man who was set for a great career. But he told them it would be risky to run a company. They knew this but they were willing to share the good and bad times with him as they regarded him as a most trustworthy friend and brother. Zhang Feng excitedly shook hands with them and embraced them warmly. He also contacted Mr. Du who said he already knew the political situation was now very favourable and he had fifty million Yuan ready to register the company: Zhang Feng just need a little more capital from his local banks.

Zhang Feng tried to apply for funding to some local banks. He did not realize that his reputation was so high in the city. People regarded him as a trustworthy and capable person and were therefore, very willing to help him. He visited the Provincial People's Bank and although the Director did not know him personally, he admired Zhang Feng for his achievements in economic reform. Listening to Zhang Feng's proposal to set up his own company and reading the details of his business plan, the Director said the chances of Zhang Feng getting capital were high. He just needed to discuss his application. Zhang Feng asked the

Director to follow the normal procedures for risk assessment of his application and not to consider his past position as the Mayor.

Two days later, the Director telephoned him with the good news that the bank would give him a low interest loan of fifty million Yuan. Hearing this, Yu Mei jumped up and declared that it was their first victory!

They were thrifty when it came to finding an administrative base for the company and found an old, two-storey building near the Song Jiang Hotel. They hired three rooms on the ground floor as offices thinking they would find a better place later on, if their business was successful. For the design and construction of the houses, Zhang Feng, with Lin Jianguo and Chen Tao, also found some reliable firms and companies.

The final thing was to find a piece of land where they would build their houses. Zhang Feng thought of Chang Zheng who had been appointed as Mayor of the city recently. Chang Zheng consulted the City Planning Bureau and found a piece of waste land in the Western suburb of the city which used to be the site of a small chemical factory. Because of the pollution on the site, no state building company wanted to use it. Therefore, the city would sell it cheaply to Zhang Feng's company but it would not be suitable for building residential apartments until the polluted soil was properly treated.

How to treat the pollution? Zhang Feng suddenly remembered his friend Huang Lei in the Chemistry Department of Jili University. He was the Deputy Director of the Chemistry Department now. Listening to Zhang Feng's request, he visited the site with Zhang Feng and took some samples of soil to analyze. Huang Lei telephoned Zhang Feng the next day to tell him the good news. The polluted soil was acidic and could be neutralized by cheap, alkaline chemicals. Afterwards, rain water would remove the smell and then the land would be safe and suitable for building residential properties. The cost of treatment would only be about several thousand Yuan.

Zhang Feng was delighted and very grateful to Huang Lei. Huang said Zhang Feng did not need to thank him, just sell him an apartment when the project was finished. Zhang Feng said that would not be a problem! He would sell him an apartment at a discount.

The funding, the right plot of land, the office and staff all looked ready. Zhang Feng felt it was time for him to resign from his official post and to register his company formally. With a relaxed and confident feeling, he walked into the Provincial Personnel Department with his resignation letter. It was just by chance that evil Deputy Governor Shen was there. Shen said to him,

"What happened to you? Are you not happy with your post and want to get a promotion? I hear you have not been working so hard recently and you are often absent from your office. If you continue in this way, you might lose your existing post."

Zhang Feng cast a contemptuous glance at him and replied,

"Deputy Governor Shen, thank you for looking after me for such a long time, leaving me to float and sink on this treacherous sea of officialdom. I have now seen through it all. Reform is almost impossible because there is always somebody blaming and attacking you. Now I will change direction and find a different way to serve my country and my people. I will run a company for the benefit of all the citizens of this city. This is my resignation letter."

Putting his letter on the table, he left the room straightaway without looking round. Shen asked the Head of Department to read Zhang Feng's letter for him and discovered that Zhang Feng was intending to run a real estate company.

"Damn! He has made the most of a good opportunity once again! If I had known this earlier, I would have told my son to open a real estate company."

His son used to be a speculator but the double-tracks system had basically finished so he could not make easy money now and had become idle.

In the corridor, Zhang Feng met his former classmate and his political enemy, Li Qiu. Li Qiu smiled grimly and said,

"My old classmate! Do you think your official career is not successful enough?"

"Yes," replied Zhang Feng. "There are so many officers who are good at flattering their superiors and informing on their colleagues. How can I possibly have a successful career here?"

Li Qiu knew Zhang Feng was criticizing him, so he tried to argue back.

"You should know the key to being a successful official is to obey your superiors. To obey your superiors means you also obey the Party."

Zhang Feng mocked him.

"Some officers do not serve the people at all and only care about their own promotion. It would be better to have fewer officers like them. I thought the students in our university class of 1977 had all experienced the real Cultural Revolution and so hated all evil informers but unfortunately, there are still some villains amongst us. It is a shame."

"You…You…" Li Qiu was too angry to speak.

"Have your dreams of promotion. I will not serve these corrupt officials anymore!"

Zhang Feng waved his hand and left. Li Qiu stamped his feet in fury.

After registration, Zhang Feng's company could formally

begin to operate. Yu Mei, Lin Jianguo and Chen Tao all resigned from their posts. Everybody was very happy preparing for the opening ceremony.

One afternoon, somebody knocked at the door. It was Dan Dan and their son, Dan Feng! Dan Dan wore a white coat and black skirt, still looking like an intelligent, mature, very beautiful, professional lady. Dan Feng was eight years old now, smart and handsome, with innocent and artless eyes. Zhang Feng picked him up in his arms and kissed him. Even though they had not seen each other for a few years, he still called Zhang Feng 'Daddy'. Putting him down, he wanted to embrace Dan Dan, out of habit, but he hesitated when he saw Yu Mei next to him. Yu Mei pushed him to show she did not mind and they hugged briefly. Then Yu Mei and Dan Dan embraced each other warmly, like sisters.

Yu Mei was moved to tears and said to Dan Dan quietly,

"Sister Dan Dan, thank you very much."

Dan Dan knew why Yu Mei was thanking her.

"No need for thanks, I am very well."

Then she pointed at Yu Mei and said to her son,

"Dan Feng, call her your 'second mother'."

Dan Feng gazed at Yu Mei with his big eyes and asked,

"Why is she my 'second mother'? All children only have one mother! Why do I have two?"

Everybody laughed. Zhang Feng and Dan Dan agreed that they would not tell Dan Feng about their divorce until he grew up and would continue to tell him they just lived apart.

Dan Dan said to the boy,

"It is good to have two mothers as you will have one more present on your birthday! "

Dan Feng happily shook hands with Yu Mei and kissed her.

It was spring, 1993. The genial sunshine enveloped the River City and the breeze swayed the weeping willows. The Song Jiang Real Estate Development Company had opened. Although it was a private company, its opening was like that of a major state company, drawing both official and public attention. Zhang Feng and Mr. Du Shan did not realize it would be so crowded. Government officials, business leaders and journalists all came to the opening ceremony. Ordinary citizens could only stand and watch from the street. Dan Dan said the reason why the ceremony attracted so many people was because both Zhang Feng and Mr. Du were well known in the city and the luxury hotel had been built by them. Also, the citizens were keen to have better and more spacious accommodation. They hoped Zhang Feng's company could help them buy their own properties.

Zhang Feng, Mr. Du, Dan Dan, Yu Mei, Lin Jianguo and Chen Tao all stood at the entrance of their office to meet the guests for the ceremony. Chang Zheng came on behalf of the City Council to congratulate them on the opening of the company. Some city and provincial officials who supported Zhang Feng also came. The appearance of retired Secretary Liu caused warm applause. A lot of managers from both state and private companies came as well. Seeing He Hua and Song Ping in the crowd, Dan Dan asked a member of staff to bring them into the building. Journalists were taking photos inside and outside.

Zhang Feng said to the people around him,

"I feel today's ceremony is more like an oath-taking event to boost free marketing for our economy."

Everybody said they felt the same.

As the space was limited inside, Zhang Feng decided to hold the ceremony outside the building. After the deafening noise of firecrackers and the performance of the band, Lin

Jianguo announced the beginning of the ceremony. Firstly, the Chairman of the Company Board, Zhang Feng, introduced the main members of the company. He picked up the loudspeaker to warm applause, and announced the establishment of the new company. Mr. Du was the main partner, Dan Dan was the General Manager, Lin Jianguo was the Manager of the Building and Construction Department, Chen Tao was the Manager of the Service Department and Yu Mei was the Manager of Sales and Public Relations.

Then Zhang Feng announced the first project of the company, which would be to build ten apartment blocks with 800, one bed and two bed flats. The price would be reasonable and citizens with some savings could afford them. Hopefully, in the near future, mortgage borrowing schemes would be introduced and more citizens would be able to buy these residential properties. He said his company promised to build high quality properties, using the best architects, designers and construction teams. Thus, the buyers could feel confident about living in these properties comfortably and safely. In addition, the company would also build one modern middle school and one primary school. His speech caused loud applause.

After the ceremony, Zhang Feng invited the distinguished guests to have some refreshments. He felt a bit hot and tired, so he asked Dan Dan and Yu Mei to accompany the guests, and he walked out of the building to rest on a bench on the river bank. Suddenly, he saw a familiar slim lady in a white skirt coming towards him, with a little girl. Qing Lian! Zhang Feng recognized her. She had gone to Da Lian City and had been politically punished following the 4th June protests.

"Brother Feng! You do not know me?" she asked, with a smile. Like Yu Mei and Dan Dan, she still looked very young.

"Qing Lian! Have you come back to visit your family? Is this your daughter?"

Seeing the nervous expression in his eyes, she said to him,

"Brother Feng, congratulations on your new company! Whatever you do, you will always be successful. I remarried in Da Lian and have a daughter."

Zhang Feng relaxed and stood up to say hello to the little girl.

"She is a very pretty princess, like her mother!"

"Really? Is her mother so beautiful then?" she asked, pleasantly.

"Of course! You are beautiful!"

"You flatter me! I am not as beautiful as Yu Mei or Dan Dan," she said, shyly.

Recalling their 'accidental' love-making a few years ago, he did not know whether he should apologize to her or comfort her. Suddenly, he noticed the jade bracelet on her wrist which he had given her before they parted. Seeing him look at this bracelet, she said with a smile,

"Wearing it makes me feel you are just next to me."

Hearing her words, Zhang Feng felt guilty again. Noticing his embarrassed expression, she changed the topic.

"Brother Feng, can you believe that I will be living once again in the beautiful River City, running a travel company with Li He."

"Really? Did you know he remarried?"

"I know. We cannot be a married couple but we can go into business together. He is going to do the internal arrangements and I am going to work outside. He has always longed to run his own business and does not want to work in a crowded hospital forever. He wants to run a private, Chinese medicine clinic, managed by his new wife who is also a doctor. He himself wants to run this travel agency with me."

"Very good! It seems we are all getting out of the official system," Zhang Feng said.

"I think a new age is coming for people like us to choose their own profession or business, using their talents and capabilities," Qing Lian replied.

"Yes, by doing this, Chinese people can eradicate poverty and become a rich nation," he said, with emotion.

He invited her to have some refreshments but she said she would not waste his time. She would consult him if she ever had problems with her business. Zhang Feng assured her that when he wanted to go on holiday, he would go to their travel company. In the end, they said goodbye to each other and parted on friendly terms.

Epilogue

In spring, 1995, the River City and the distant mountains were bathed in light green. People enjoyed this enchanting scenery with its green water, blue sky and white clouds. Spring is a season of hope and yearning for a bright future. At a weekend, the mighty North Mountain attracts throngs of visitors and among them, we see the main character in our story, Zhang Feng, with his lovers and friends, enjoying the scenery there. The group included Zhang Feng, his wife, Yu Mei, his ex-wife, Dan Dan, his friend, Wang Hai, Li He, and Li He's ex-wife, Qing Lian. They did not bring their children with them.

When they met at the entrance of the park, Wang Hai asked Zhang Feng,

"Brother Feng, brother-in–law, for what reason have you invited us here today? You have your wife and ex-wife with you so why can't we have our partners with us? Have you just invited those of us on the future-telling picture?"

"What future-telling picture?" the three women asked.

Li He knew Zhang Feng did not want them to know anything about the picture, so he quickly smoothed things over.

"Do not listen to Wang Hai's nonsense! Today is a classmates' rally! We were all in one class in middle school."

"What about Yu Mei?" Qing Lian asked.

"She is the wife of one of our class," replied Wang Hai.

Anyway, everybody was in a good mood and ready to visit the mountain today as they had achieved great success in their business in the past few years.

The six of them climbed up to the top of the mountain. They sat on a big rock in front of the Taoist temple and enjoyed the enchanting scenery, with the three men sitting in the front row and the three women behind them. Looking to the distance, they could see the ten apartment blocks built by Zhang Feng's company, which were all sold a year ago. With modern interiors and spacious rooms, the flats were very popular with buyers. Zhang Feng, Dan Dan and Yu Mei excitedly talked about their successful business and yearned to build more blocks and houses for the city. Zhang Feng said,

"We are preparing to build some luxurious villas at the end of this year. Please start saving up now if you want to live in one!"

Wang Hai could not wait to talk about his business.

"Oh, don't just boast about your own business! My factory has also had a good year. We now have more modern makes of cars and trucks. Brother Feng and Li He, get rid of your Japanese Charade cars and drive our VW Jetta instead! It drives fast with a sleek body design!"

After free marketing was legalized two years ago, the state enterprises were also reformed by company law. With the separation between the political administration and business management and clear ownership, his factory's output doubled. Then Li He said,

"Is today a rally for successful businessmen? Let me and Qing Lian also report on our business then. My private clinic is not worth talking about, but the holidays offered through our travel company now cover most of the national parks and ancient attractions from the South to the North. We have employed ten new staff as it is too busy to manage ourselves. They are all college graduates. We will start offering international holidays next year. You can book now if you want to have your holiday in Greece, Italy and Egypt, with a 20% discount!"

Zhang Feng said with emotion,

"I used to think if you wanted to contribute to your country, you had to go into political circles but now I realize that running a business and boosting the economy is a practical way to do this."

Everybody agreed with him. Wang Hai asked Dan Dan what were the differences in living conditions between the West and developing countries, like China. She said,

"One of the most important differences is that people in developed countries not only have enough food and clothes, but also, own properties, cars and can afford holidays."

Wang Hai rubbed his forehead and said, excitedly,

"Interestingly, by chance, our businesses are providing properties, cars and holidays!"

They all nodded in agreement.

"I discussed this with Dan Dan before," said Zhang Feng. "If more people become middle class, owning properties and cars, it will lay the foundation for a democratic system. Poor people who are struggling with basic living conditions, do not know how to use their democratic rights, even if they have them. Only those who are comfortable, with good living conditions, an education and independent thought, have the luxury of judging the policies made by the leaders in power. The good thing is, our universities are also carrying out educational reforms and expanding student recruitment. It will not be like 1977, when the universities had just re-opened after the Cultural Revolution, and only 5% of candidates could get a place." Then he continued,

"I heard that some people said, 'Mao Zedong made Chinese people stand up in the international community in 1949. But Deng Xiaoping has made Chinese people get rich now.' You may have different opinion about this idea. But I think Deng's economic policy to introduce free market indeed has helped to develop our economy very rapidly, and to improve our living condition greatly."

Everyone agreed with him.

The three ladies were all in a good mood today. They had stopped being competitive and jealous after their experiences, both happy and sad, in the past. They felt like they were real sisters. Qing Lian suggested they should pick some wild vegetables and make stir fried dumplings when they returned home.

The three men sat on the rock, watching these three lovely, busy women and Zhang Feng's heart filled with many emotions. Yu Mei was his lover whom he loved most of all. The love between them was like the surging waves of the sea. Dan Dan used to be his beloved wife. Because he had regarded her as his sister for many years in the past, the love between them was more like the love between family members. Like a tranquil lake, she had given him the warmth and happiness of a family. With Qing Lian, they had saved each other's lives and he had 'accidentally', once made love to her. His love for her encompassed care and responsibility, like a relaxing, garden stream which also needed attention from time to time.

While Zhang Feng was gazing at the three women, Wang Hai remembered the future-telling picture, interpreted by the old Taoist monk, thirty years ago. Fifteen years ago, in 1980, when they had looked at the picture again, they thought the Taoist monk had made a very accurate prediction. Wang Hai had again hidden the picture in a gap between the bricks.

"Brother Feng, I am going to search for that picture to see whether it is still there or not."

"It must be damaged after 30 years," Zhang Feng replied but Wang Hai still stood and went over to the brick wall of the temple.

"Brother Feng, you are lucky to have three women loving you at the same time," said Li He.

"But Qing Lian is your own ex-wife!" Zhang Feng exclaimed, immediately.

"Yes, but she loved you early on in middle school and even kept loving you during the Cultural Revolution. She was reluctant to marry me and divorced me after one year. Then she moved to Da Lian and married another man, and had a daughter but she has never told me who her husband is. Now, we have a good relationship and run our business together. She also has a good relationship with my new wife. We can be successful business partners but not a married couple."

Zhang Feng said that his situation was not too bad.

Wang Hai returned to them quite soon and showed an old and shabby piece of paper to Zhang Feng and Li He.

"Look! I found it!"

Then, as usual, he began to analyze the picture. He pointed to the objects and details in the picture, saying,

"Look! All the things in the picture stand for seven people. The high peak in the middle is Brother Feng and the two lower peaks stand for me and Li He which means we are his loyal friends. The three flowers at the foot of the mountain represent Brother Feng's lovers: Plum Blossom, Peony and Lotus, the meanings of Yu Mei, Dan Dan and Qing Lian. This shows there are three ladies who love him. We thought that this vine, twisting round the peak, represented a snake which could be Brother Feng's enemy. Fifteen years ago, we realized that it was the evil Cai Wenge who framed Brother Feng and sent him to the execution ground. He also broke up the relationship between Brother Feng and Yu Mei. He cheated Yu Mei into marrying him and then abandoned her later. He was punished after the Red Storm and was sentenced to 12 years in prison. Actually, he should have been released from jail two years ago. I hope Brother Feng never sees him again."

"The Cultural Revolution is over. He is just a released prisoner and dare not frame anyone anymore." Li He said.

Listening to Wang Hai's analysis of the picture, Zhang Feng said,

"You still like your old superstitions! Qing Lian is Li He's ex-wife and has no relationship with me."

"Since she is in the picture, she must have some connection to you," Wang Hai replied.

Thinking of their 'accidental' love-making, Zhang Feng stopped arguing with him.

Wang Hai remembered that they had verified this picture fifteen years ago, right here.

"Do you remember, when we checked this picture fifteen years ago in 1980, all seven persons in the picture were here on the day? Three of us, plus Dan Dan and Qing Lian. That snake, Cai Wenge, was digging a trench with other prisoners at the foot of the mountain. Only Yu Mei was absent. We thought the future-telling was not too accurate but in the end, we knew Brother Feng had hidden the truth that Yu Mei was actually living in the temple as a nun on the day. What do you think about the prediction of the Taoist monk now? It was really spot on!"

"So what about today?" Li He asked. "Six of us are here, but not Cai Wenge."

"Wait a while!" replied Wang Hai. "He might magically appear!"

Both Zhang Feng and Li He shook their heads and said that would be impossible.

Just then, the three ladies returned happily with bags full of fresh, wild vegetables and talked about how to cook dinner that evening. Suddenly, Yu Mei grabbed hold of Zhang Feng's arm, and trembling all over, she pointed to a man wearing sunglasses.

"He…He…"

Zhang Feng and everyone else looked at this approaching man and felt he was very familiar. The man walked slowly towards them and stopped, about ten metres away. He then took off his sunglasses.

"Cai Wenge!"

Everybody shouted with surprise. Yes, it was him, the wicked man who became a high ranking official as an active Red Guard during the Cultural Revolution: the man who framed Zhang Feng and ruined Yu Mei. Twelve years of jail had made him thinner with some gray hair but the vicious expression still shone in his eyes. Zhang Feng, Wang Hai and Li He stood up to defend the ladies.

Cai Wenge walked a few more steps nearer and grinned, hideously.

"Gentlemen… and ladies! It looks like you still recognize me. You probably thought I died in prison. Fortunately, I have survived and was released two years ago. Now, I have equal status with you – I am a legal citizen. It looks like you are going to attack me but I can call the police now."

Wang Hai shouted at him,

"Why are you looking so arrogant? You are only a released prisoner. Nobody will want to give you a job."

Cai smiled and said,

"You don't realize that Deng Xiaoping may have sent me to jail but his new economic policy has now saved me. Like all of you, I have my own company and I am a manager now."

Seeing Zhang Feng and his friends were not going to punish him, he looked even more pleased with himself.

"Zhang Feng, I had have competed with you over the last thirty years to see who is more successful. In the end, you lost in the Cultural Revolution but I won with a high ranking, official post. After the Revolution, I lost, with a twelve year prison sentence and you won with a professorship and a high ranking post as the Mayor. But now, we draw as both of us are company directors. We will have more competition in the future. Ha, ha!"

He looked at Yu Mei, lasciviously, and said,

"As for private affairs, you have lost to me again. I heard you had married Yu Mei but she is my ex-wife. I had her first and you only got a second-hand woman, Ha, ha, ha!"

Yu Mei almost started to cry. Dan Dan and Qing Lian cursed Cai fiercely. Zhang Feng and Wang Hai were so angry they were ready to beat him up. Cai Wenge was frightened and started to retreat, step by step.

Seeing they had stopped, he pretended to be brave and shouted,

"Let's wait to see who will win in commercial circles!" and then he quickly ran back down the mountain.

Meeting this villain made the group angry and disappointed.

Zhang Feng said,

"Do not worry. This evil man can only come to a disgraceful end, unless he changes his nature, like Hei Hou. Forget him! Let's enjoy ourselves again."

Dan Dan and Qing Lian tried to comfort Yu Mei and gradually, their happy mood was restored.

Wang Hai said quietly to Zhang Feng and Li He,

"What do you think now? The magic of the Taoist monk is really powerful! Just like fifteen years ago, all seven people in the picture have been here today! I am going to learn how to predict the future when I retire and then I will become a millionaire!"

Both Zhang Feng and Li He mocked him.

Soon, they saw the lingering glow of the setting sun. They were reluctant to say goodbye to the enchanting scenery of the mountain top. Zhang Feng said,

"Let's look forward to our future. We are full of pride and enthusiasm. We will battle with the wind and waves on this sea of commerce and sail smoothly to a brighter destination."

"Yes, we will!"

Everybody responded to his words.

Under the beautiful glow of the setting sun, these middle aged friends and lovers walked forwards, side by side, to face whatever future challenges lay ahead of them.